*Rose Moss*

Rose Moss was born and grew up in South Africa and emigrated to the United States in 1964, a few days before Nelson Mandela was sentenced to Robben Island. In New England, she worked as a writer, teacher, and management consultant. She has published one other novel, *The Family Reunion*, and a non-fiction book about the Delmas Trial and the changes brought about in South Africa in the 1980s, *Shouting at the Crocodile*. Her writing has received a number of honours, including the Quill Prize for Fiction, a PEN Syndicated Fiction Award, short listing for a National Book Award and Fellowships at Yaddo and MacDowell. *The Schoolmaster*, published in Britain as *The Terrorist*, was featured by the New Fiction Society on its first publication.

She teaches at Harvard and is currently writing about South Africa and other themes. Her preoccupations remain revolutions and revelations.

*By the same author*
The Family Reunion

# The Schoolmaster

## Rose Moss

**Ravan Writers Series**

Published by Ravan Press
PO Box 145 Randburg 2125
South Africa

© Rose Moss

All rights reserved. No part of this publication may be reproduced, stored in a retrieval system, or transmitted in any form or by any means, electronic, mechanical, photocopying, recording, or otherwise, without the prior permission of the copyright owners.

First published as *The Terrorist* in Great Britain in 1979 by Harvester Press Ltd
First published in South Africa by Ravan Press 1981
Second edition 1995

ISBN 0 86975 470 X

Cover design: Insight Graphics Pretoria
Cover photograph: Used with the kind permission of *The Star* Johannesburg

Printed by Galvin & Sales, Cape Town

for Duncan

*Solitary*

THE voice that connected him to what he had done faded, but before he lost it he heard the news. The music stopped with pips like those that used to interrupt programmes during the war. The announcer's voice sounded controlled, but David was sure it was frightened too. Boom. His was no distant act of sabotage. They knew that his act meant real danger to them. The voice, hiding its fright, said, 'The area around the station has been cordoned off.' Ha! They were taking notice now. Police and ambulances were being rushed in. Joy made his hands tremble. He gripped the steering wheel more firmly. Nothing was known about the cause of the explosion. Ha, Ha! he shouted to the voice. The police suspected a bomb. I did it. I did it. The city was trickling away behind him. The voice gave way to crackle and static. He switched it off. At last. He had done it. It had been done. Boom. At last the dam of tyranny and pent up rage had been blasted. Water would flow over all the land. When he had phoned *The Star*, he had said, 'This is the beginning.' Now they would all wait for more acts of terror. They would not sleep their fat and insolent sleep. They would know that the misery they poured every day on the suffering and the poor was about to be poured on them. They were being brought to justice. And he was the one who had done it.

The sunny road sped under him. He started to sing a passage from the *Messiah*. 'Thou shalt break them. Thou shalt break them with a rod of iron.' Crash, the cymbals met. Boom. He heard this joyful act. Boom. 'Thou shalt dash them in pieces like a potter's vessel. In pieces. In pieces.' The deep male voice would sing that promise of justice. Joan would be sitting there in the orchestra, ready to bring her cello to voice too, to sing the praise of justice. 'In pieces. In pieces.' He had no truck with Joan's God who never got round to doing the job, all promises. He, David, had started it. Boom. He had made the bomb and planted it. Now it had burst, and now the seed was scattered, flashed in terror over the whole land.

Cumulus clouds were gathering over the green fields of mealies, building high baroque structures in the blue sky. They matched the grandeur he felt. Their majesty calmed him.

He would reach the border by evening. He would meet Philip. He hadn't told Philip. There had been no time for discussion. But Philip would see it had been right. Once they had Francois and Trevor anyhow, it was right. There was no more time for patience.

The villages he passed through looked peaceful, as though the news hadn't touched them yet. It would. A slow dust stirred the stoep of the Grand Hotel, the reflection of his car in the window of a café where there might be a customer drinking a cup of coffee at this hour, or blasting a pinball machine. Everything looked as though nothing had happened. But it had. He had started the end. Boom.

He passed a single African walking it seemed from nowhere to nowhere. The man wore his shoes dangling at his shoulders, the laces tied around his neck. He wanted to stop and confide in him. For your sake . . . So that it would not in future be only whites who could own and ride cars. So that there would be some other lot for them than this barefoot trudging in the heat, the emptiness, breathing in the dust of the white man's car that swept past him. Curbing the pity and joy that welled in him, he drove without stopping. He must get to the Basutoland border by night.

It would probably take some time to arrange the security measures and the manhunt they would set up after him. If he could make it to the border in good time there would be no problem. He would go to the house where Philip would be waiting for him. Once out of South Africa it would be possible to get to England.

The clouds had piled up, and the south he was driving to looked dark. It would rain before he reached the border. The weather matched his exultation and sense of power. Mabotoana had taught him that in Basutoland the blessing given at farewell was *Pula hantle*. Rain well. It was beginning to come down now, the first heavy drops, another beginning, breaking the curse of drought that cursed his country. He was right. He had done the right thing. The others would see it. The rain was blessing. He put his arm out of the window to feel it and spread his wet fingers. His fingers were wet. He cupped his palm and brought it to his face, pressing the water to his forehead and wiped his cheeks. He had forgotten the feel of his skin. He reached out again for more water to pour over his hair until his scalp and face were wet. The rain was coming down so quickly he could not see the road ahead. He slowed. The warm liquid was pouring through the window, but he kept it open. His shirts and pants were clinging to his chest and thighs. He reached outside for more rain and brought it to his lips and tasted it. Lightning flashed ahead. The purified air yielded the smell of veld woken by rain. There was no dust, only air smelling of a power for life. He breathed it, expanding and relaxing.

That first year with Joan the spring rains had come late. The day of the first storm she stopped practising, and put her 'cello aside. They went walking. Rain poured off their hair and faces. When the power of the storm was spent, large globes of water dripped from the trees. They came home and made love, and slept, and ate supper, and went out again into the moist night, and came home again and made love.

They had had only one year of happiness like that. Then the country's bitterness and rage began to divorce them. First, in the middle of summer, there had been the Coalbrook mine disaster. Then, at the end of March, the street of corpses at Sharpeville. Immediately there had followed the state of emergency, and the arrests in the middle of the night. Michael and other friends had been imprisoned, and Pratt had tried to assassinate Verwoerd. Then had come the sequence of laws that brought everything back to where it had been before. Only now with more suffocating power.

Nothing in their lives or in South Africa remained unmarked by Sharpeville. Its weight had fallen into their lives like a rockfall, and crushed them. But now he had thrown that impotence and pity off. He would write to Joan from England. There the misery that had divorced them would lie behind them. He would get a job teaching and would not have to be part of the system of Christian National Education. In England, he would love Joan again and she would love him. He would listen to her playing the 'cello without feeling that music should not be allowed in the world. They would be among friends. Michael was in England already. Philip would be there. Joan would see what a friend Philip had become. And when François and Trevor were released from prison, they would also come to England. They would be together as they had never been, not even at the beginning when he had first loved Joan, and she had been the one who knew that South Africa could not exist without its prisons, when he knew nothing.

A white stroke of lightning glared on a fence just ahead of him. He swerved at the clap. Boom, he answered the thunder. Boom. He closed the window and pressed through the torrent. Even if lightning struck the car, he would be safe. He was invulnerable and potent. He drove through the darkness that the storm made. It would not last long.

The storm eased. Bars of afternoon light caught rain still falling, and pieces of rainbow appeared. It was a day of extraordinary weather.

At the border the sentries took him for a missionary and he went through without trouble. Now there was just the last lap of the journey to the house in Teyateyaneng where Philip was waiting for him. He would arrive there after dark, and the road was running with mud, but he was safe. He had done what had to be done. He was past the border. He would change into dry clothes. Philip would give him some food to eat. If there was time before the message came from Mabotoana's friend, he would sleep. Driving was slow in the wet mud of the twisting road. Until sunset, fragments of rainbow appeared and disappeared among the mountains.

When he arrived and knocked, Philip opened the door but did not move to let him in. He stood in the threshold. David's senses opened to the night. Philip stepped back. His eyes held

David as though to outstare a dangerous animal.

'What do you want?' said Philip. David's stomach tightened.

'You're mad.' David stood still.

'We agreed not to do it.' Philip had moved behind the round table that filled the room. 'You're a mad dog.' A paraffin lamp exaggerated the lights and darks of his neck, the cleft in his chin, and black grapes of hair. His eyes locked on David's.

'Get out, or I'll call the police.'

The police? Philip?

Philip's stare bemused him.

A movement of Philip's hand drew his eyes towards a telephone on the sideboard behind him.

'I'm sorry we ever trusted you.' Philip's hatred pulled his attention back. 'I trusted you.' Philip repeated with a grin of rage, 'I trusted you!'

He found the door and put himself outside the house. Leaning over the car, he felt the engine still warm. He put his cheek against the metal as though it could offer him a human comfort. He heard Philip lock the door of the house. It was dark, he was cold, and his clothes were wet. He climbed into the car.

Whatever had happened to enrage Philip, he must drive away. The police were after him, and if they found him here, they would find Philip too.

The British police would let the South African police in, past the border into Basutoland. Philip and François had never imagined Basutoland could be a haven for long. He would have to go back into South Africa.

There was nowhere else – other roads would be even more hopeless than the muddy track that had taken him here. But he must leave. This place was too dangerous, for both of them. Too bad. He must get himself away from Philip.

When he reached for the car key, he couldn't find it. He had lost hold of everything. Then he found the key in his left pocket and started the car, heading for the border post at Maseru this time, instead of the one at Ladybrand he'd taken this afternoon. It was too soon to go through that one again. They'd recognize him immediately.

In any case, this place was too near Philip. When they

arrested him, it should be far away and they must think he was going somewhere else. He should aim for the coast. A memory of Sweetwaters came to him – the warm valley and cool hills where Joan's family lived, the smooth green lawns and nourishing mists of that green place. He would get out at Maseru, head west for a while until he came to a good road, and then turn back towards Natal and Sweetwaters. They'd get him before he reached the coast and Durban, but that's where he could seem to be heading.

So he would never get to England with Joan after all.

There were no roadsigns, and where the road forked, he chose randomly.

He didn't know where he was. In the sleeping villages general stores carried the names of owners, missions carried the names of saints. They wouldn't tell him where to go.

Towards dawn, he blundered into a border post. He waited for the Basuto police to question him, but they were not suspicious. His years as a schoolteacher must have marked him with respectability.

He drove back to South Africa. He began to recognize place names and headed west. Later he would turn north and east towards Sweetwaters and the coast.

In Thaba Nchu he stopped for petrol. The African attendant took no notice of his number plates. If the manhunt had started, it was none of his business to enforce the white man's law. Brown teeth showed as he accepted David's tip with a wide smile.

'Dankie, baas,' he bobbed, a touch of clowning in his gratitude.

'I'm not your baas.'

'Why should any white man be your baas?'

'Baas?'

'It doesn't matter.' David smiled, winning another vision of the rotted teeth. As he drove away, he waved. It was an unexpected gesture. Diminishing in the rearview mirror, the African stared at the car. Perhaps he would remember David's face when he saw the photograph in the white man's newspaper. Perhaps he would understand that this white man had stood with him, ready to suffer from apartheid. Would he have the sense not to talk about the man he'd served? If he seemed to know David he would be punished. You're a mad dog. He was afraid of himself. He shouldn't have attracted the man's attention. I trusted you, you know. He should turn south soon, get away from Basutoland.

Driving through the spacious veld and wide sky in the sunrise, he slipped into euphoria again. The veld was still wet from yesterday's rain. Birds flew out of the grass at the roadside. When he came to a shallow bridge he stopped the car to wash his face in an eroded spruit. He drank. The water tasted of mud.

He climbed back into the car. The taste of mud in his mouth made him gloomy.

He was going to die. He was tired. He had two nights without sleep behind him. They would get him. His eyes felt sore with strain. When they got him they would hang him. He might as well die. He was a mad dog.

He stopped the car and got out. He took off his jacket and rolled it into a pillow. He picked a stem of grass. It glittered with brown seeds like tiny beetles. Shrivelled filaments and pollen hung on the seeds, relics of an earlier stage of life. He pulled the stem between his teeth. The juice tasted sweet. This would be the last time he would touch the soil alive. He lay down on it, looking at the dumb pebbles and grasses. Damp from yesterday's rain rose into him. The wool of his jacket itched through the lining.

An Afrikaans voice shouted at him to get up. He tried to turn away from it. Something hard prodded him, a foot pushed him over. A brown face loomed in the sky. David scrambled up.

'What's the matter with you? Who are you?'

'I was too tired to drive.'

The farmer's broad and hard face was cut for anger. He carried a rifle.

'Take him to the house,' he ordered a barefoot African standing at a respectful distance behind him. His green eyes jabbed at David. 'Walk. Don't make trouble.'

They came to the house exposed in a barren yard. One rangy rose in the front yard stood for a garden. A woman watched them from the door, and as they drew near, she retreated. The farmer commanded David into a parlour. Standing behind her husband, the wife watched him from a face as blank as a skull.

In the dark and spotless room the floor and furniture glistened. Tight embroidered cushions perched on the sofa's tight leather seat. Two high wooden chairs faced the window.

'Sit.'

David sat on one of them.

'Watch him.' He heard the phone click. The farmer's voice, now intimate and practical, asked for the police.

David twisted to look round the back of his chair. The woman was watching him from the door. The gun in her hands, competently held, made her look like one of those stalwart women of the Great Trek. She would see him dead without wincing. As he would her. He turned back to look into the room.

Facing the window, he could see out into the dry yard and the blank road. Impervious to anything he had done, the barren sight assured him that nothing had changed, nothing had happened. The scraggly rose bush offered two blooms, one blown and fading. The sun stared harshly at them. This was no country for European luxuries. Let the English have their gardens, cool and leafy and consoling, like the one Joan's mother tended. Joan's family pretended that they still lived in England. They played polo and rode out to hunt fox – if they rode far enough, they'd find baboon and hyena instead. How unreal their world had seemed to him, green and easy. Like the world he had been dreaming of yesterday, when he longed to go to England with Joan and love her again and be happy with her. England could not be like the place they imagined in Sweetwaters or the place he'd imagined, able to heal the dusty ferocity that burned and dried him, and divorced him from Joan.

A stream he had seen somewhere was calling him with flickering water. As he tried to reach it, stones grew round him and he could not cross the caked and jagged earth.

Three white constables handcuffed him and hustled him to a pickup van. They didn't ask his name. They didn't speak to him. They slammed the door and locked it. They went back into the house.

The African constables who guarded the van were standing in the dry yard talking solemnly. The darker, a man of about forty-five, had large earlobes pierced and distended where he had once worn earplugs. David was thirsty but he didn't want to ask for water in the language of the oppressor. He didn't know whether the kitchen kaffir word his mother had used for water when she spoke to servants came from Zulu or Sesuto. It was an old bitterness that he had never learned to talk with Africans in their language. But a few weeks ago Mabotoana had started to teach him a few words.

'*Dumela, Ntate.*' Greetings, father. Mabotoana had taught him the salutation of respect. The constable came to the van, staring.

'*Manze, Ntate.*' The African stared as if he didn't understand. 'I'm thirsty.' He mimed drinking, to show what he needed. The African shook his head, smiling, but turned away.

A bench was fixed to one side of his cage. He lay down on it and stared through the wire mesh. The sky blanched as the day grew hotter.

Emptiness closed round him. When he was a boy they had lived in the southern suburbs near the gold mines. The dumps lolled under the sun. He wasn't allowed to play on their dry white sand, so loose and slippery anyone could slide to death there. Even the older dumps where the mine sand was less poisoned and straggly clumps of grass held the recovering earth gave no sure foothold. The dumps were hollow, people said, and could crack. Anyone could fall in.

They had him now. They would hang him.

An electric light burned all the time. There was no day. There was no night. He knew what was up and what was down. Up was the ceiling painted black, where a naked electric filament danced a red illusion in his eyes after he looked at it. Down was the floor, the coir mattress, the grey blanket, the corner where the bucket stood stinking quietly. Around were the four walls painted green. In one, a door and a judas for them to look through. Above the door, a ventilation brick.

Sometimes a warder came with stew and then another with tea and bread and jam. They would not answer when he asked the time or date. Sometimes he saw the hands on a warder's watch, but his sense of duration wandered and he could not tell how long it had been between this ten past three and the last quarter of eight he had seen. A day? Half a day? Which half? Sometimes he felt cold, but it was summer outside. Was it?

He knew where he was. In police headquarters, Marshall Square. He had recognized the area as they drove into Johannesburg through heavy evening traffic. They had passed near the Stock Exchange.

Perhaps shares had fallen yesterday after his act. Tomorrow they would rise again because he had been caught, and would soon be hanged. Everything would go back to what it had been before. As though he had never existed. And South Africa would be safe again.

He didn't care about the shares on the Stock Exchange and whether they had risen or fallen. Apartheid was not maintained or broken by South Africa's prosperity. That was one of the ways he hadn't agreed with Michael's Communist friends. Disagreeing with them, he had found himself agreeing with Philip. Who called him a mad dog.

He was caged now.

As the van came in to the city where the streets were full of secretaries and businessmen going home, he saw picannins selling newspapers. He couldn't read the paper banners they tied to light poles, but as the van turned in to Marshall Square he caught one glimpse. ATION BOM RREST. That must be himself, the station bomber, arrested.

They took him to an office high above the street. The heavy man with the red face questioned him. He told them that he had been trying to get to the coast and they wrote down what he said. Silly flowered curtains too small for the window, allowed him to see the sky becoming deeper until it became black. Van Der Merwe, the man with the red face, drank coffee. David knew that he should be hungry and thirsty but he felt nothing, only that he must concentrate on their questions. He was finding it hard to lie and remember the lies he told, to tell them what they asked without telling them about the others. He tried to lean against the filing cabinet behind him. One of the three warders in the room pushed David away, and the other drew a chalk circle on the ground.

'Stand here, hey,' the tall warder with pinched eyes and black hairs in his ears pushed David into the circle. David stood, and the world grew smaller. It shrank into the room and to the circle where he was standing. It shrank to his head and his head filled everything. Throbbing. The floor was soft and would let him sleep.

So if they had not taken him anywhere else while he was unconscious, he was still in Marshall Square, police headquarters, and outside in the streets near the Stock Exchange and the library there were secretaries wearing flowered dresses, and picannins selling newspapers with his name in them.

His father had said, 'One day the whole world will know your name, David. You'll be a great man, like General Smuts. I never had a chance myself, but you'll do it, David. You'll go down in history.' David was going to be a leader and a discoverer, a new Cecil Rhodes opening up the belly of the dark continent to take out gold and diamonds and empire. That was what a man needed. That was what life was for. Those millions who lived unknown by history lived, in a way, but not like men. Their lives had a dubious, shadowy quality. Who knew them? Who could believe in them? A man wanted something solid. Immortality. David was going to win it and give it to his father.

The night the Nationalists had come into power in the 1948 elections, his father sat up till sunrise listening to the returns come in. He had spread newspapers and charts all over the round dining-room table. Whenever pips interrupted the music his father stopped the game of patience he had been playing, and listened intently to the figures, wrote them down, and exclaimed at them. When the figures surprised him, and there were many surprises that night of the Nationalist victory, he exclaimed aloud, 'Aha!' or 'My God!' or 'The bastards!' David heard him from his room. Long after his mother had gone to bed and there was no one with his father but the sound of the wireless, the election charts, the pack of cards for games of patience, the calculations, the smoke filled air, David still heard his father exclaim aloud at the portentous figures.

Some time during the night David woke and went to the bathroom. His father heard him and, coming out of the dishevelled room, took David by the shoulders and said, 'One day, David, when you're a great man like Smuts, people will sit up all night to hear what happened to you.' He released David with a slight shove, and went back to the harsh light of the dining room. David couldn't fall asleep again. He heard the trains, he heard the milk boys, and later it seemed to him that he had heard lions roaring in the zoo.

He stopped pacing up and down the closed cell. He put his hurt cheek to the wall. Its indifferent surface did not take up his anger. It asked nothing of him. It was itself. It was hard. Definite and supporting. It would be, and let him be.

Waiting for David to make him real by entering history, his father had accommodated. Although he did not make history himself, he participated in the manner of a Greek chorus, reading the newspapers, fighting in the war, and feeling that he knew what was going on. When anything specially important happened, an election or a cricket test match, he stopped strangers in the street to ask the results, and felt united to all those who participated as he did. At such moments, David felt, his father's life was borne on a great surge of meaning, as happy as in the best moments of the war.

After the war, and the elections that handed the country over to the Nationalists who had stayed home and supported Hitler, his father had joined the Torch Commando to protest against the Nationalist's policies. He marched in Torch Commando processions and talked with other men who had fought up north with him, and now felt angry like him.

Later, he had seen how, in the meaningless interstices between elections and important events, his father grew shifty about his own hopelessness, disappointed, not despairing, comfortable, accommodated. Curbed rages showed in his face, and in the unexpected outbursts that alternated with his impotent silences, themselves full of rage.

He pushed the wall away.

'Well, fuck you!' he cursed his father.

In the solitary cell his voice sounded strange to him, echoing in a nimbus of resonances in his own head. He would go mad here. He needed some other person's voice, separate from himself.

He must keep control, or he would become a mad dog. Like his father.

Pinchface came in and found David lying on the mattress. He loomed over David, but David would not move and give him the victory of noticing his presence. Pinchface stooped to set an enamel plate of food on the floor. David noticed the material of his khaki uniform stretched tight and pulling a fold to the corner of the armpit. They shouldn't allow that, he thought. I could get him in a moment like that and overpower him. But then there would be getting out of Marshall Square. Out of Johannesburg. Another trip to Basutoland?

He did not show that he noticed when Pinchface stood straight again, a threat in his eyes, dry as stone. He waited for the sound of the key in the lock before he turned, stood, went to the judas to see whether an eye looked into his, picked up the plate, and started to eat.

The next day (or the same?) a new warder brought food. This man was young, no older than David himself, slender, his brown face lumpy, like a walnut, his eyes curious and disingenuous. He spoke, 'Hullo.'

David stared, as though he had forgotten that he could hear another person speak and could use his own voice to answer.

Then he remembered. 'Hullo.'

'Here's your lunch.'

'Thanks.' He stepped forwards to take it. His eyes met the warder's observing him with inquisitive candour. A human being. Another person. Sanity and relief flooded back. And caution.

'Are you new on this section?'

'I'm not allowed to talk to you.'

'Thanks for saying hullo, then.'

'That's O.K. man.'

The youth went out and locked the door.

He couldn't tell any more when he was dreaming, when awake. He often found himself rehearsing conversations, half remembered, half dream. He asked Mabotoana what he thought of the bomb. Had it been a success? Would it encourage the Africans? Their conversation turned with the relevance of dreams to a pool in the mountains near Rustenberg where a vein of malachite showed under the clear water. But Mabotoana knew nothing of that pool. It was Michael who had known of the place, and they'd all gone swimming there. Michael, Aviva, Edward, Ann. They had camped the weekend in the mountains and climbed and swam, and at night, sitting round the fire, they talked until the stars and the night silenced them. Joan had leaned her head on his shoulder, and space without limit had become part of his mind and memory of her. Ten paces forward. Wall. Ten paces. Wall. This cell was even tighter than the wall they had built for the whole country, to make everyone inside it mad with their own madness. Ever since Joan and her friends had brought him to the point where he read newspapers as they did, and saw what happened in South Africa, he had craved for a voice from outside. He needed to know that there was someone who recognized that this world in South Africa was mad.

In Pretoria his craving for a newspaper from England had become, at times, like physical hunger, and as soon as he got to Johannesburg he would go to a bookshop in Hillbrow that would have the London *Times*, or *Observer*, or *New Statesman*. Bookstores in Pretoria wouldn't keep these papers.

But the government knew about his craving and that they must silence the voice from outside that could keep people sane. At first David had laughed at the new censorship laws as though they were only ridiculous. He laughed at the funny articles Michael wrote for the English newspapers when *Black Beauty* was banned (pornographic), and *The Red and the Black* (political), and Dostoievsky's *Notes from Underground*. But what was the use of laughing? In the end the government had all the power, and recently, when he had bought English newspapers, there had been pages missing or blocks of print cut out. They had locked him in a prison as big as the whole country. They made the world. It obeyed their laws, and it was impossible to tell whether it was they who were crazy, or himself. No one laughed when they put Muller on trial, saying that he taught heresy about the Father and the Son. No one seemed to notice what they did in the prison at Bitterspruit. No one said that the country where these things happened was mad.

No one thought it monstrous that apartheid should always exist, in every act of every life. Only he balked that men should always be called European, and with their own names, and native, without names.

Perhaps there was neither cruelty nor madness. Perhaps white South Africans were really kind. In spite of group areas removals and pass arrests, they pleaded for donations of blankets in winter, and collected money to buy milk for children. They pleaded for exceptions when the law would separate a child from its parents, and a husband from his wife – when these looked like exceptional cases. To the laws as a whole they resigned themselves. They accepted them and voted for them.

After all, no country is perfect.

But he had not been able to resign himself. He was mad, and found it monstrous. He could not resign himself to the prison at Bitterspruit, or the children in the mission hospital at St Thérèse's, where he had gone with Joan and talked with Edward. She had played the 'cello for them.

He must not think of Joan. That way madness lies. Other faces. A gnomish man with pointed nose – he'd seen him on a bus; and a woman wearing a green dress suffering a big goitre in her neck. The dress pulled tight over her back. Like Pinchface's uniform. He couldn't keep his memories coherent.

Long before St Thérèse's there had been another night when Joan had played and he and Edward had listened. That had been the night of the Treason Trial arrests, when he hardly knew Joan and he had been astonished when she had spoken of "those in prison for our sake." Did she think him now in prison for her sake? It wasn't true. He was in prison for the sake of the Africans. But for the whites too, so that they could say the country belonged to them too, at least one white man had given his life for justice. How did it work? He was forgetting that too. Children starving. They had been in the hospital at St Thérèse's. He had had to do something. The bomb. The bomb seemed incoherent. Boom. He couldn't get the connection. The passion of the time before the bomb lurched away, became mental and metallic.

Van der Merwe came to his cell. David stood facing him, feeling the ache that made his right cheek stiff, and stubble pushing through the bruises, ashamed of the untidy mattress on the floor that showed he nearly grovelled when he slept. Van der Merwe's red face looked like the thick faces of people in Pretoria, and blond fur grew between the knuckles of his fingers. Pinchface behind him slouched slightly. It would be a long session.

'How are you, Miller?'
'Bored.'
'You'll soon find things more interesting.'
Fright jumped at David's chest like a large dog. 'Are you letting me out?'
Van der Merwe grinned. 'Not yet, Miller. We need more information.'
'I've made a statement.'
'Yes.' Van der Merwe paused. David knew that game. He waited too.
'Where did you get the dynamite?'
'I stole it.'
'Where?'
'From de Bruyn's quarry near Rustenberg.'
'There's no quarry belonging to a de Bruyn in Rustenberg.'
'It was there last year.'
'Did you keep it a year?'
'No.'
'How long do you think you've been here, Miller?'

So they knew. They were trying to drive him mad. He must mislead them. He still knew the time. His body ached and his beard itched. His body told time. He still had his body. He still had his mind.

'Only a few days.'

Van der Merwe smiled. Without turning, he ordered Pinch-face to bring a chair. When he sat, David noticed how his thick thighs spread.

'Who was in this with you?'

'I worked alone.'

'Where did you get the dynamite?'

'I stole it in Rustenberg.'


The session felt as if it had taken hours. The game couldn't last. They could do anything they liked. They could smash him in pieces. In pieces. They could torture him.

The day they learnt how to handle dynamite, all four of them had worked together, closer than brothers. Philip, François, Trevor, himself. Trevor's sure painter's hands had tamped the detonators with neat authority but Trevor's imagination was less obedient. That night, the police in his dreams banged on his door, swearing. François woke him.

'It's all right, Trevor. It's only a dream.' Afterwards they all lay awake and could hear each other breathing. They were all alone.

Nothing had worked. They did not follow their own plans, and now Trevor and François were in prison. Perhaps in this very building.


The young warder came again, and again seemed willing to give him a few words. So he hadn't dreamed the human warmth of that ingenuous and lively face. Philip had warned them that friendly warders could be a trap. Madness was another trap. David thanked the warder for the soup he brought.

'You needn't thank me. It's just my job.' The boy looked

more fit for a farm than a prison.

'Do you like it?' He didn't answer.

'I bet you used to think you'd do something better with your life.' Brown eyes went away without another word, and David felt, what's the matter with me? He is what he is – it's too late for me to do anything about the way people live in this country. And anyhow, I'm a mad dog.

But the next time brown eyes came, he still seemed friendly, a simple young man slow to take offence. David asked, 'What's your name?'

'Petrus Hugo.' Their eyes met.

'I'm David Miller.'

'Ja.' The smile that went between them had a strangely rueful feeling, as though they might have wanted to be friends, in some other time, in some other country.

Van der Merwe came again with two warders following him. One was Petrus Hugo. But David looked only at the handcuffed figure between them.

They had shaved off Trevor's beard, and the whiter chin accented his sick cast of face. His cheeks seemed eaten away, and the veins on his forehead protruded. His eyes, looking out of slits between heavy curtains of flesh, did not meet David's. David had become a thing, an obstruction one must not walk into.

Neither David nor Trevor spoke, but van der Merwe seemed satisfied. He pushed Trevor round and shoved him toward the door. Trevor's hand dangled behind his back, hanging from metal wrists.

Before he went out, van der Merwe looked at David.

'I'll see you later,' he promised jovially.

For a long time after that visit David found himself rubbing his hands strenuously against his thighs and upper arms, as though he could press some evil out of himself by the action.

Suddenly exhausted, he lay down and pulled the blanket over his head like a shroud. It hid him from the electric light, it itched and smelt of rot and past prisoners, but the smell and thin warmth comforted him as though the cheap material held him close to something alive.

When Sina died his father didn't want David to know what was going on. He wanted David to go on swotting for the matric prelims so that he could do well enough to win a Rhodes scholarship and immortality.

After supper his mother went out to Sina's room at the end of the yard. At the dining-room table, with Latin books in front of him, David could hear Samuel still washing up in the kitchen. His father was sitting at the table smoking, watching David work. His fingers were stained with nicotine.

Not limp, like Trevor's hands. What had van der Merwe learned? Trevor's hands had done everything with such command and pleasure, that day near Hartebeestpoort dam. They had exchanged exultant glances – yes, they were going to do something at last, something that had to be done. But now the police had Trevor before he had been able to do anything, and it looked as though the police had done whatever it was Trevor had dreamed of in that nightmare.

It was a hopeless business they had tried – to bring down the fort built by more than two hundred years of white obstinacy and madness. They had hoped for too much, and now Trevor was smashed, and soon he too would be smashed. In pieces.

Wiry strands of coir from the rough prison mattress pricked his face.

Perhaps they had tortured François too, one of their own, an Afrikaner of the Afrikaners, and therefore the worse traitor. It was hard to breathe, taking in the smell of fear and hopelessness that clung to his coarse blanket like sweat.

Sina's room had a complicated smell. He knew it from the times he'd been there to give her a message of her day off. The smell seemed to come from everything in her room – her starched embroidered pillow cases and big Bible, candles, paraffin lamp, the red polish on the concrete floor, the soap in a saucer on the box next to her bed, her clothes. Perhaps there were witchdoctor medicines too adding their note. The night she was dying, smells of white medicines overcame everything else.

Samuel, finished with the dishes, had come with a message that his mother wanted him in Sina's room.

'I wish your mother wouldn't interrupt when you've got to study,' his father complained. 'You've got a Latin exam tomorrow.' He lit another cigarette.

It had been cold that night, the middle of winter. David had pulled on a jersey before crossing the windy yard. When he opened the door, his mother pulled him in quickly. The sombre room was swathed in the light of the paraffin lamp, and it smelled of Dettol and Friar's Balsam. He saw the sheet Sina had embroidered to cover the soap box under the lamp. He saw the light high as a vault, over the bed. There was a structure made of blankets and sheets and bones. There was a pair of eyes shining, alive, not seeing. An arm hung down the sheet, straight, dark on white. His mother held its hand.

'David, close the door quickly.' He hid the windy night behind the door.

'Phone Dr Leighton, David. I want him to come immediately. I think it's serious.'

Dr Leighton advised Friar's Balsam and warmth.

'No, my mother wants you to come to the house. She says its serious.'

'Tell your mother I don't attend to natives. If she's not satisfied with Friar's Balsam, I'll give her a prescription for something stronger, but she'll have to come here to fetch it and then she'll have to go to the all night pharmacy.'

When he gave the message to his mother, she was furious. 'Is that so? He's breaking his Hippocratic oath. I can have him struck off the rolls for this. Phone Dr Green and ask him to come. Then you can phone Dr Leighton and tell him I'm going to complain to the Medical Association.'

Dr Green didn't make calls at night to new patients.

'Phone Dr Harvey.' Dr Harvey couldn't promise to come at once. He had several other urgent cases. He promised to come in the morning if he was still wanted.

'Go through the Medical section in the phone book. Try nearby doctors first.'

He phoned until he came to a Dr Getz who turned out to be newly qualified, aggressive and nervous. David was surprised and preoccupied, because Dr Getz had not sent them out of the room when he bared Sina's chest. He lifted a breast and put the stethoscope to the ribs. He held the wrist to take the pulse. He pushed her abdomen. He lifted her legs one by one.

The prickling mattress had its own smell. He turned over again, away from it, and stared at the electric light.

He had helped to wrap Sina in blankets and carried her through the lane at the side of the house, to the doctor's Studebaker. He felt clumsy in the dark, bumping against the gate with Sina's docile body on his arm. Dr Getz put her on the back seat. When he drove away the street looked dark and empty.

'Go to bed, David, it's late.'

There was no time left for swotting. It was the first time he had been close to extreme suffering and the first time he had seen a woman's breasts naked. He couldn't make anything of these facts. They seemed closed and dull. The acute sensual impressions told him nothing. There was the windy ferocious night, the naked light on the kitchen steps, the smell of Dettol, the black arm on the white sheet, the answers to Dr Getz's questions that came as distorted breaths, not voice. There were the lolling breasts hanging on each side of the ribs, the warm weight on his arm, the blanket flapping at his ankles. His sexual fantasies had never been pressed by such insistent detail, or so barren. And suffering had never seemed so mechanical.

He could not make anything of the hopeless things that happened, Sina's death and Trevor's hands. That night before his Latin exam he had tried to understand. At school they had read Tennyson's "Crossing the Bar," and he had learned if off by heart as a sure question in the exams – but it seemed to be about an experience of death he was too shallow to imagine. He listened to the wind outside dragging leaves and papers along the street with a thin scraping sound.

In the morning, waking with a headache, he felt annoyed that, of all times, Sina had to be sick before his prelims. Everything was out of order. He didn't have a clean shirt ironed, breakfast was late, and his mother had to give him money to buy something at the tuck shop because there were no sandwiches.

'Phone me when you come out and tell me how it goes,' his mother said. 'Good luck.'

'Good luck, David. You just show them,' his father echoed.

After the exam and its immediate autopsy ('Wasn't the Virgil a stinker!' 'Did you get the unseen?') some of David's friends decided to see a film at the café bioscope, but David, suddenly flourishing a mysterious importance, said he couldn't come. 'I've got to see someone in hospital,' he announced. 'Someone who's dying.' He refused to explain more and enjoyed his special status riding the bus with his friends as far as Hospital Hill, where he climbed off. He bought a large slab of chocolate with the money his mother had given him. He walked down Kotze Street to the Non-European Hospital. Once there, he wasn't quite sure what to do. He didn't even know Sina's surname. He tried the out-patient door. The wooden benches were crowded, but an old native man near the door saw David standing confused. He stood for him. He was wearing a blue jacket so old it bulged where the old man hunched and flopped where he shrank. 'Sit, baasie, sit.'

David felt embarrassed, but before he could decide what to do, a European nurse with the air of a Girl Guide came to them and said, 'Yes. What do you want?' She must have taken David for a very light Coloured.

'Er, I want to visit someone.'

'A relative?'

'Er, no. Our servant girl.'

The nurse's tone changed to a new voice, because now she was speaking to a European. 'When was she admitted?'

After a few more questions she directed David to an information desk in another room. The old native man had retreated unobtrusively and was sitting again.

In the appropriate wing, another European nurse talked to David.

'Visiting hours aren't until one-thirty, but I think we can make an exception,' she smiled. 'Miss Ismail,' she called to a nurse in a small office behind her. 'Take this man to Ward Eighteen. Sina Buthelezi.'

As they walked through the hospital and Ward Eighteen,

David felt an aura of silence and wonder move with him like an enclosing radiance that made him conspicuous. He hardly dared look at the patients in beds and on mattresses on the floor between beds, or the nurses giving injections and helping the sick on bedpans. The nakedness that had opened him to every impression in Sina's room had stripped him of blindness. Now every time he thought 'hospital' it was that hospital. Even the hospital at St Thérèse's, where the children died, had been filled in his mind with these crowded sick. As though he was guilty of them all.

The Indian nurse pointed to Sina sitting on a stoep outside, and left. Several patients were sitting in the sun like dry chrysanthemums abandoned in a winter garden. Some sat in partial shade on the concrete floor against the parapet wall, some, like Sina, in the full sun. She had pulled her knees up, and her thin grey blanket pulled away from her naked feet.

He saw white cracks on her soles, callouses, chapped ankles. Her breathing was quick and shallow; she was panting like a tired dog.

'How are you, Sina?'
She nodded, looking at him.
'Are you comfortable?'
She nodded.
'Is there anything I can bring you?'
She shook her head and looked down at her hands.
He stood. He didn't know what to do. He looked at his shadow on the grey concrete. He took the chocolate out of his blazer pocket and held it out to her, but she shook her head, and he put it back.
'I hope you'll be feeling better soon.'
Again she nodded, not looking at him.
'Well then, I'll be saying goodbye now.'
She waited, saying nothing. He turned to leave, feeling foolish as he found his way through the wards and hospital passages.

Sina had made him a thing.
He still had the afternoon all empty and could easily have

gone to a film with his friends. Instead he went to see Sunset Boulevard by himself.

Everything said no to him.

He turned to face the wall and touch its still, indifferent surface. So that was why seeing Trevor had brought Sina to his mind. With averted eyes.

The night after his visit to the hospital, a policeman had come to the house, and his parents, fearful, signed papers that said that Sina had worked as their servant, and had resided at their address for nine years. His parents did not know where her husband lived, or who would pay for the funeral, but Samuel knew all about it; he knew where her children lived – there were two – living with their grandmother near Bethel, and that Sina had been paying weekly instalments on a plan that guaranteed a good funeral and a coffin with brass handles.

He dropped his hand from the still wall and pulled the blanket tight over his back. Did they still bind the dead in grave cloths, or was it only a loose shroud?


When he woke, his eyes were so caked with dried tears that at first he could not open them. He had been dreaming about Joan. His grief about Trevor and Sina had put out a bulbous, swollen pressure, like old potatoes and onions that sprout in sacks. His dreams had been raw and tender. He pulled the blanket away, and went to the bucket. Hot piss poured out of him.


Van der Merwe had promised to come back. The dark walls of the cell had, ominously, been newly painted and showed no record of the other prisoners who must have been in this room before him, no name or mark on the floor. Their censorship was total. No one could know what they wanted to hide.

If they tortured him it would be better to break quickly, the way Philip had advised. That way you might not tell everything.

He must stop thinking about torture. That business when he had fainted in van der Merwe's office had been nothing to what they could do. They had shocks. They had water. That's how they'd killed Zwane in Bitterspruit. He should let himself think about Joan. He would die soon, and should allow himself to remember her, especially when it had still seemed so awesome and endless and full of light – like that first day, that enormous day, when he first come to know her.

Door, wall, wall, wall, door, wall.

In the library that distant afternoon she had seemed to be a source of light. They had been sitting at the same table, and she had been copying a picture from an art book. He could see her thighs rounding under her cotton dress and her bare arm with the golden hairs on it, the hollow where her thumb curved into her wrist. He could hear the hssh, hssh of her pencil on the sketchpad. When he looked at her hand she saw his glance and said, 'Isn't it wonderful?' She pushed over the glossy art book and he saw the picture she was copying, a Pietà. In the centre of the composition Christ's dead arm hung straight and angular from the severe and naked body, small in its bed of voluminous folds, Mary's robes. Like Sina's arm.

'Yes.' The memory clouded his voice with a sadness he had not recognized on the day itself, when he had stood so awkwardly in front of Sina, and she had refused his chocolate, or the night in her room where everything had seemed so strange to him, Joan looked at him with a question in her eyes, and he added. 'That's what it really looks like, when a person's dead.' Though Sina had been dying, not dead yet, that night in the room where he had seen her arm hanging among voluminous folds. 'Everyone else looks so . . . clothed.'

'I love this Pietà. It's in the Louvre. One day I'm going to go to Europe to see it.'

'Of course.'

After that he couldn't concentrate on Plato. He listened to the sounds made by the starched cotton of her dress when she moved and the sound her hand made when she pulled it across the sheet of paper where she'd started to write notes. Whenever she turned the pages of the art book he heard a firm, muted, glazed crackle. He imagined that he could her breathing, under the masking sounds of steps to the catalogues, chairs scraping, whispers, pages, and the librarians behind the desk talking softly as they stamped books and challenged overdues. He had never heard so many sounds in stillness.

When Joan shifted in her chair as though she'd studied enough, he invited her to coffee.

'Wonderful idea. I'm getting so stale. You walk up the hill, don't you?'

It had seemed astonishing to him that she had noticed who he was and what he did. 'Yes, I take the bus there.'

'Let's go to the Florian.'

So she knew her way around Hillbrow. To David it seemed the area of Johannesburg that seemed to show a world like Europe, a heightened life. Vivid people walked among the small shops and cafés, florists, fruit shops and boutiques in Kotze Street. He heard people passing by speaking Greek and Spanish. Bookshops kept newspapers from England, and copies of *Match* and *du*. Hillbrow seemed like the world where history happened.

In Hillbrow there were women who looked like those who come to places where gold lies underfoot. Perhaps Hillbrow was more brilliant than Europe itself because Europe and Africa met there. Among its shops, and Europeans really from Europe, dandified natives paraded in purple suits and smart felt hats, and Indian women walked with subtle insinuation in their flowing saris, servants shouted conversations to boys on delivery bicycles, and Indian shopkeepers set tins of flowers on the pavement.

The glamour of Hillbrow clung to Joan. She would go to Europe and see her Pietà in the Louvre.

More and more as the day showed her to him, he felt that she belonged in the luminous living world of art and music and history, leading a life higher than his own.

They stood together at the desk to have their books stamped, and went out into the shining afternoon. Joan wanted to leave her books at Women's Residence, so they walked past the bay trees near the swimming pool, and through a rocky short cut where everything was golden, the rocks, the grass, and Joan's hair twining the afternoon sun into its fine wires.

He waited in the formidable lobby until she came back and they went out into the sun again.

As they crossed the street towards the bus stop outside the Lion's Brewery, Joan pointed to the neon sigh, 'Do you know the story they used to tell about that?'

'No.'

'People round Women's Residence used to say that if the lion ever stopped waving his tail, someone at Res would fall pregnant. Last year when they took the sign down, there were wild rumours, and when they put up a new sign, it was this, lioness, cub and all.' They both laughed.

As they passed a thin cluster of students waiting for the bus to town, they both fell silent. The brewery smelled of yeast. Grass and weeds sprouted through cracks in the pavement. The sun twisted into Joan's hair. Everything was clear, everything was important, everything was itself and part of a whole.

'I like to look into the houses,' he told her, 'Don't you? Sometimes I stay late at varsity, and when I walk back the lights are on and I can see women making supper and children sitting round the table.'

'Yes,' she answered, 'It always feels so strange to do that. I feel it when I look into houses, especially from the train. Sometimes in the houses I can see that the family's poor, but it looks so warm and close in the light, and outside it's all dark.'

'Do you travel often by train?'

'Yes, when I come to varsity and go home. My family lives in Natal, in a place called Sweetwaters. Do you know Natal at all? Sweetwaters is near Pietermaritzburg.'

'We used to go to Durban for the winter holidays, and the train stopped at Pietermaritzburg in the early morning.' It had always seemed misty and loud with the clatter of milk cans being loaded on the morning platform, tribute from the rolling and soft countryside. Natal had never seemed like the rest of South Africa to him, and he had understood how it was possible for homesick Englishmen to make green Natal another England, ridiculous, royalist, more English than the

English now could be. In Natal, framed photographs of the Royal Family looked down from the walls in tea rooms, and the Union Jack flew from the flagpoles of private clubs. People talked of 'home' meaning England, even if they had not been born there.

He wondered whether Joan's family was like that.

'I used to feel excited when we stopped there because then we were only two hours from Durban and the sea,' he told Joan.

'Sweetwaters is in the hills round Maritzburg. It's really beautiful.'

'Have you always lived there?'

'My family came to Natal nearly two hundred years ago, almost with the first settlers.'

'Why did they come?'

'You're a history major, aren't you?'

'How do you know?'

'Michael Henderson told me.'

Pleasure swept him with giddy force. She had been talking about him.

'Why do you ask?'

'Some of the stories in my family would amuse you. The Prince Imperial was in love with my great grandmother, and perhaps they'd've married, but he was killed in the Zulu wars. The way my family talks about it, we might as well have really had a Napoleonic marriage.'

Immediately he felt how vain his happiness had been. Joan came from a family deep rooted in history, and in a part of South Africa he hardly knew at all. Compared to hers, his own family was as shallow as a reflection, almost invisible, not quite real. He did not know who his grandparents had been, or who they had loved. His father had come from London thirty-five years ago, a young man dreaming of gold. He had not found it in the city, and for eight years he had tried to farm in the Orange Free State. The Afrikaners had always called him a *rooineck* and an *uitlander*, and after four years of drought and losses he had known he was beaten, and moved back to Johannesburg. Ever since then it had been clerical jobs, in a bank, in an importing business, and in a factory producing plastic raincoats. David felt no tradition in his family, and no stories of tragic or passionate love except the novels his mother read. How could Joan come to know him, a thin phantasmagoric creature with no real past?

That was when he knew that what he wanted more than anything in the world was for her to love him.

There had been nothing to fear then. Joan had not forgotten him. Misery for her. He had married her and left her, and come back to her and left her again. He was a mad dog. He hurt everybody. The green wall said nothing. It examined him. Thinking of Joan only brought him back to himself, in this trap where there was nothing but himself. Sina, Trevor. Philip. They all knew he was a mad dog.

Guarded by Petrus Hugo.

He felt for Petrus Hugo some of the tenderness he had felt that afternoon for the children they passed, playing in the small and dusty yards. The children ran and called to each other. Sun had browned their faces and legs, faded their shirts and bleached their blond hair. Their lives seemed pitiful and innocent. Their fathers must have been farmers driven, like his own, from the harsh land. But his father knew how to live in a city. These had been swept into Johannesburg like waste before a broom, leaves before a wind.

On that day with Joan, walking up the hill from Braamfontein to Hillbrown, Afrikaners were not those who caged him. Not those who would come to hold him and the whole land in a mean grip of angry power.

To the judas, from the judas. They could watch him and exterminate him. Van der Merwe could torture him and he would talk. If they put electrodes on his ears, his penis. . . .

They would send someone to clean up the shit and blood. Perhaps Petrus Hugo.

'Does your family still call itself English?'

She laughed. 'Well, actually, yes. I don't think we know any Afrikaners.'

'My father feels very bitter about the Afrikaners because

they wouldn't fight in the war.'

'Well, of course, they didn't think it was their war. They thought it was ours – to defend the British Empire. Why should they defend that? They want to get out of the Commonwealth and make this country a republic as soon as they can.'

'What will your family do, if they succeed?'

'Oh, we'll just go on pretending that Natal's England, I suppose,' Joan said.

'My father's only bitter when he thinks about Afrikaners in general, really. Nationalists. When it comes to people he knows, he's different. He used to have a farm in the Free State, and then there was a terrible drought so he came back to Jo'burg. Some of his neighbours came too. The Barends couldn't manage after the vultures started to settle on cows that hadn't even died yet. Dad was sorry for the Barends. When they came to Jo'burg he tried to help them out. They couldn't read and didn't know how to catch buses or anything. Dad said they lived a kaffir's life. So he lent them money, even though we didn't have much ourselves, and showed them round a bit.'

'Do you still see them?'

'No. We stopped after Mrs Barend died. We went to their house after the funeral. I must've been about twelve then, and it was awful. It was hot and crowded – they lived in a corrugated iron shack – and there were children and relatives, mostly sitting around, and men going out for a nip of brandy.' He didn't tell Joan about the way they went out to piss against the trunk of a stunted peach tree in the yard.

'Was the coffin there? Did you see the body?'

Perhaps she recognized that her questions surprised him. 'I mean, how did you know when you looked at the Pietà?'

'I haven't really seen anyone dead, but when our native girl was dying I went to see her in hospital.'

'You did? I've never known anyone who'd do that kind of thing. Was she your nanny?'

'No . . . but she'd worked for us for years. I suppose it was funny. The nurse at the hospital seemed surprised.'

'When did your maid die?'

'Last year. The seventeenth of June.'
'You remember the date.'
'Yes.'

Joan's word had startled him. 'Your maid.' It didn't sound the same as 'girl.' He'd thought 'maid' was a word used only in old fashioned poems or the detective stories his mother liked, set in big country houses where there would be a butler and a maid. Not Sina.

Perhaps that was when it had started. Joan had taken something in him that no one else knew about, and showed it to him in her light until he saw too much, until it became unendurable.

Their walk up the hill had brought them to a fenced yard where a large pepper tree grew in a corner. Joan stooped to pick up a twig of berries that had fallen onto the pavement, and was rubbing their pink, papery skins off absent mindedly, as she asked, 'Is this the hospital you came to?'

Perhaps because he had never spoken to anyone about Sina, perhaps because the entrance he had used had been from another street, he had never connected that visit to this daily walk to and from the university, or to the natives he always saw sitting there on the pavement, leaning their backs against the wall – that afternoon, an old man whose crushed and angular face looked like a ball of crumpled newspaper, two fat women wearing black shawls tightly knotted over their breasts, talking and laughing, and a young woman, her face like a classical statue's, smooth and oval, nursing her baby. He saw the exposed breast, and the steady movement of the child's mouth. He saw that the woman looked at Joan and Joan at her, as though there was something they both knew. He saw everything that day.

But he still did not see what he saw.

Opposite the hospital was the Fort. He had not even glanced at it. He did not see the prison that straddled the city and looked down at it, like van der Merwe standing with his legs apart, looking down at the man on the floor. Every day he walked past the Fort opposite the Non-European Hospital as though his eyes were closed and he could see nothing but the official city, Johannesburg, the shops and offices of the city in the valley to the south, and the mine dumps beyond them, those pale hills where he had not been allowed to play as a child; and to the north, under the Fort's protecting eye, the northern suburbs, their gardens, their peace and luxury. All sunned under the golden evil eye of the Fort, the prison set on a hill, on the very crest of the Ridge of White Waters, the gold-bearing Witwatersrand. That blind day he had not known yet that all South Africa was a prison.

Though he was coming to see. That very day he would meet Philip, and soon he would hear Joan count Philip among 'those in prison for our sake,' and hear her say the Fort was among the worst of prisons. Did she know about this black and green cell in Marshall Square where the electric light never slept?

Petrus Hugo came and did not speak to him. He handed David an enamel plate of soup and a brick of brown bread. The door locked behind him.

David sat on the mattress. He was hungry and the soup tasted good. He still believed that they would do what he dared not think of, but it was easier now to feel human, remembering that day with Joan when time had seemed endless, sweet and clear.

When they had reached Hillbrow they found that a change of mood had dimmed the streets. Pedestrians clotted intersections where newspaper boys were selling the *Star*. An old man sitting at a tram stop stooped over a paper in his lap, muttering. A woman swinging her handbag impatiently had the bereft look of a child playing alone in a time of grief.

'Something's happened,' Joan said.

'I'll get a paper.'

David attached himself to the crowd pressing around a picannin who was sorting out change and handing out newspapers with stiff, hurried movements. SOVIET TROOPS MASSACRE HUNGARIANS. TANKS IN BUDAPEST.

Handing the paper to Joan he wondered why Kotze Street seemed so shaken by an event that seemed no worse than the usual thing in the papers. Because his father listened to the news and talked about things at table, he had been dimly aware that there was trouble in Poland and the Middle East, perhaps in Hungary too. But how did that become a calamity here, so many thousands of miles away?

"I can't believe it,' Joan said, shocked like other readers.

'Come.' He took her elbow and led her to the Florian.

On a balcony overlooking Twist Street she read, turning to see whether he was ready for the next page, pushing the paper towards him so that he could see the pictures, a street full of corpses like dead leaves scattered. At tables around them, others were reading, some talking to each other in foreign languages. Below, in the street, secretaries and shoppers were climbing off the crowded trams. They too would know soon about the tanks in Budapest. He felt that now he was living a moment of history.

'They're so ruthless. How can they be so ruthless?' Joan's mouth made a straight line as though she were putting on ruthlessness to feel what it was. She noticed that he was looking at her and smiled. Her eyes changed from a deep grey-green, and seemed to be full of light.

'I'm sorry to be such bad company.'

'No. You're not bad company at all.' He looked away, confused, at the afternoon crowds below, then back at her. Their eyes met.

Outside, they turned to each other uncertainly.

'If you're going somewhere near, I'll walk with you,' he offered.

'A friend's invited me to supper. We sometimes play chamber music together. She's a violinist.' Joan laughed in a short, pained burst. 'She's Hungarian.'

'Oh, you're upset for her.'

'Come with me. I'm sure she won't mind.'

Hours ago, in another century, before he was alive, he had opened a book next to her in the library. Fire ran from him to her, from her to him, through their joined hands.

Evening was drawing in. Silver watches and engagement rings glittered in the windows of jewellery shops. Glows of neon led them through diffuse volumes of colour. Here and there a line of orange on the chrome of a car showed that the sun was still about. They came to the end of Kotze Street. Hillbrow opened over Nugget Hill to a view of dim houses in the valley, warehouses and factories in Troy street, the city's office buildings, and pale mine dumps swimming like whales towards the horizon.

The earth shook, and they felt the tremor of a rockfall in one of the mines.

'That must've been a heavy one,' she said.

At the top of Nugget Hill an Indian flower seller was still transacting the small exchanges that transmuted her perishable goods into rent and food. A boy, about eight, was preparing to end the day's work, packing flowers from different jam tins together.

'Abdool,' the woman called in a high, singing voice. 'Show the baas the flowers.' David scanned the bright display, and shied away from roses. Joan tucked the twig of grey mimosa leaves and feathery orbs of pollen into the neck of her dress, smiling.

Another rockfall shook the hill.


Eugenie lived in an old block of flats in Abel Road, where the trams turned in from Kotze Street.

'It's a relief to share this time with friends. I've been longing to see you, Joan. I'll give you something to drink, and you'll both tell me what you think of the news. I feel so cut off from others who understand what this means to me.'

He could see that she was watching to see who he was, and how he was connected to Joan. He was looking at the walls and bookcases encrusted with pictures and ornaments, the antique tables and mirrors, and plants in handpainted pots. And at Eugenie. She had shaved her eyebrows and, over the arch of bone where they would have grown, but with a slightly different curve, she had pencilled dark brown lines. She had marked the shape of a mouth with lipstick over her thin lips. She looked both bald and painted. Seeing himself observed by her intelligent brown eyes, David felt that her European, experienced style was something he had never known until this afternoon and the walk with Joan. Everything he had seen with her belonged to a heightened life, the world of art and music and history.

'Now everyone will see who these Russians are! They are barbarians. Brutes, peasants! Mongols! I'm even glad they've done this, because now everyone will know.'

Eugenie gave them sherry and switched on the wireless. From Europe came the slow chimes of Big Ben striking four o'clock in England, sixteen hours Greenwich mean time. Then the neutral voice of a British announcer said that Russian troops had entered Budapest and were patrolling the streets. Heavy fighting continued, and refugees were streaming to the border. An emergency meeting of the United Nations would convene that evening. Student uprisings in Poland were meeting with strong official resistance. The American ambassador had voiced a protest. Two men had been killed on the border between Jordan and Israel. Prime Minister Eden had summoned the cabinet.

Eugenie switched the wireless off.

'It's hateful to be able to do nothing. And to be so far away. I find it degrading, like being raped.'

David wondered how she knew what that was like.

'The people there can't do anything either.'

'I know. I know. But they're there, and share my country's suffering. It's hideous to be an exile at a time like this.'

Joan walked over to Eugenie and kissed her cheek. Then she sat on the floor near Eugenie's chair, where she could hold her hand. She looked at David. How complicated it was to be alive, to feel sympathy with Eugenie's sadness, and this enormous happiness growing between himself and Joan.

After a while he felt it must be time to leave, but Eugenie insisted that he stay to supper. They all went into the kitchen, and David felt again how Eugenie was unlike anyone he had ever met. His mother never allowed guests into the kitchen, and here he was, helping to slice beans and wash tomatoes.

'In Budapest they must be running out of food now. It always happens.'

She knew about history, he thought.

'Do you still have family there?' Joan asked.

When Mabotoana was arrested, Trevor went to visit his wife. Keep away, Francois warned. It won't do her any good when they see that white people visit her. And when Didi Patel was arrested, Munira had been anxious that David should not be seen coming in a taxi.

If anyone knew that he'd been arrested, someone would come to visit Joan, and the police would be watching to see who it was. Someone would have come to share the shock with her, to eat with her. And the police would be watching every move.

During the meal Eugenie went to the next room to turn the news on again. They did not eat as the British voice recited what they had already heard. Then there was a South Africa newscast. Students in Stellenbosch were volunteering to go to Vienna, where refugee camps were being established. Prime Minister Malan had issued a statement saying that Hungarian refugees would be welcome in South Africa. A European worker, Mr Karl du Plessis, had been killed by a rockfall in the City Deep mine. Three natives were killed in the same accident.

Eugenie went to turn the wireless off.

Before they left, there was a moment when Joan had gone to the bathroom and David was alone with Eugenie in the kitchen.

'Joan's a very unusual person,' she said to him.

'Yes, I think she is.'

'Good. I'm glad you see it. I care for her very deeply.'

Then Eugenie released him from the grip with which her eyes commanded him.

Joan had arranged to attend a meeting that evening. As they walked down the stairs from Eugenie's flat he took her hand again. And in the almost empty tram that rattled loudly and held them in a long capsule of light he felt the sweetness of this long day.

He had been feeling the call of other people's lives, of all he had seen that afternoon, the woman feeding her baby on the pavement outside the Non-European Hospital, the old man sleeping with his back against the wall like Sina, Ward Eighteen, the memory of that hospital, and of the Barends coming into the city so ignorant, Eugenie connected to those lumps lying in the streets of Budapest. He had woken up. He had started to see.

All he had started to see had turned into the anger that had fouled his marriage, and twisted his bitterness against Joan.

He threw the blanket aside and recognized what he had not noticed in his insistent and torrential dreams about her. He was still angry. His mind turned on her because she could live as though she did not see what she had taught him to see. When he came out of the City Hall after her concerts, he tripped over beggars sitting on the steps. 'Penny baas. Have pity baas.' Picannins danced on the pavement. "Honger, baas, honger.' In the lobby the white audience, dressed in pink satin and dark suits weighed the musicianship of the performers. Why didn't she hear, his musician wife?

He paced the green frightful cell, clenching and unclenching his fists. He was completely alone. To Trevor he didn't exist. To Philip he was a mad dog. To Joan . . .? He stared into the naked light until the jagged filament danced in his eyes leaving a red mark in his retina and his mind. No one knew what he saw.

Before the key turned, he heard the noise they made and scrambled up. Van der Merwe waited for one of the two new warders to bring him a chair.

'How are you today?'

'Just fine!'

'Good.' He looked up at David trustfully. 'Your friend has given us a complete statement.'

They tortured him, David reminded himself. And anyhow, that ploy was an old one, that about the friend's confession.

'We'd just like to clear up a few points.' Again each waited for the other to speak, like an outstaring game. When van der

Merwe spoke first David thought, he can afford to.
'Where did you get the dynamite?'
'I stole it from a farm in the Orange Free State.'
'Last time you said you bought it in Rustenberg.'
'Who sells dynamite? I must have been mad.'
'That's what you said.'
'Did I? I can't remember.'
'Where did you really get it?'
'In the Free State, like I told you.' David marvelled at his cheeky tone. He sounded like one of his own pupils caught cheating. Van der Merwe's hand caught his eye. It was stroking the thick thigh with an unobtrusive slow gesture. Van der Merwe would feel anger like tumescence. His release must be terrible.
'What was the name of the farm?'
'Totsiens. It's near Kroonstad.'
'What's your friend's name?'
'Christopher Columbus.'
The hands stopped their obscure caress. 'Don't be funny.'
'We all had code names. I don't know any other.'
The fingers resumed stroking. 'What's your code name?'
'Vasco da Gama.'
'And the others?'
'We had only one name each.' David could smell his own fear.
'I mean the others in your group.'
'There were only two of us.'
'You're lying Miller, and you'll be sorry.' Light shone on the glossy bulges in van der Merwe's forehead.

He felt cold again. Why weren't they torturing him? He paced the gloomy cell, nauseous as though he'd been handling dynamite and had picked up that familiar chemical headache. He could smell himself. Sweat and fear. They'd have to let him shower some time. He rubbed the lengthening stubble on his cheek, tender where the skin had broken.

Exercise time. He worked through the pushups he had set himself. Then he sat on the mattress looking at his feet. He started to put on his socks. They were about to perish. He took them off and made a ball of them and stuffed it between the mattress and the wall, feeling a spiteful triumph that he could hide something from them. Unless they were watching him through the judas.

Monica's house was large and full of glass, light, dazzling and threatening. Monica greeted them at the door and gestured them towards the living room. He felt swallowed by the crowded luxury, and all the people Joan knew, sitting on the floor in groups, and on chairs near the walls. He recognized some of the crowd from university. He had always found their gestures and argot as foreign as the languages that threaded Kotze Street. Why was Joan part of this crowd? Again he felt himself thinner than a reflection wavering on the skin of water.

Michael had saved a place, and immediately asked Joan whether she had come with Aviva.

'She's coming with Philip.'

'We thought you were going along, to help.'

'How could I help? I mean, if they notice, it's not going to make it any better if I'm in on it.' Their secret conversation left him out.

'I dunno. They could think he's fucking you instead.'

David saw that Michael was amused at the reaction he was getting from David.

'I'm sure Aviva's parents have no idea she's having an affair.'

'Even if she's just friends with a Coloured.' Michael was still watching David, 'Do they want their daughter to . . .? That's what it always leads to, you know.' Looking for another reaction from him.

'Oh, shut up Michael. Philip's been passing for years. They'll never guess. Anyhow, I didn't know anything about it. She's silly to have him to dinner if she doesn't want trouble. They're going to ask questions. I mean parents always do.'

'We told her.'

'Well don't gloat, Michael. It's complicated enough, isn't it.'

Edward changed the subject for her. 'Did you come by car?'

'No. Did you?'

'Yes. I'll take you home.'

David burned. He hadn't bothered to wonder whether Joan had a boyfriend. Far less a lover. Edward might be her lover. She hadn't spoken as though to have an affair was itself momentous or disgraceful. It might be worse. He had never thought of a friend or anyone he knew who would really be friends with a Coloured. Suddenly, he felt overwhelmed by the presence of people he had never paused to think of. He had heard that there were white liberals who associated with Coloureds and natives, but these people would never have anything to do with him. Least of all with what he was feeling for Joan.

A large picture on the wall opposite him accused him. It showed the figure of a man bent under a huge basket of pink flowers. He felt accused for the Indian flower seller at the top of Nugget Hill, and her son Abdool. Joan had pinned the mimosa he'd bought under the collar of her dress. It was beginning to shrivel and brown.

Aviva came, her cheeks flushed. Michael stood and waved. There were more people now, and waves of contrary impulse sent looser members from one group to another. Aviva looked over the crowd, holding her chin high. A little pad of fat at her neck belied her slim waist and hips. She came towards them picking her way over legs, and slowing to greet friends. The man following her, his sallow face composed and private; looked thoughtful and distinguished, no more Coloured than Michael with his olive skin and thick black curls.

'Hullo' Michael greeted them, 'How did it go?'

'What? Oh my parents? Goodness, I don't know what you're making such a fuss about. Of course it was all right, wasn't it Philip?'

'It was all right.' Aviva's voice had betrayed pleasure in its coolness. Philip's was grim.

Aviva turned to David, 'Hullo.' Her voice was set at an artificially high pitch, 'I didn't know you were interested in the theatre.'

Again David realised that they had talked about him.

Before he needed to answer, the speaker arrived, but he heard Edward say to Aviva, 'Don't bitch, Viv. He came with Joan.'

Harry's face had the soft, used quality David later came to associate with actors, writers, painters, pervasively wrinkled with deep and quavering lines. His talk was about how everything in South Africa's cultural life was distorted by concern about race.

'Last year I wanted to stage a production of *Othello* with Ronald Mbatha in the lead. We were three weeks into production when the Special Branch honoured us by attending a rehearsal.' Someone on the floor giggled at Harry's sarcasm. 'I would have been delighted to believe that there had been a change of heart and a new appreciation of the arts among these gentlemen. But alas, it was no such thing. Apparently we have a statute that forbids actors of different races to appear on the stage at the same time. I'm sure everyone here appreciates the importance of laws like these to our way of life. I could, of course, produce *Othello* without contravening the Immorality Act or any other such law. But that would be rather missing the point of the play, don't you think?' Harry developed his argument to its conclusion. 'Unless thought and art in this country allies itself with the struggle of the black masses, it becomes an instrument of cultural, and eventually of political oppression. There is no way for an artist, or anyone else, to stand aside from the Africans' struggle for freedom.'

Again David felt coerced and accused. He recognized the jargon Harry was using, that stuff about the struggle of the black masses. David associated it with simple minded explanations of history as an effect of class warfare, or of the relation of the workers to the means of production. It all seemed terribly false, in a way that denied things for which he had no words, but things that were part of him and, although he couldn't understand or explain, more important than anything else. The look of Joan's hair when the sun had caught it, the way muscles of water going down the plughole twisted like a sheet Sina would hang up to dry, and pigeons descending in an evening sky came in a spiral that twisted from light to dark. What did Joan have to do with these people? Could her sense of life be like their's? Where was there a place in this schema and this jargon for her to play the cello with her friend Eugenie? With the callous blindness of the oppressors? And her amused stories about the Prince Imperial's beloved? With the oppressors.

He glanced at her, sitting straight and with her hands in her lap. He would learn that it was part of her training as 'cellist to sit like that. Immediately, looking at her, he felt again the sure independence of her spirit. She was not the dupe of this language. She was alive, responding, golden and quietly centred on some inner peace that seemed to make her life more full and peaceful than this petty moil of envious political bickering her friends enjoyed.

How simple it had seemed to him then to divorce her from their errors. And to hear everything they said as a lie. Now he had become a mad dog and also believed that nothing in South Africa remained untouched by the bitterness of race, and that Joan's music needed a wall of callous indifference around it.

The bucket in the corner stank. He still felt his old anger at the Congress line, the righteousness of their tone and the division he had felt them make between all whites who were oppressors, and all blacks who were the noble people struggling for freedom. As though he still wanted a world impossibly true.

In the end he had turned to Michael for help, and discovered that very few of them really believed the jargon they used. But that night he had felt all alone in his aloof contempt for their language, and disdainful when a man he would come to know as Gerald, thanked Harry saying, 'You are one artist who will always inspire us with your integrity.'

After the talk there were questions. A long legged man sitting on the floor began. 'Harry, I think we're all pretty concerned about today's news. I wonder what you think about it.'

Harry frowned, 'Well Simon, I came to talk about the theatre, and I'd really rather keep to that.'

But Simon, hugging his knees, persisted. 'You've just been saying that art can't ignore politics.'

'Yes, of course, but what can we get out of discussing today's news here?' Harry tapped the arm of his chair impatiently. 'I don't know any more than you do, and from the same sources,' he gave an empty stage laugh. 'We know how reliable the BBC and the SABC are.' Another laugh. 'All we can be sure of is that we're hearing lies.'

'You mean you don't think Russian tanks entered Budapest today?'

'No. Of course I believe the pictures in the papers and all that. What I mean,' Harry's voice became very patient, 'Is that we don't know what they mean, and we're in no position to find out until we have more information.'

Another voice challenged Harry. 'You mean you're prepared to justify the invasion when you know what the party line is.'

Harry raised an eyebrow. 'If you care to misrepresent my position like that, you may. However, it cannot lead to fruitful discussion.' He stubbed out a cigarette. David looked at the others. He could not see what they thought of this exchange.

Gerald took up the argument. 'I think, Harry, once the topic's been raised, we have to talk about today's news. But I want to say that I agree with Harry.' His voice was flat and blunt. 'We don't know what's going on, yet. We can't believe all the propaganda we're going to hear now. It's all going to be brave little Hungary against big bad Russia. We won't hear a word about tanks in the streets of Latin America, or the peaceful intentions of the United States. Let's remember the Rosenbergs when we hear all these tears about Hungary.' David didn't know who the Rosenbergs were, but he felt that he got the gist of Gerald's argument.

As the discussion turned to further orthodoxies and personalities, and politics dissolved into names, Beria, Nagy, Gomulka, Khruschev, he couldn't understand why Joan had come to this meeting. He looked for her eyes, and saw Aviva's assessing him. Then he saw Joan, and there was nothing but the connection between them.

When their glance broke, he remembered Aviva, but now she was watching Philip who had joined the discussion.

'This evening's meeting has been fascinating.' David wondered where Philip had learned to speak with such an English voice and intonation. Had he passed for white at a school like St John's? No wonder he'd been able to fool Aviva's parents. 'We came here to hear about the theatre, didn't we. But only

Harry has spoken about it. We are incensed about something far more important – twenty white people were killed in Budapest today. Or was it twenty-five? Now let's see. How many Africans were killed in South Africa today? There were three in the City Deep rockfall, a few stabbed in Alexandra Township, a few children with kwashiokor. I'm sure we could find twenty-five Africans dead today because of our own political situation. But what we're worked up about is Hungary. Why?'

Philip's speech chilled the meeting, but Gerald broke the silence to say, 'Don't be ridiculous, Philip. You know that we're all terribly concerned about the things you've been talking about, but millions of people die all the time and we don't think it politically significant. You know that Hungary is significant. England and America are going to use it as an hysterical diversion from the real problem.'

'Like us?'

'I don't know what you're trying to say, Philip.'

'Let me clarify. First, the invasion of Hungary is atrocious – whatever the party line turns out to be. Second, it's the same atrocity we see here. The only terms that make it different are ideology. The ideological struggle of the United States and Russia is irrelevant to this country, and if we won't consider anything significant except in their terms, we'll never achieve a revolution in this country. Never. Hungary is here, and has been here for hundreds of years, ever since the first settler party went out to hunt Hottentots.'

Gerald answered plaintively, 'I cannot believe, Philip, that you are so completely naive.'

It had seemed too silly to take seriously. Philip was right, they were pretending to be students in Europe. Aviva seemed to enjoy this game as much as her game with Philip and her parents. When the question time gave way to tea, she asked David, 'Were you interested?'

'Some of the time.'

'You're pretty cryptic.' But then she continued in a new tone, 'I like being cryptic.'

Joan joined them.

'Oh, I don't know.' He edged towards the table and put his

cup down so that it wouldn't betray him.

'Ah,' Aviva's intonation was full of meaning. 'Don't you enjoy secrets?' He looked into her grey eyes, feeling suspicion in her question.

'I've never been to a meeting like this.'

'Ah.'

She turned away abruptly. Philip was standing near them. Without acknowledging him, Aviva walked away into the other room. Joan smiled at Philip, and then followed Aviva. David felt confused, but he couldn't very well leave Philip as though his presence had sent everyone off, so he said 'I think you're right about Hungary.'

But Philip was irritable. Later, Joan would tell David about the quarrel with Aviva.

'Yes? Why?' His tone sneered.

'It doesn't make sense to judge everything in South Africa in terms of foreign ideologies.'

'Hmm.' Then Philip asked abruptly. 'Who are you?'

'My name's David Miller.'

'That's not what I asked.'

'I don't know what you mean.'

'Tell me what you do, then.'

'I'm a student at Wits.'

'What do you study?'

'I'm doing a B.A.'

'Oh, you don't really study; you're getting a degree.'

Now David felt angry. 'Actually I study history, and I think that stuff about Hottentot hunts is just another kind of propaganda.'

'Of course. I'd hardly expect you to think otherwise. However, the records are there. Do some research some time.'

'What do you do?' David asked.

'I live.'

'Other people do too.'

'It takes them less effort.'

'You can't really know that.'

'I do know, actually.' Philip said. 'Rather well. Ever read population statistics? An invaluable historical source. You'll see who dies. People like me. Non-Europeans.'

47

'You mean Hottentot hunts?'

'I mean you white people live off my blood.'

'You sound as if you're accusing me.'

'Yes, I mean that. I'm glad you understand me.'

'I don't see why you're talking to me this way. What d'you expect me to do?'

'Oh hell man. Do what you like. I don't trust white people.'

David surprised himself by his answer. 'Neither do I.' But he knew, having said it, that he meant it.

Philip looked at him, perhaps surprised too. What had he meant by it? It was the time before he knew anything. But he had said it, in an inexplicable prescience about what he would come to feel later. Philip had remembered that remark and repeated it to François. Perhaps that was why they had trusted his seriousness. Perhaps, without it, Philip would never have come to call him mad dog, never said, I'm sorry I ever met you.

Philip hated him now. Later there would be a reason. They would torture him and he would tell them whatever they wanted to know. About Philip. About François. Anyone. Van der Merwe might do it, with the blond furred hands that had stroked his thighs. One touch of the electrodes. You shit and pissed. Then perhaps they'd let him wash. They wouldn't leave him stinking, his beard growing out of him like the beard of a corpse. He might as well be dead, all alone like this. Waiting to be tortured. These cells were made to make men mad.

He faced the wall and started to beat his head against it. Rhythmically. Beat, one, two, beat, one, two. Reassuring pain filled his skull.

He woke, appalled to remember how he had put himself to sleep like a lunatic. His forehead felt tender to his touch.

Crouching over the bucket, not allowing his flesh to touch the crusted rim, he could not release the lump that clogged him. Was it another day? The soup plate on the floor and the hunk of bread in it stared at him like a dirty eye. It was horrible to live like this, without any connection to the world outside.

He pulled his pants up and stood. They must bring it to an end. He could not go on like this forever. If only something in the cell could connect him to another person. There must have been other prisoners before him, but the walls had been newly painted and he could find no mark on the floor or the black glaring ceiling. He pulled his mattress away hoping for a mark underneath it. The socks he had hidden rolled out, and the sight cheered him. He hid them again.

Thinking about Joan had become like a duty now, his attachment to sanity.

After his curious conversation with Philip, he had seen her in the next room, and gone to speak to her. First they stood silently next to each other. Then she asked. 'What did you think of the meeting.'

'I didn't know you were a political person.'

'I'm not. Musicians are terrible that way, completely apolitical. But some of my friends feel involved.'

'I notice. Aviva's been practically interrogating me.'

'Oh, Aviva's impossible, but it doesn't mean anything. She's had a row with Philip, and they're both rather upset and nasty. I'll tell you about it some other time.'

Their eyes met on the promise.

In Edward's car, taking Philip home, his thigh burned against hers. Light from the street and darkness flowed by as vacantly as when he was little and fell asleep at the back of the car, drifting, sticks under a bridge, waves, here, near, far, forward, here, near.

He had never before been to Fordsburg, where Philip lived. Small shops and crowded old buildings shone in a yellow light. Groups of Coloureds and Indians talked in the street and glaring cafés. Lights showed behind cheap print curtains. Fordsburg was as alive as Hillbrow at this late hour, though the rest of the city was dark and sleeping. Philip left them, and Aviva, in the front seat, put her head on Edward's shoulder. 'Christ, I'm tired.' David again jerked at the little volt of shock, as when Eugenie said rape.

At Women's Residence he got out with Joan and watched

the car drive up the road they'd walked that afternoon. He took her hand and lead her to the amphitheatre near the swimming pool. They looked at the water glancing here and there with reflections of electric light. She was sitting on his jacket and he held his arm around her. They sat so still the thin blur of city noise reached them. It was coming from Fordsburg and Hillbrow and the railway. He felt that he was alive and knew every blade of lawn and every stone in the darkness, the bay trees they sat under and the wild grass behind them, the koppie path to Women's Residence and the straight path to the Arts Buildings; the library where they had worked, Kotze Street, and Nugget Hill. As if flying, he surveyed the dumps beyond the city, the veld beyond the dumps, the plateau, the escarpment, the coastal plain, the shore, the sea, Tristan da Cunha on the way to the Pole, the earth turning back, the peninsulas of New Zealand and Tierra del Fuego, the antipodes, the earth, the air, the burning core, the sun in the earth's belly. He held Joan and knew her to be another close and secret universe.

He kissed her and she kissed him. He stroked her hand, wondering at its power to make music, to write, to be Joan. His hands found her breasts. His body was burning and his mind was pouring with joy.

As he walked home afterwards, he knew that the joy he had felt would change his life. Another moment of prescience had warned him how his parents would feel if he felt serious about a girl. He would not give her up, and he would not tell them anything about her. He was no longer the child he had been when he read *The Wonders of Science*.

That book had changed everything he saw when he was a child. He knew what things were made of. Everything was made of atoms, too small to see, but the human mind could know more than it could see. There was light that could take photographs of things no one could see. And no one could see that light itself. There were sounds only dogs could hear, but humans could whistle to them at those high pitches. There were so many things in the world.

He had taken *The Wonders of Science* out of the library as one of the two books he was supposed to read every week to increase his vocabulary and prepare him to be a Rhodes scholar and a great man like Smuts. The pictures showed galaxies and whirlpools, dust storms, and water running out of the bath. One law made all their spirals. The planetary system echoed the structure of atoms. There was one law.

He had tried to feel atoms in his own hands and searched for them in the wood of the polished dining room table. He expected a feeling of fine granules, but the veneer remained smooth. It was hard to believe the book.

He read that all the colours of the rainbow were in plain white light, that solid colours mixed together made black. He did the experiments the book suggested, and looked into a drop of rain where the world was held upside down, as explained in the chapter. 'How We See' and he believed the book.

He began to feel that everything had its own being and inner secret, and this knowledge felt like an image of something he knew about his own self. Even then he must have felt that his parents did not know, could not know, all that was in him. As early as that? Yes. He must have been about eight.

At that time he used to suck nigger balls bought after school. After every house he walked past he took the nigger ball out of his mouth to see what colour it was now. It would change from the black licorice outside to pink, green, yellow, orange, until nothing was left but a greyish dot at the centre and a sugar taste in his mouth. He used to wonder about the insides of the houses too. Mr Schillermacher's had a sign near the gate, 'Music Lessons.' Scales and exercises flowed over the neglected roses and khakiweed. Ninety-six had a low yellow brick wall, a yellow dry lawn, a facade of yellow brick. Ninety-four was also yellow brick, but blurred by tides of flowering trees and shrubs. At its wire fence he stopped to look at a rose. Red buds swelled out of their green clasps, opening and curling backwards. *The Wonders of Science* said that the same basic patterns reappeared constantly in nature and now David saw, starting out of the rose as if underlined by a diagram, a spiral. He didn't need a lens to see it. It was plain. The pattern of galaxies and snail shells. He followed the line furling in towards the minuteness of atoms, reaching out towards the

Milky Way. It was more thrilling than the infinity of the baking powder box on the baking powder box on the baking powder box.

He pulled the rose towards him to examine it more closely and found that it was the centre of sweetness in the air, the warm smell he had not specifically noticed until he pulled the flower near. He touched a petal. He turned it down and saw the base, thick and pale, and the veins that netted from it, becoming finer and more invisible until they disappeared at the curling edge. He saw how that network of veins dividing gave the petal its shape. The whole world could be clear to the human mind, and lovely to the senses. He felt that the world was full of wonders and his mind was blazing with intellectual joy.

Joan and the rose came together in his mind. Each was a universe formed by its own life and being, expressing itself in its own history. History. Marc Bloch had found history in the shapes of fields because nothing could remain entirely unmarked by what had happened to it, not even this cell. He turned to face the wall. He touched it. Carefully, like a blind man. Nothing. He moved a few steps to the right. He felt. The featrues of the wall touched his fingers. A bump. It was only a knot in the paint. He moved on, searching, the way he had tried to feel atoms after reading *The Wonders of Science*.

While he was making a third circuit, lower yet, he heard a noise at the door. He jumped away from the wall and pretended he'd been pacing. It was Petrus Hugo again, bringing a plate of porridge, and a mug of tea covered with a thick slice of brown bread and jam. He put the food on the floor. 'Thank you.' But Petrus did not talk to him any more. He went out, locking the door. David took the plate quickly, standing up, and ate the mielie meal hurriedly, as though he had no time, he must get on with it before they interrupted. Still swallowing the last mouthful, he came back to the wall. He felt its surface gently, so gently. He ran his fingers around in careful, overlapping circles. Not an inch would escape.

Perhaps they were watching him through the judas. They

wouldn't know what he was doing. They would think he was mad at last.

He was crouching, on his sixth circuit, when he found it. Under his breath he sounded out the letters as his fingers traced them Ffff. Yes, that was it. U. Yes, of course, that was the thing to say. Fuck the cops. It came quickly when he was sure of the first letters. He stood up, his heart beating. Euphoria, wild as fear, swept over him. There was someone else in the world. Fuck the cops! Once more. His energy was too much for him. He ran in one spot pulling his legs up high. Fuck the cops! Fuck the cops! FUCK THE COPS!

He went to the judas. Nothing to see. He took the spoon from his plate and licked it. With his back to the door, shielding his hand from view, he started to scratch. He agreed. Fuck the cops! His hand trembled so much he could not get the letters straight, so he made them big instead. The work was surprisingly difficult. Spent with effort and promising himself more, he wiped the spoon carefully with a remnant of sock so that they wouldn't see the paint.

If he could, he would have thanked Joan for the power of that night's joy. It still connected him to other sources of joy, his love for Marc Bloch's writing about history, and now, other people. Sanity.

He could not sleep for joy that night after kissing Joan near the door of Women's Residence. He was prevented by joy and the sense that he would have to fight his parents for what Joan meant to him.

It was after two when he reached home. There had been no buses so late, and he had walked through the sleeping, tree lined streets of the northern suburbs, the still emptiness of Louis Botha Avenue, and the barren new developments beginning to reach Alexandra Township. When he opened the door his mother called.

'David.'

'Yes Ma.'

'Why're you so late?'

'I missed the last bus.'

'Where've you been?'

'To a lecture.'

'Don't lie. You've been with a girl.'
'We both went to the lecture.'
'Who's she?'
'Ah, Ma, let me go to sleep.'
'David, come here.' He came to the side of her bed.
'Yes?'
'Don't you cheek me.'
'O.K. Ma.'
'Who's this girl?'
'She's just a girl at varsity.'
'Tell me about her.'
'There's nothing to tell.'
'All right, but I want to talk to you tomorrow.'
'Don't think you'll get away with it,' his father warned.

He heard every sound he made in the night house. His shoes on the floor, the click of the bathroom door, urine hitting water, brush on teeth, water in basin. It must have been about four o'clock when he rose and dressed again, holding his shoes. He crept out by the kitchen door, and tied the laces of his shoes in the yard. The deep air was prickling with morning sounds, distant milk bottles, a cockcrow. He was walking quickly, his eyes giddy with the immense depth of the sky, and his mind singing. The morning star was huge and brilliant. He had never seen it before. He had never been out so early.

'Oh, Venus,' he sent it a message, 'Venus.' A line of red showed between houses and trees. Birds were stirring and cheeping. A dazzle trickled over the silhouettes of roofs and trees. When the unutterable sun rose he tried to stare in its radiant face, but he couldn't. Blind and drunk with joy, he saw what his eyes could bear, a pine branch spraying light, fat spring buds on the Christmas-flower bushes, peach blossoms hanging over a whitewashed wall.

He came on another sight, at first unintelligible and surprising. A migration of metal insects. Louis Botha Avenue was whirring with the sound of bicycle wheels. The natives were coming in to work from Alexandra Township. They filled the whole street as far as he could see with a thick and speechless stream. It was so early, hardly five in the morning. There were so many. He didn't know what to make of the sight, the hundreds, these thousands coming into the city. They passed in front of him like an army from another world. He turned back home, suddenly feeling the exhaustion of the sleepless night.

At breakfast his father asked.

'Where'd you go in the middle of the night?'

'I didn't go anywhere.'

'Don't lie to me. Caroline saw you coming in.'

'I went for a walk.'

'In the middle of the night? Who d'you think I am?'

David spread fishpaste on his toast.

'You'll answer me, d'you hear!'

'You're my father.'

'That's right.' Having scored this victory, his father changed his tune.

'Listen David, you're my son. I'm not against you, but I'm older and I know more. You can't afford to mess around with girls at this time of your life. You've got exams in three weeks. You've got to concentrate. Listen, I know it's not easy, but there's a way to handle it. I've been in the army, and you know your mother. I'm sure you've guessed she's not an easy woman. Just keep up with the tennis. And, a man's got hands. Know what I mean? Your whole future's still in front of you, but you've got to start right. Look at your matric results – you're going to be a great man. You can't spoil everything now. No girls, no walks in the middle of the night. You need to sleep and to work.'

But, going out to work, his father stopped to slap David on the back, 'You're growing into a man, David.' If he had been able, David would have cut away the place where that hand had touched him.

The year he had read *The Wonders of Science* his father had been out of work. It seemed to have something to do with that Nationalist victory he had sat up all night to hear. After that election, his father used to say, 'They're keeping all the jobs for their own now. Look what's happening on the railways. Every Afrikaner gets a job. Just us bloody fools who went to

55

fight the war get nothing.'

His mother didn't answer these tirades, but she had taken to rebuking David for talking out of turn. 'Shallow streams babble all the way: still waters run deep.' 'Speech may be silver but silence is golden.' As though to strike his father through him.

When he asked for sixpence to buy sweets, or half a crown, to go to the bioscope she compressed her lips and said. 'No, we haven't got the money. You'll have to do without extras.' If his father heard her, he seemed to shrink, and keep quiet. But later, alone with David, he would add his own stroke of advice, 'Don't ever talk about politics. It only gets you into trouble.'

David felt flattered to receive this grownup warning. He sensed a submerged suffering in his father, and his father, feeling that David's sympathy stood with him, told about his childhood in England, the hard years of the Depression, his ignorance when he came to South Africa and bought that farm in the northern Free State that was promised to be a gold mine because the soil was so rich. It must have been the years of drought there that had laid a hard anger into his face and voice, an anger that exploded intermittently for years after, especially when the Nationalists spoke as though they were the only real South Africans, and the English were *uitlanders, rooinecks* who didn't understand the land. 'They've suffered for the land — well so've I, and I've as much right here as any of them. Where'd they think they've come from anyway? They're Europeans, like the rest of us, and they never forget it either when it comes to the kaffirs. They're on top now, but they're scum, just scum. Bloody Nazis! Stayed here while we were up north getting killed, and then when we come back they kicked Smuts out! It's enough to break a man's heart.'

The day before his father's birthday, David got off the bus early, near the shops. He liked to look in the windows of the fishmonger's and the outfitter's and the florist's, feeling that each was different inside. It was like nigger balls.

In the florist's, buckets of flowers stood on the floor, and fancy vases filled the glass counters.

'Good afternoon, my young man. May I help you?'

'Yes, please. How much do roses cost?'
'Ten shillings a dozen for the roses.'
He didn't know what to say. While he was trying to find the right words for the dignified refusal, she added, 'I have got some smaller roses of the sweetheart type for five shillings. You could take half a dozen for a half-crown.' She paused and then accommodated still further.
'And we sometimes sell a single rose for a shilling. We wrap it specially. It makes a very handsome gift.'
'Yes please miss. Can I buy a red one?' She wrapped the flower with a bit of fern and baby's breath in a cone of green waxed paper.
'A present for your mother? Roses make a lovely gift.'
'It's for my father. It's his birthday tomorrow.'
'Oh.' David didn't understand the expression in her face, though he reverted to it afterwards with the same kind of bitterness with which his father learned that his farm in the Free State had, after all, been a gold mine, but in the mining rather than agricultural sense.
The next morning he set the rose at the side of his father's plate the way his mother set birthday presents, and waited for it to be unwrapped and seen, the flower, the spiral, the wonders of the world. He went to the kitchen to ask Sina what she was putting on his sandwiches, and to the back door to watch Samuel polishing the stoep. Out in the yard a scattering of sparrows pecked for food, and the sky was a deep, immense blue.
At the table his father unfurled the green cone with a look of foreboding. 'What do you mean by this?' he saw his father's cheeks flush and swell, the minute stubble left after shaving darkening them like dirt.
'How dare you taunt me, you pipsqueak?' He turned on his wife, 'You put him up to this! It's not enough to criticize me in public — you teach him to taunt me! You bitch! You slut!'
'I don't know what you're talking about, and I think you should mind your language in front of the child.'
You don't know! You make me laugh! As for my language, I'll teach the boy!' He turned to David, 'Just you come with me.' As he stood up, his chair fell over. He pulled David

from his seat and towards the door.

'What are you doing, George?'

'I'll teach you! I'll teach you both. You won't mock me and you won't teach my son to mock me. I'm a man still.' He dragged David to the bedroom. 'Pull down your pants and get onto the bed.'

'George, you're mad! What are you doing to the boy? He gave you a birthday present! Where would he get an idea like that himself?' He turned to David on the bed, 'Cry baby, I'll give you something to cry about!' His hand smacked David's buttock with a loud clap.

'Don't touch the boy,' his mother tugged to pull them apart.

'Don't provoke me, or I'll show him who's the man in this family!' He pulled her down onto the bed.

'If you touch me, George, I'll call the police. Help! Help!'

The servants had heard the whole explosion, standing at the kitchen door, uncertain whether they dared become embroiled. At the cry for help, Sina ran in.

'Baas, baas' she implored and, obviously terrified by her own daring, touched his father.

'Get out you black devil!'

Sina retreated to the door, 'Baas, baas.'

He rushed towards her, pushed her away, and slammed the door. He turned and leaned against the wall.

'Get up, both of you. You make me sick.' Pulling himself up in a military stance he shouted louder, 'Sick, you hear.' He turned and banged out. They heard the front door slam.

'Go wash your face David, and get ready for school. You're probably late.'

After school that day, his mother took him to town and treated him to a milkshake and a cream doughnut. She told him he had a poet's soul and loved beauty.

A sick taste stayed from that day, like a grease mark on a book.


All the angers flowed together. The new drew up the old. As the old joy had drawn the new. He went to the place where he had found the words under the paint. He felt around it, searching for a name. Irrationally, for a moment, he was convinced that he would find François's name and know that they had shared this cell. The thought filled him with joy and horror, he could not find any name. He moved along the wall, feeling it. The light, stroking action of his hands disturbed him. It confused emotions about Joan and van der Merwe in one gesture. He stopped and began pacing again.

What he had seen with Joan transformed everything he saw. On the walk down the hill to the university he saw the woman at the Non-European hospital who had smiled at Joan. She was still sitting against the wall. Her baby was sleeping. Had she been there all night? She couldn't have — there was a curfew for natives, and she would have been arrested. Sina had always needed a note from his mother or father if she was going to be out after eleven o'clock. She couldn't have slept all night with the baby in her lap. There must be a native hotel somewhere, perhaps in Alexandra Township or some new other location. He remembered the locust stream that had filled Louis Botha Avenue, the natives bicycling to work before the sun was fully up. He had never seen anything like it. Or like the hospital Sina had died in, sitting outside on the concrete though it was winter. He felt that he had never seen the city around him, had not been walking on solid ground. Now he felt that only a thin layer separated him from hollow chambers, tunnels, and mines, and this was the first time he had felt their tremor.

He didn't see Joan at the English lecture, in the canteen or the library. He looked for her on the steps at eleven o'clock, but no one from her set was there. He couldn't find her at lunchtime or in the afternoon.

At home in the evening, his mother took him aside, 'David, I want you to tell me about this girl.'

'There's nothing to tell.'

'You can't come home at all hours of the night without any explanation.'

'I missed the last bus.'

'Why? What was going on? Were you alone with her?'

'Ma, I can't answer all these questions.'

'You have to. I'm your mother, and I've got a right to know.'

'I can't answer and I won't.'

'We'll see about that.'

The contest with his parents began after supper when he went to the front door.

'Where are you going, David?' his father asked.

'For a walk.'

'Don't you have to study?'

'I'll do it when I come back.'

'I want you to stay home and work.'

'I'll do it when I come back.'

'I'm not allowing you out.'

'Ugh, hell.'

'Don't you swear at me. You'll show respect, understand?'

'For Godsake leave me alone.'

His father hit him over the head. David slammed the door and walked quickly. He couldn't think about his father. At a Greek café in Louis Botha Avenue, he tried to phone, but the line to Women's Residence was continually engaged. After a while he tried another café, then he looked for a public phone booth, but the phone was broken. At the third café he got through, but Joan wasn't in.

'That was quite a walk you took,' his father accused. 'How was the weather in Timbuctoo?'

'Fine. The sun was shining.'

'All right, that's enough cheek. You're not going out of the house again without permission. You're still a minor, and I can call the police if I like. I tried kindness this morning. You don't bloodywell know what kindness is.' David didn't answer. He went to his room and fell asleep without another word.

The next day too he couldn't find Joan or her friends anywhere. He came home early and tried to phone her. This time it was easy to get through to Women's Residence, but she wasn't in. He left no message.

His mother came home before his father. She came to his room. 'David, I want to talk to you.'

'Yes.'

'You can't treat your father like that. You know how sensitive he is.'

'I'm not his prisoner.'

'Don't test him, David. You know his temper.' She sat on his bed. 'And I want to talk to you about something else. What kind of girl is this Joan Hamilton?'

'Who told you her name?'

'Caroline.'

He had forgotten that Caroline would hear his conversations. Natives were still invisible to him.

'You'd love it. Rich, Natal English. They hunt and play polo.'

'You're joking?'

'Where does she live?'

'Didn't Caroline tell you she's at Women's Residence? They lock the door before twelve every night, so you've got nothing to be afraid of.'

'I'm not afraid of anything David. I'll be very happy if you find a girl you love, but you're still very innocent and I think it's my duty to find out who you're seeing and what you're doing. I don't want to pry, but I've got to know.'

'There. You know.'

He did not see Joan all week, and the next week, despairing of seeing her or understanding her disappearance, he went into town to study at the main library.

She was sitting on the library steps.

'David! What's the matter? You've gone absolutely white.'

He laughed. 'I've been trying to get hold of you. Where'd you disappear to?'

'I tried to get in touch with you, but I don't know where you live.'

'Bramley. You haven't been at varsity.'

'I've been staying with Aviva. Her parents are in a fantastic stew about that newspaper story, and they're hardly letting her out of the house, so we've all been going there. But she's swotting here today. It was getting too much.'

'What newspaper story?'

'Didn't you see it?'

'No.'

'About the Special Branch calls after the meeting?'
'No. I never read newspapers.'
'But you've got to.'
'If it's important I'll hear about it anyway.'
'Well this is important and you didn't.'
'Tell me what happened.'
'I can't tell you everything. There must've been a spy at the meeting. The Special Branch phoned everyone who had a car outside Monica's house, I mean, in the middle of the night. Edward's parent said he was with Michael and Aviva and me, so they phoned Aviva's parents too, but not Michael's and we're trying to work out why . . .'
'And you?' he interrupted.
'They haven't done anything about me either. Just Edward and Aviva. And Aviva's parents are terribly upset, there's going to be a war in Israel and they have to go out to meetings every night, so they won't let Aviva go out, and she's had a fight with Philip. It's been awful. So I've been staying there. I got permission from Miss Grundy.'
'What did the Special Branch want to know?'
'They've been citing the Suppression of Communism Act when anyone asks. They're so silly.'
'Some of them sounded like Communists to me.'
'Don't be silly David, I can't bear it. You think they were going to start a revolution in the middle of the night because of something that Harry told them? Or anything anyone said at that meeting?'
'No.'
'Well that's the point. They just want to scare people like Aviva's parents. They think she won't get a passport and she's supposed to go to Europe for Christmas.'
'But they *are* Communists,' David said.
'I suppose some of them are. Harry is. He's been for years. So what? He's not going to start a revolution. It's just too silly. I can't bear to argue with you about such nonsense.'
'What about the others?'
'I don't know, but I think it's just a fad, the way it is for Aviva and Michael.'
'And for you?' he asked.

'I don't know anything about politics. It doesn't interest me.'

He took her hand, feeling, as he had before, how mysterious its power, how unknown her life was to him.

'Are you swotting?'

'Ja. We all are. I suppose we'd better go in.'

'Ja.' They didn't move.

'Aviva thinks you might be the spy at the meeting.'

'Why?'

'She says you were watching everything.'

He didn't ask whether she thought him a spy.

The library hush held them in artificially silent hours, interrupted only by quiet requests for rubber or red pencil, offers of Lifesavers or toffees, chairs that scraped as someone rose to fetch a book from the shelves or request one from the stacks, enveloped them in a privacy that David felt drawing him into Joan's everyday life as quietly as air, and as intimately. He was sorry to go out when they decided to break for lunch. At the small café near the library, he felt still not one of them.

The day wore into afternoon. They all fell into a reading stupor and worked slowly until Aviva whispered, 'I can't stand this any more. Let's go to my place and swim.'

Arid city glare gave way to suburban gardens. A few jacarandahs had started to flower and late fruit trees still held blossoms. Aviva's house was set off from the street by oaks and pines, and beyond them, a sunny lawn flowering with imported daffodils. When they had changed, and gone to the pool, Michael short and heavy-built, but moving gracefully like a dancer, and Edward, skinny and lank, protecting himself with a loose shirt against the burn that showed red where he had been careless before, a fat native girl brought them a jug of Oros and a plate of biscuits. Michael rubbed oil onto his legs and asked Edward to do his back.

'That's sublime. Positively erotic. Try some on your legs.'

Edward shook his head. 'It won't help.'

'Shall I do you, David.'

'No' He didn't feel comfortable at the thought of Michael's

naked touch and insinuating wit.

Joan and Aviva came out of the front door and the native girl again emerged from the kitchen, bringing tea and sandwiches cut into small triangles with the crusts removed. Joan's collar bone and shoulder blades showed near the surface of her skin and he saw her notched supple spine as she sat holding her knees. Their gossip worried at exam questions and anecdotes about lecturers. Edward and Michael were going to Cape Town for the long holidays, and Aviva would go to Europe if she got her passport. 'Let's not talk about it,' she said.

In the silence, they all began to swim. Aviva threw a ball; they caught and threw and pursued, splashing bright drops. Sometimes, in the uncanny medium that blunted his sense of touch, David brushed by Joan and knew that he had felt her flesh, innocent and distant as if he touched her in an aquarian underworld. Mermaid and human at last, Joan climbed out of the water. They lay on their backs feeling blades of grass prickling through their towels. David closed his eyes and saw the red corpuscles swim among haloes and translucent colours.

He made no effort to follow their conversation. It always tended towards politics in those days, as though their buoyancy was tugged by the injustice that held them up so light. Aviva said, 'It's so awful. We've got no right to be living like this.'

'There's nothing wrong with enjoying ourselves,' Michael countered. 'What's wrong is that no one else's allowed to. That's what we're going to change.'

'We can't keep our privileges,' Edward warned, 'If we really want the revolution.'

Perhaps Aviva still thought David might be a spy and the conversation too risky for him to hear. She asked in a low voice, 'Is David asleep?'

'No.' He sat up and clasped his knees in his arms, 'Just dreaming.'

'What about?'

'Nothing.' The day itself, awake for them, had taken on for him the luminosity of a dream.

'Don't be so cryptic. Tell us,' Aviva teased. 'You know I like

other people's secrets.'
'It's no secret.'
'Hmmm.'
'You're right, David.' Michael had his own game. 'If you tell Aviva a dream she'll psychoanalyse it to death. Though in the end there's only one interpretation. Sex. Whatever you dreamt, it's about sex.'
'But he was,' Aviva crowed, 'Look at him. You hit it first shot, Michael.'


Caroline reported that he hadn't come home until after five. His father wanted to know where he'd been.
'Swotting in the library.'
'How'd you get sunburnt in the library?'
'Are we going to have another fight, Dad?' They turned away from each other, holding the break for another time. The next day and the next, David's sunburn went unchallenged.


When Petrus Hugo came, he brought a bucket, a towel, and a piece of soap chopped from one of those yellow bars Sina had used for laundry.
The touch of water on his face startled him. In the relief of washing, he allowed the tears to flow out onto his furry face, as though the water and lather would hide them even from himself.
He remembered that he hadn't finished making his own mark yet. He took the spoon and set to it. The chips and grains of paint fell in a thin waste onto the floor.


No one told him why They gave him his shoes. They handcuffed him between them like Trevor and walked him through the corridors with casual brutality, pulling him to their pace. They locked him and pushed him into the Black Maria with a shove that made him hit the floor with his face.

New rage made him screw his eyes so that he didn't at first look out at the buildings of the city, but soon, Rissik Street caught his eye. He stood to look out of the fenced window at the back. At the railway station a barricade marked off the place where a wall was being rebuilt. Boom. His rage flashed deeper. The police van moved. It rolled past summer trees and Indian flower sellers outside the European hospital. Further up the hill Africans were still sitting against the wall of the Non-European Hospital. The pepper-tree was still growing in the corner of the yard. As the van turned, he caught a glimpse of Hillbrow's flats. He heard metal doors open. A red-and-white bus passed before the Fort's doors shut.

*The Fort*

He could hear the life of others in the Fort, footsteps, and keys, doors opened and shut, a clatter of pails. There were other people in the world.

As they brought him through the corridors he saw a gang of African prisoners on their knees. He was still in the larger prison where he would never be free of service from Africans. His bomb had not changed the privileges apartheid forced on him, heavy as a rock.

His cell had a bed under the mattress. There was a box he could sit on. There was a basin of water for washing.

The prisoner in the next cell introduced himself.

'Hullo. My name's Gericke. Hendrick Gericke.'

He went to the door to stand near the grating, where he could hear better. 'I'm David Miller.'

'Ja. I heard about you. Hell, what's the idea man?'

'Oh, I dunno.' Boom. Even here they had heard the explosion. Perhaps it had not been in vain.

'The fellow before you was also here for murder.' David put his hands on the wall for support. He could feel his heart beating huge and terrified. Murder. So someone had been killed in the explosion. Gericke was still talking. 'His wife was running round with another man. Hell! they gave him a hard time in court, you know. He was also running round. *Jirre!* Why should a guy like that get into trouble? He wasn't hurting anyone. Jus this wife, she comes to him one day in a jealous rage. So he clouts her one. What d'you expect? So she falls in the sea, man, en drowns. You think a dame could swim. Anyhow, it's O.K. He got off with manslaughter, ten years en good behaviour. He's got a terrific lawyer. Nothing but the best. Man. Who've you got?'

Murder.

'I haven't got a lawyer.'

'Jesus man, you better hurry up! You got money? Get Thompson if you got money.'

'I haven't got any money.'

'Well then you jus got to take what you can get, like me man. It's no good man. When I get out, I'm going to get money so next time I can get a good lawyer, none of this cheap rubbish.'

Murder. That was why Philip had called him a mad dog. They'd spoken about it, how people one might call innocent could be killed. He'd said he didn't believe any white person was innocent in this country. Every white was loaded with privileges acquired by murder. But murder! Of course. He'd intended it, expected it. But never expected it to sound like this. Murder.

'So someone was killed in the explosion. Who was it?'

'Jesus! Don't you know?'

'I was on the run. I didn't hear.' Though he should have understood something from Philip.

'Mrs Blackmun. She was a widow. Jesus, man, you're in trouble.'

'Anyone else?'

'There's none of your chommies here. I heard there's one of them in England. You know François Marais?'

'François in England? I thought he was in prison.'

'That's him. He's in over there.'

'In prison?'

'Of course man. Accessory before.'

'Not here?'

'Not him, *jong!* he's jus walking roun, en he sees trouble. Next thing he hops on a plane, en *blitzjong,* that's the end of him.'

So what Philip had told him in Pretoria had been wrong. Perhaps Trevor had also been free, and arrested only after David. His hands . . .

'Was anyone else killed?'

70

'You're a bladdy cool customer!'
'Well, tell me.'
'Nobody else has died yet.'
'What d'you mean, yet?'
'There's a little girl, about eight, in hopsital, en a typist. She lost a leg. You got it in for women, hey!'

David left the grating and found the bed. There was nothing he could do about it now. In any case, he had accepted it long ago that the innocent die with the guilty. There was no way to separate them. Other children had died and died of injustice. He couldn't say that he hadn't killed them. He was white.

A warder brought him food and said he wasn't allowed to sit on the bed. He paced the cell and measured it. Ten paces by six. Big. He read the names scratched on the wall. Piet Kreer, Tertius Keyter, Hans Breitenbach, Jacob Arndt, Louis Spaarman, Pretorius Eybers, Peter Venter, Andrew Smith, in different scripts and sizes, some skew and crooked, some firm and broad. All in for murder? No, some listed their crimes with their names. Rape, Burglary. Immorality.

While he was fitting the wires to the clock, he had imagined how it would appear in the newspapers and what the Africans would think of what he had done. Would Luthuli say something? Even though nothing Luthuli said could be published, because he was banned, he would hear about the bomb. What had he said? And Sobukwe? He wanted them to know that one white man had given his life for justice. He wanted it to be possible for the new government after the revolution to be something better than a racial tyranny pushing over the old like a huge boulder, while worms and slugs and things without names scrambled away from the sunlight and weak things crouched in the path of a weight they could neither escape nor survive. He had known that these things would happen. There was no revolution the innocent didn't pay for. He had known and had fit the wires to the minute and the hour hand to touch at noon.

He was here for murder, murder, murder, murder, murder. If he said the word often enough, it wouldn't mean anything.

Mabotoana must have been drunk to boast that way at Edward's party, so many years ago, that he was in the P.A.C. shadow cabinet.

'Come the revolution, man, I'll be Minister of Interior. Man, I'll move into one of those big houses in Houghton, and I'll send the madam to live in Soweto where the whites have given us such good housing and cleaned up the slums. I can just see her in a charming little house with no water and no lights. Oh boy! She can come and be my *meid* if she doesn't like Soweto, and she can live in the girl's room. I'll be good to her and won't tell the police if her husband comes at night. But no children. Come the revolution, man. I'll have a swimming pool and a tennis court, and I'm not joking, man, the whites are going to live in Soweto.' He laughed.

'Revolutions aren't that easy.' David had answered him, altogether green and full of history out of books. 'By the end of a revolution life gets so bad, places like Soweto seem like Houghton to the people who're still alive.'

'Ugh sis, man! You don't know what you're talking about. You come and live in Soweto for a week. Or make it a week-end. If the tsotsis haven't stabbed you by Monday morning, we'll hear what you have to say then.'

'O.K. I don't know Soweto, but you don't know revolutions. Who cares. Have your revolution. You may be right that things can't get much worse.'

Edward, the peacemaker, had listened silently, and Michael had been dancing with Aviva. The lights of Johannesburg sparkled outside the wide windows that opened onto the terrace of Edward's home. Late summer. Between Coalbrook and Sharpeville. At Cato Manor near Durban, African women had rushed on a group of policemen coming to search their houses for illegal liquor and men, and had killed them. David believed the rage in Mabotoana.

Joan didn't. Driving home, he told her what Mabotoana had said.

'He wouldn't do it. It's too petty for him. He's beating up his courage for the pass protests next month. If he really felt that way about whites he wouldn't come to Edward's party.'

Those were the pass protests they later called Sharpeville.

'You don't really believe there's got to be a revolution, do you?'

'Why does that sound like an accusation, David?'

'I feel as if you don't care.'

'I don't, in a way. If revolution brings only a reversal of white and black in Soweto and Houghton, it's not worth hoping for.'

'How can you stand it, Joan, how can you stand living the way we do?'

She took his hand on the steering wheel and held it. He saw her face, the long firm curve of cheek, the line of white around her mouth, sad.

A few months ago Mabotoana had been at François's flat.

'This is a surprise,' he said. 'I didn't think you had the guts for real work. You wanted revolution without trouble. Maybe no revolution. Changed your mind, hey?'

'O.K. I've changed my mind. You still want to live in Houghton?'

'Why should I change my mind?'

Pieces of the past lay flat on the surface of his mind like pennies on the ground.

Eight years old. His own age when he read *The Wonders of Science*.


Exercising in the courtyard, he saw Gericke, middle aged and drooping in every feature, the eyelids over the eyes, the jowls over the jaw, the lips over the chin.

'That's Prinsloo,' Gericke looked at the warder and spoke out of the corner of his mouth. 'We're chommies. Anything you want, jus ask me en I'll fix it with Prinsloo.'

'Thanks.'

'That's O.K. *boet*. We're in this together.'

Involuntarily, he recoiled. As though he was not Gericke's

brother, in anything together. Not a murderer. The glare of open sunlight was hurting his eyes. He closed them and saw the red tissue, blood moving between his eyes and the light. He opened his eyes.

'What's the child's name?'

Gericke looked at him askance.

'Freda Bekker.'

His pleasure, hunger, tiredness, were all a murderer's. He must be the same man he had been yesterday in that dark cell in Marshall Square, the same who had driven through the clear dawn of the Orange Free State. Who, the dawn before that, had heard the birds begin to sing as he cleared away evidence of his night's work making the bomb. So it must be he who had hurt the child and murdered the old women. He tried to imagine her, swathed in bandages, in the Children's Hospital, only a few blocks away from the Fort. The picture ran into that other, the children at St Thérèse's. There was no way to separate the guilty from the innocent.

The sunshine, the joyful play of air on his skin, the heat, clouds forming huge balls in the sky, sounds of traffic bringing the city's life over the embankment and walls of the Fort. Secretaries would be coming home now in crowded buses. The plane trees would be in full leaf, newsboys selling their papers in Kotze Street. Just outside the Fort. The longing and joy of being free enough to move in the sun and know the city's life overwhelmed him. He could not repel the incongruous happiness of being alive.

The warder who came to shave him, a skinny boy, pocked with acne on a pallid skin, told him that there was a lawyer to see him. It was not a matter he could argue with this gawky barber, but he was not going to allow them to pretend they could bring legality as a semblance of justice against him. He had murdered because the law murdered: they were equal. Snyman's gentle awkwardness reminded David of Edward. Perhaps he had fallen into this work as guilelessly as he might have fallen into a position at a bank or selling shirts in a department store if he had been English instead of Afrikaans.

When they set out for the office, Synman said, 'I must handcuff you.' David noticed that he expressed his act of coercion as a coerced act, imprisoned himself. They walked along concrete corridors lined with other men's cells. David felt numbed by the possibility that they knew who he was. The murderer. He knew that his expression was haughty. He was their peer, whatever their crimes.

In the small office, the lawyer stood to greet him. 'Maurice Kaplan,' he stretched out a pudgy hand. David felt that he recognized the quick brown eyes behind thick glasses, the face under a pate fringed like a medieval monk's. Perhaps Kaplan had been a music-lover at Joan's concerts.

'Take the handcuffs off, please,' he said to Synman, who looked dubious but did as he was told. Kaplan smiled, and his cheeks formed little red apples like those David had liked as a child.

'You can leave us alone now,' and Synman left. Kaplan gestured to a chair facing his own across the cheap varnished table, and David sat.

'Now where shall we begin?' David shrugged, and Kaplan gave him a quick glance.

'All right. I've been asked to take your case, so of course that's why I'm here. I'd like you to tell me as much as you can, and then we'll work out a defence.'

'Were you appointed by the court?'

'No, but my client would like to remain anonymous. I have been instructed to tell you that you can choose another lawyer if you prefer.'

'Is my wife paying you?'

'No. I was instructed to tell you that too.'

'Why can't you tell me then?'

Kaplan did not answer him. Then, 'Would you prefer someone else?'

'I've got only one preference.'

'Yes.'

'Not to be represented at all.'

'What do you mean?'

'I don't want to stand trial.'

'That, I'm afraid, is not up to you.'

'I don't want to defend myself, or to be defended.'
'And why not?'
'I don't want to pretend that we have a system of justice here.'
'I'm afraid your scheme is impossible. You have to stand trial in court.'

He looked at the square window of the small office. It obscured the outside world with bars. Dust on the glass made the sunlight opaque. Freda Bekker. Eight years old.

'You know that there is nothing I can say in my defence.'
'Let me see what I can do, Mr Miller.'

Mr Miller. And he had stood up to take his hand as though David could be not only a mad dog, but still a man.

'What can you do?'

Kaplan shifted on his hard wooden chair and smiled, as though he had achieved the first victory.

'First I must find out as much as I can, of course, then we can construct a defence.'

'I'm sure you know as much as I can tell. I gave a complete statement to the police. They'll probably let you see it.'

'I have seen it. I've got a copy here.' Kaplan handed him his own confession. Noticing the quality of chubbiness on Kaplan's hands, David wondered whether Kaplan was a man who dieted all the time instead of allowing the comfortable rotundity he would have had as a medieval monk, with that bald pate.

'There's nothing more to tell.'
'Not quite nothing, Mr Miller. You leave a great deal unexplained — where you got the dynamite, how many others you worked with, whether anyone else was involved. A great deal.'

'All right. No one else was involved in the station explosion. I was the only one. Is that clear?'

'Then how did you get hold of dynamite?'

'Van der Merwe's been asking me the same thing. Do you know van der Merwe?'

'Come, come, Mr Miller. I'm on the defence side, not the prosecution.'

'Then you don't need to know how I got hold of dynamite. I

had it. How I used it was my own decision and my own work.'

'Let me say that Trevor Reed has given a complete statement to the police and will be testifying for the state, so it is known that others are implicated.'

'Has he given any names?'

'I don't know.'

'Can you find out?'

'I doubt it.'

'Well then you don't need them from me. Trevor knew I had dynamite. He had nothing else to do with the station explosion. It was all my own work.'

'It only makes it harder for you, Mr Miller, if you take the whole burden on yourself.'

'It won't help me if they hang other people too.'

Kaplan did not answer him. 'Is Trevor still in prison?'

'No, he's out on bail, charged with being an accessory before the fact, and he's under surveillance, but I think the charges against him will be dropped if he testifies at your trial. Is there anything damaging he can say against you?'

David laughed.

'Do you think it'll make any difference?'

'Then there's François Marais in England.'

François. David looked down at the varnished table between them, a cheap wood, like the desks at school. All government buildings had the same kind of furniture, and walls painted dark green or dark brown below hand level and some mistrustful colour above to match it. But in the Cape the old homesteads were whitewashed and cool. Inside, the wood and furniture were dark, polished, and shining. The air moved freely. In François's home in the Long Kloof, the kitchen floor had been made of peach pits set in *mis*, like a mosaic, and then polished smooth by Africans on their knees, like the prisoners here at the Fort. What was it like there for François in an English prison?

'François is like Trevor.' He stared Kaplan in the eye. Brown and deep. 'He knew that I had dynamite. That's all. What're they going to do about François?'

'His case is causing some stir in England where he's fighting extradition. If the court can be persuaded that his involvement was purely political, not criminal, he'll be released.'

'Can I make any difference? I mean, can I say that it was purely political?'

'And commit perjury?'

David raised his chin and stared at Kaplan angrily.

'It won't be perjury. I tell the truth.'

'Frankly, Mr Miller, it's a delicate situation.'

'In other words, contact with me can only bring harm.' David looked down at the table again, and then at Kaplan, who had raised a thin, uneven eyebrow at this comment.

'So why are you willing to take my case?'

'It isn't really relevant to discuss that, Mr Miller. We have only a short time today.'


'So you got a lawyer,' Gericke said.

'Yes.' Impervious to David's brevity, Gericke chattered.

'Ja man, it makes a man feel better, you know, when you got someone to talk for you. Take me. If I didn't have a good lawyer I wouldn't hev a snowball's chance in hell. I'm in for rape you know, but reduced to immorality, cause she's only a *koelie meid*. But Jesus, what a sweet cunt, fifteen en still juicy. Hell. Ag man! but they could have me for the works, man, jus like you. We was jus having a sweet time, man, you know, en nex' thing I know they got me locked up on a hanging charge. Without a lawyer, man! *Jirre*!'

Sometimes in Pretoria, when he was shaving, his father's face had risen to the surface of his own like the face of a drowned man. In prison he would not have to see that face. No mirrors here to show him who he was like, except Gericke. He would never attain his father's face, or Gericke's. He was going to die young. Kaplan's talk about a defence was nonsense; they would let Gericke off because she was only a *koelie meid*, and they had let off the constables who made Zwane drink so much water at Bitterspruit, and then beat him with a rubber hose so that his stomach exploded. They would not find an excuse for him. Fifteen and still juicy.

Innocent of David's anger, Gericke asked. 'You like curry? Every Tuesday we get curry. The food here's so boring, man, en it makes me constipated. I'll tell you what, it's because we don't get enough exercise. Sometimes I think the kaffirs is the lucky ones, at least they get a chance to move, they cleans the floors, they works in the kitchen.'

'Ask your friend Prinsloo to let you clean some floors.'

'Jesus, you sour. What'chou got to be so sour for?'

He wanted a newspaper to tell him an outrage, something like Zwane's death at Bitterspruit — or the hill of rotting oranges when there was a glut on the market and the children at St Thérèse's were dying of starvation. He needed the narcotic, alien suffering of men he did not know, children he had never dandled. Without the clamour of their cries his act seemed meaningless. He wanted to remember why he had risked his life and would lose it now, why he had made the bomb and planted it, so that it had killed Mrs Blackmun, a widow, and brought the child Freda Bekker to hospital. It had seemed necessary. That it had to be done.

He could hear Gericke farting and groaning, and wondered whether Gericke could hear him walking. Piet Kreer, Tertius Keyter, Hans Breitenbach, Jacob Arndt, Louis Spaarman, Pretorius Eybers, Peter Venter, Andrew Smith. Perhaps there were walls somewhere in the Fort reading Mohandas Ghandi, Albert Luthuli. Not in these white cells. Among the capitals and lower case, some large, some crooked, some small, in scripts as various and confusing as the crimes and their dates, other words addressed him. I'm sick of clink. Money is the root of all evil. A line drawn through money, and women written above. Perhaps there were other walls inscribed Michael Henderson, Philip Brink.

By the time Michael had been arrested during the state of emergency after Sharpeville, David had known that these things happened; the innocent jumbled with the guilty. When Philip was arrested with the others accused of treason, he had not known how to understand his shock until the opening days. Blood. Joan. The police beating at the crowd. The gates pressed so that the vans of prisoners couldn't get out. Philip must have been in one of those vans. In the Non-European section of the Fort, he might have read those names, Mohandas Ghandi, Albert Luthuli. Those in prison for our sake.

More than four years later, in Pretoria and separated from Joan, he had seen them the day they were released, that thin group left of all the accused. Crossing Church Street near the Square where official buildings of the stone state stared at each other, and President Kruger's bronze eyes surveyed the heart of his dry republic, he saw a small crowd outside the building called the Palace of Justice. He had not realised who they were, scattered and small in the hostile space, until he read in the evening paper that all the remaining defendants in the Treason Trail had been acquitted. More four years.

The whole business had seemed so implausible. Aviva had said from the first that the charges were trumped up. At that time, so green and ignorant, he hadn't understood her reference to the Reichstag fire.

He had never felt one of that group around Aviva, though Joan was among them and so he was drawn in, finding his way among first year exams, and Joan's friends, still wary, and his parents fearful that he was still seeing this girl, Joan Hamilton. Every day he saw her at the library, in town or at Wits; every afternoon they swam at Aviva's house. Aviva's parents were never at home now. Israel had erupted into war, and they had Zionist meetings to attend. The protest in Hungary had failed. Suddenly, in a way he had never noticed before, the streets were filled with newspaper boys hawking special editions. For the first time he saw the world racked by history. Had there always been times like these when calamities cracked like dam walls, pouring their consequences on appalled civilians who had not caused them? The years of his childhood must have been like that, but the only portentous events he remembered were the night the Nationalists won the election and Smuts lost his seat, and the Torch Commando marches his father had marched in.

To celebrate the end of exams they had gone to see a Hitchcock film at the Empire, and when they came out the street was thick with readers again. Michael bought a paper, and the others all clustered around him.

'It's just like Nazi Germany.' Aviva's eyes blazed with a hot temper of life. He hadn't been able to tell, that day, whether she was angry or happy.

They read snatches of the story to each other, adding coals to each other's fire. To him it had still seemed a story about distant people.

'They haven't finished the arrests yet.'

People going home after work pressed past the clot they made on the pavement.

'John's been taken.'

'And Philip.'

That had shocked him. Although he had met Philip only that once at the Discussion Club meeting nearly a month before, he couldn't connect threat with that sensitive face and slight figure. Philip had criticized the way the others played at ideology. He couldn't be a Communist.

So he had been drawn in by sympathy with Philip. A mad dog. I trusted you. They had gone round each other in a circle. *I* trusted *you*. Like a dog chasing its tail.

'Let me see.' Aviva took the paper from Michael's hands.

'Under Coloureds,' he showed her.

'Fuck and damn,' she swore. 'If my parents recognize his name they'll kill me!'

'Don't worry, they're too busy with Israel,' Michael promised.

'Where is he?' Joan asked.

'In the Fort.'

'Oh no! The Fort's one of the worst,' Joan said.

And David had been shocked that she should know which prisons were the worst.

The Fort clacked around him. Doors opened and closed. He had fallen into the habit he had allowed in solitary, thinking about Joan in that time when it was still sweet. Before he was a murderer.

He had gone along with the others, suspicious of their excitement and pleasure, but following them when they agreed to phone Monica. They trailed to the library because there was a phone in the lobby, and when no one answered at Monica's house, they called Gerald. Edward warned, 'No names on the phone. Gerald's tapped,' and David was appalled again at the things they knew.

Aviva reported what Gerald had said.

'He wants me to phone back in a few minutes. He says I should check at home first in case something's happened there.' Her eyes were burning with the joy of being in the centre of things, like his father in history.

But Joan and Edward seemed to know that this time it wasn't a game, although they didn't know what it was.

'I can't get the hang of it,' Edward said, 'It looks like a lot of Congress people, but I can't see then why they've taken Philip. He's not Congress.'

'What're they going to charge them with?'

'It doesn't say. They can cook up something. They can do anything they like.'

A shadow had fallen across Michael's face as he bent his head toward Aviva in the telephone booth and then put an arm around her shoulder, Edward's face was pale as he said, 'This feels more serious than random intimidation. I can't see the point. Why now? Why arrests in the middle of the night?'

Joan was standing like a flower in the sheath of her green dress.

'Let's hear what Aviva's got to say,' as Aviva came out into the dim library lobby.

'It doesn't look as though anything's happening at my house. Gerald says he'll come over tonight. He wants to talk to us.'

Edward went to the phone booth with Joan, and David felt cut off from them. He didn't even know what Congress was, and felt jealous of this danger and experience drawing them all together.

No one had come for Edward or Joan. 'Let's go.' Aviva sounded impatient, although there was nothing for them to do.

They walked to the car, Edward with Michael and Aviva, Joan with David.

'What does Congress do, Joan?'

'Nothing. Its's all like the meeting you came to. Talk.'

'Nothing else?'

'You heard Philip at that meeting. Congress is a lot of talk.'

'Are you a member?'
'No.'
'And Edward and Michael?'
'I think so.'
'And Aviva?'
'Also.'
'Why?'
'Why don't you ask them?' she sounded angry and scornful.

When they reached the car, he felt the issue between them unconcluded. Taking the first step away from his parents' control and dreams, he climbed into the car and sat next to Joan.

Caroline answered his phone call from Aviva's house. 'I'm not coming home for supper. Please tell my mother.'

'Madam's here baas. I'll call her to the phone.'

'No, I don't want to talk to her. Just give her the message.'

'You speak to her, baas.'

'No.' He hung up with a sense of victory.

At the swimming pool, they were all drinking sherry and talking, because Aviva's parents were there, about the weather, and the drought that Mrs Solomon said was ruining the lawn. Then Mrs Solomon touched on the day's events.

'We're lucky the police caught them in time.'

'In time for what?' Aviva challenged.

'There must've been something going on, darling. They don't arrest people in the middle of the night for doing nothing.'

'How do you know? They did it in Germany.'

'Don't be ridiculous darling. The situation here's completely different.'

'How?'

'Well, darling, I'm sure when you learn more you'll see that these people have been up to something.'

'What, for example?'

'I knew you'd disagree with me, darling, but you're young and idealistic, and I'm afraid it'll get you into trouble. I just wish you'd be more sensible and careful. I don't just mean your passport. You just don't know how you can damage your whole life by something you do now. I mean that for all of you,' she addressed them. 'You're a lovely group of friends, but you don't know where your ideas will carry you. You'll learn as you grow older. I just hope it won't be too late.' She looked at their faces, noncommittal and polite. 'Well, every genereration has to learn from its own mistakes.'

Michael signalled to Aviva to shut up, and her parents left for their Zionist meeting.

'Why do parents have to be so silly! Aviva exploded as their car pulled out of the driveway.

They felt together, a band sharing the secret of danger and Gerald's impending visit.

At dinner Michael engaged Aviva's younger sister, Cynthia, in questions about a swimming gala to be held in the last week of school. When the phone rang they heard Aviva's end of the conversation. 'We're all fine . . . All of us. I can't mention names . . . I can't talk to you now . . . No . . . I'll phone you . . . *Please* don't mention names on the phone.' Cynthia was not even intrigued. She had been kept out of her older sister's secrets too often to take particular notice this time.

After dinner, Joan said, 'I'm going to practise for a while until Gerald comes. I've got a *Messiah* rehearsal on Thursday.'

The sound of her exercises overlaid the servants' talking and washing up in the kitchen, and Michael and Aviva and Edward in the study speculating on the meaning of the arrests and what Gerald would tell them.


David was moved by Joan's constancy. He loved her for the discipline he felt then as a true effect of civilization, preserving art against the destructive instrusion of crises. It was the same habit of work he had come to feel as a vice of atrocious indifference. He couldn't resolve the knot of his feeling.

The dilemma had come to them that very night. When Joan finished her exercises, she brought her 'cello to the study, and Michael carried a straight-backed chair towards the empty hearth so that she could sit in front of them and play. For a moment before putting bow to strings, she sat with her eyes closed, collecting herself. Looking at her pale lids, David felt again the mystery of her separateness, the inward life she closed from them and communicated to herself. He felt that having seen her this way, he would never be the same again. Light from the lamp caught her golden hair and deep glints in the wood of her instrument. He felt himself fixed to a vision of something he could not name, alter, or escape. The sweetness of an ideal Europe entered the room, veiled by the summer crickets in the garden where the air was heavy with the scent of stocks, and the last clink of dishes and murmur of conversation from the servants in the kitchen. For the moment it was as if they need not wait to hear more about who was in jail, in danger, in flight.

At the pause between the first movement and the second, Edward said, 'Please stop, Joan. It's too incongruous. I can't take it.'

She set the bow on a small table and looked at him, waiting.

'I hope I'm not offending you Joan, but I can't listen today, and I can't even understand how you can play.'

'I play every day. It's not something I make new choices about. I do it the way I breathe. That doesn't mean you have to listen.'

'But today . . . I mean, it's not like every day. All those people in prison.'

'That's just like every day.'

'I don't see how you can go on playing as though nothing's happened.' Again Joan paused, her eyes downcast and her lids fringed with short golden hair, 'What happened today is what happens all the time in this country. Today's different for us because we know the names of those in prison for our sake, and they're our friends.'

Edward heard the danger in her words.

'What do you mean, for our sake?'

'Everything here,' she had raised her golden green eyes to look at Edward, and moved her hand at the wrist in a cramped gesture that showed the room around them, perhaps the whole house and garden, perhaps more. 'Everything is this way for us because of the people in prison. If someone didn't put them in prison, we couldn't be here. We couldn't even be who we are. I know why you don't want to listen to music when you think of them, but music is the same as everything else in our lives.'

'How can you go on living like this then, if that's how you feel?' Edward leaned forward as though he couldn't afford to lose a fraction of her answer.

Joan looked him in the face.

'I could ask the same of you. How can you go on living here? What do you want me to do when you ask how I can go on living?'

'I don't want you to do a damn thing. I want to know for myself. Perhaps we should go overseas. But I'd always know that the same things are going on here: I'd just feel I was turning my back on it.'

Joan's tone, accepting and realistic, patient in a way David had come to know so well, but not to understand, shaped her voice. 'If it destroys you, you must turn your back on it.'

'I don't know whether it will destroy me.'

Aviva broke the bubble of concentration that enclosed the two of them.

'You're both geting awfully cryptic.' Cryptic had been Aviva's word that season.

'You can't go overseas, Edward. We've all agreed that liberals have been doing that for years, just leaving the rest of us more isolated. Sometimes I think liberals have done this country more harm than the Nationalists. We've all agreed we must stay, and work for the revolution.'

'I don't think we can say everyone must do the same thing,' Joan rebutted in an aloof tone.

'Everyone's different.'

'Oh Joan, you're incurably bourgeois,' Michael sided with Aviva. 'You can't excuse individuals from an inevitable historical process.'

'If it's inevitable, we don't have to do anything about it. It'll happen whatever our opinion.'

'That isn't so, Joan. We can shape the way the revolution goes.'

'That's not *my* vocation, and perhaps not Edward's.'

'Of course, if you're going to be Catholic about it . . .'

Edward forestalled a religious squabble by saying, 'It's eleven o'clock, let's listen to the news.'

Arrests were still being made all over the country.

A few minutes later, Gerald arrived.

'Thank God you're here,' Aviva greeted him. 'We've been feeling absolutely cut off, Gerald. Tell us everything.'

Later, they wondered where he had been. Rumours pointed to Gerald as a spy. They recognized discrepancies in his stories, and remembered that he had wanted to hear what everyone would say about the Discussion Club meeting.

But the evening of the Treason Trial arrests they did not suspect him. Rather, he wanted to know who David was.

'Where've we met before?'

'At the Discussion Club when Harry Gordon was talking.'

'Of course.' Gerald settled into a leather chair. 'I'd love some coffee, Aviva.'

When she came back from the kitchen, he said, 'This is the situation. Almost all the Congress leaders have been arrested. There are a few left — no one knows why. Probably just inefficiency. They aren't interested in liberals. Alan Paton's free. So are most of the smaller leadership in Congress. There seem to be some mix-ups. They've arrested Marge."

'Marge! But that's ridiculous," Aviva protested. "She's not even political. I bet she's never even handed out leaflets.'

Aviva still didn't know that they could do anything they liked.

'She's Ben's girlfriend,' Gerald told her.

'I didn't know that.' Aviva sounded chagrined.

'They've been living together for the last month,' Michael confirmed.

'How do you know?'

'I had dinner with them.'

'When?'

'About a month ago.'

'And you didn't even tell me . . .' Michael did not answer her accusation. 'Anyhow, just being a girlfriend's no reason to be in jail.'

'She *is* in jail,' Edward's voice was quiet, but his lips had disappeared into a straight line.

Aviva looked at him for a moment, and then turned back to Gerald, 'We couldn't get hold of Monica.'

'She's all right. No one's been to her place.'

They did not talk about Philip. Joan had told David that the quarrel with Aviva had become increasingly bitter.

'We'll have to see what happens next.' Gerald seemed to be instructing them. 'It looks as though they'll all be charged with treason.'

'Treason! You can't be serious.' This charge was too heavy for Aviva to treat like a game.

In retrospect it seemed strange that Gerald knew the charges so early. 'There've been a lot of scare stories in the Afrikaans press during the last few months — plots to poison the wells, bomb the railways, that kind of thing. Now they'll say they found the plotters.'

'But they can't do that without evidence,' Aviva protested, as though she had forgotten her earlier suspicions.

'They can do anything they like, my dear. For all we know, they've prepared evidence. Or perhaps they don't care whether the charges stick or not. It suits them to have everyone under lock and key, and people praising the government for saving them from God knows what. The smear'll stick.'

'Charming.' Michael had always turned to irony to vent his rage at apartheid. He praised the government for its bumbling and folly — at least stupidity sometimes mitigated its laws. When the Extension of University Education Act was passed to keep Africans out of the universities, he wrote an article for the *Star* on how many laws in South Africa could be called Extension of Freedom Acts. The London *Observer* printed a ribald piece on the Immorality Act, and another on how the Orange Free State lived up to its name. Michael made apartheid, so far as he could, an object that could be criticized or praised as though it had no human consequences. That was how he tried to survive without becoming a mad dog.

When Snyman brought the day's soup David began to eat it hungrily, holding the warm taste in his mouth. He did not know how to connect himself with who he had been. He felt as separate from that day as from the spoon now fallen idle in his lap. Everything had dried out. The country had not changed. It had ignored them and beaten them. Michael to England; Aviva into complaisance, Edward to quixotry. Joan had always accepted it all, in a way David could not understand. Now he was here in the Fort, and soon they would hang him. It would be as though he had never lived. Except for Mrs Blackmun, Freda Bekker, Lettie du Toit the typist. And Joan, the murderer's wife. He could smell the food. He put it away from him.

Somewhere when he was a child he had seen three picannins scavenging in rubbish bins for bread and rotten fruit. They ran away when they saw that he was watching, so he pretended not to look. He turned his back and played behind a tree, and when they weren't looking, he watched them. They found some half eaten mealies and buns, and chased flies off a piece of meat, and ran away when they saw him looking again.

It was his adult mind that turned at the thought. He hadn't thought about it at the time.

There was nothing to think about. The prison made metal noises, billy cans. Someone outside in the sunshine slammed a car door.

A soft snore came from Gericke's cell. Then a panting sound, and blurred words struggling through sleep.

'Hullo, Gericke. You all right?'

'Huh. Huh.' The voice struggled to become words. 'What?'

'You all right?'

A pause, then 'Course I'm all right. Why shouldn I be?'

'I thought you were having a bad dream.'

'No, hell man, there's nothing wrong with me.'

'I was in a bad mood before lunch.'

'*Jirre* you were. It's O.K. We all get in bad moods here.'

'How long have you been here?'

'Two months, this time, but I was here two years once. That was for a fight. I nearly killed the bastard, but I was lucky. One of my chommies knocked me out before I could do anything serious. Otherwise, man, I'd be roped by now. My wife always tells me I got a terrible temper.'

At exercise time he noticed the deep and endless blue of the sky, pure and thoughtless. Sina used to air his parents' mattresses in the backyard. When he came home from school he jumped on them until she told him to stop, and then he lay kicking his legs, feeling the sun, sometimes opening his eyes to stare into the blue behind blue, until he was giddy with distance. Sometimes he fell asleep and woke in the late afternoon to see bulbous clouds pressing against a pane of air, about to come down in heavy rain. By the time the storm broke he would be inside again doing his homework in time for his father to check it.

'How is my wife?'

Kaplan tapped a yellow pencil on the table between them; it sounded like a wooden heartbeat.

'She hasn't been well. She doesn't want to see you for a while.'

'How long? Since the bomb?'

'No, longer than that. She's been overstrained since November.'

So. After their visit to Aviva.

'She went to visit a friend in Uniondale.'

'Oh, Tannie van Zyl.'

The summer before Sharpeville the apples had ripened, the wheat had been reaped, they rode horses, they swam. They forgot the quarrels erupting into their marriage. There were no newspapers, no news. He put aside the extension of the pass laws to women, and the women killed protesting them. There were only their own bodies, the sun, the sweetness of life. Visiting Tannie van Zyl, Joan's friend in the Long Kloof, he had begun to recover the affection he could once feel for Afrikaners. Tannie told them stories about the local eccentrics. There was seventy-three year old Kritzinger, who climbed every mountain in the Long Kloof to plant a single Lombady poplar on its summit. There was du Plessis, who fed his prize hogs wheat from the rolling lands northeast of the valley and wine from the peninsula. 'A hog's human, like anyone else,' he used to say. Then there were the mad Marais. The maddest of them was Lord Ford, the first man east of Cape Town to buy a car. Lord Ford was dazzled by the world beyond the Long Kloof. Every year he sent a case of his finest apples to the Queen of England, the President of the United States, the Aga Khan, and Charles de Gaulle. He kept his collection of thank you letters signed by these mythic beings next to his bed, locked in a steel box. Tannie said that he read them every night before saying his prayers — they put him in a reverent mood. When the Royal Family visited South Africa, Lord Ford was invited to entertain them. 'Just lay out the red carpet for them,' a member of the Visit Committee told him. So Lord Ford ordered a mile and a half of red carpet to be delivered from the nearest town, Port Elizabeth, two hundred miles away, and laid it over the dirt road from his two whitewashed gate pillars to the entrance step of his farmhouse.

Tannie had taken them to visit some other Marais in the valley. The kitchen floor in their Cape Dutch homestead was made of peach pits set in *mis*, and on the living room wall he had noticed a pastel sketch of a young boy with dark curls and large intelligent eyes. It had been François. Lord Ford was his uncle.

After that summer in the Long Kloof they had gone to Cape Town. The newspapers told them about the miners choking to death in the Coalbrook disaster and the women who rose up with sticks and ululations to kill the policemen at Cato Manor.

'Is my wife still at Uniondale?'

'No, she's back, preparing for a concert next month.'

'I suppose all this will hurt her career.'

Kaplan did not answer. He tapped the pencil and looked at the table.

'I see. Is she living alone?'

'No, she's with friends.'

'Who? Eugenie Tikos?'

'Mr and Mrs Rosen.'

'Oh.' Aviva and her husband. 'They have a baby now,' said David.

'Not yet. It hasn't been such a long time, you know.'

'Of course.'

'Can we talk about your case?' Kaplan was as gentle as a doctor. He asked how David had been feeling before the bomb, when he met Joan, when he met François, when he learnt about explosives, about teaching at the school in Pretoria, about the principal, and the other teachers. David answered absently, not caring what the point of the questions might be.

Perversity made him hold on to his sick headache as though nausea would reassure him that he was still alive. It felt like the headache that came from handling dynamite too long. Work quickly and keep cool, François said.

When the miners died at Coalbrook, Joan played at a benefit for their familes.

'The owners will thank you, Joan,' David said. 'Show sympathy and rally when there's a disaster. Then they won't have to do anything serious about working conditions.'

'I can't force them to do more. But I won't do less because I can't do more.'

When a truck on the surface changed gear and the earth opened at Carletonville and people and houses fell through into the mine below, Joan played for these victims and their families.

'Damn Nationalists. Why the hell do you raise money for them?'

'Can't you see, David, that they're people, just like us? There's more to a person than a label.'

'That's not what they say. They say look at your ideas, we're going to kill you. Or they say, black skin, kaffir, dirt, you better die. It's not a label, Joan, its a disease they give to other people to die of if they're not white.'

Gericke said, 'No man, that's not the way to carry on. You'll get sick if you mopes. Clink's not such a bad place if you know how to handle it.'

David heard the sounds of Prinsloo's visit in the next cell. Then Prinsloo came to his door. 'Gericke told me to look after you, hey, so you can ask me if there's something you want. O.K.?'

'I'd like some books.'

'Tomorrow. I can't do nothing about that now.'
'How about a newspaper?'
'Newspapers isn't allowed. You want cigarettes?'
'If you get some, please give them to Gericke. I don't smoke.'
'O.K. I don't know nothing about it, hey?'
'Of course.'

When he thanked Gericke, he answered. 'Ag man, you needn thank me. You do the same for me man, if you knew the ropes.'

When Snyman said, 'You gonna get sick if you don't eat,' David answered. 'I don't mind. I feel sick already.'

'I'll get you Aspro.'

'Come on, leave me alone. I bet your mother nags you to eat and you don't listen.'

Snyman flushed.

'Listen, it's O.K. I'm O.K.'


'No one can force you to eat, David,' Kaplan rebuked him, 'but you won't be able to get through this business if you're sick.'

'You talk as if you expect me to get out.'

'There's a chance, but not if you carry on like this.'

'Why do you think there's a chance?'

'I want you to plead insanity.'

'I'm about as insane as you are, and no insult intended.'

'I'll give you time to think about the choices. You're sane enough to know what they are.'

'If I'm sane, how're you going to make me insane? Who's going to commit perjury to save my neck?'

'It won't be perjury. I've been discussing your case with Dr Lippert. He'll give you some tests, you'll talk to him a bit, and we'll see.'

'I won't have anything to do with Lippert. He's a collaborator. When we had a one-hour strike at Wits to protest the Extension of Universities Education Act, he kept telling us to be more moderate. People were talking about the rape of civilization, but he said one hour was too extreme, that we couldn't achieve anything without moderation. You can tell him from me that I think he's mad. Or worse. Who does he think we deal with in this country? People amenable to reason? If he wants lunatics, let him look to the government.'

'If you're amenable to reason, you should forget petty old grudges, David.'

'Do you think I'm mad?'

A look of grief and misery pulled Kaplan's mouth so that he seemed like a child about to cry. 'I never said you were. I'm looking for a legal way out.'

'You know the sane government that passed a law to prevent interracial blood transfusions because it's better to die than be saved by a kaffir's blood — well, Lippert's got the wrong colour blood for me.'

'All right, David.'


'Jesus, that guy puts you in a bad mood man. Listen, did Prinsloo get you those books.'

'It's O.K. I've got everything I want.'

'Jesus, I wish I could say the same. You wait. When I get out, first thing I'm going down to Kerk Street, I'm going to take a blonde . . . Jesus!' Overwhelmed, he fell silent for a moment. 'You like blondes?'

'I don't mind the colour.'

'You're right man. *Jirre*, when you comes right down to it . . . Hell man, I ever tell you about my first bruintjie on my brother's farm? *Jirre*! You can't beat those Coloured girls.'


For a few interviews Kaplan did not raise the topic of insanity, but then he said, 'I've been wondering about your father.'

'Yes? Have you seen him?'

'I have. He wanted to talk to me. But I wanted to know something else.'

'Yes?'

'You ran away from home.'

'I didn't run. I decided, and left.'

'Why?'

'We had a difference of opinion.'

'Every family has differences of opinion. Tell me more.'

'What's it got to do with my case?'

Kaplan gave him a strong look, defying contradiction. 'All right. You left home, you left your wife, you hate the government, you hate the principal of your school, you're suspicious of me. It makes a pattern.'

'I see. We're still going to play that I'm crazy.' Again that hurt and nearly crying look. 'Lunatic asylums have that effect on the inmates. But really, the only thing crazy about what I did is that it didn't work, and I should've known it wouldn't. I wouldn't be mad if more people resisted the government at its own level of violence. We'd get somewhere then, and it wouldn't be mad to go out of your mind trying to get justice.'

'I'd like you to trust me, David.'

'How can I, if you think I'm mad. It's bad enough without your help.'

Kaplan was looking down at the table, rolling a yellow pencil between his fingers. 'I know that, but what's your choice? It's insanity or death.'

'In a nutshell.'

Kaplan looked up at David, 'It's better to live than to die.'

'Not for me.'

'You're too young to say that. You can't know what the future holds. I want you to live.'

'Why?'

Again Kaplan looked down at the table. 'A great uncle of mine was involved in the assassination of Plehve in Russia. He was executed.'

David contemplated Kaplan's hands. The pencil between his fingers was still.

'I don't know why you told me this, but it doesn't matter to me. Obviously it matters to you, but it can't possibly persuade me to perjure my whole life by pretending that I am or was mad. South Africa isn't pre-revolutionary Russia. One of the reasons I never joined the Congress was that I felt everyone there was trying to play a repeat performance.'

'No, I agree. I didn't intend to tell you about my great-uncle. It's not important.'

They looked at each other emptily. Then Kaplan spoke. 'Actually you've helped justify greater repression. The ninety-day bill has just been enacted.'

'What's the point of this? I've got no illusions about my effectiveness. Their repressivenss is not my fault. They've done beautifully for years without me. And I can't do anything about it by pretending I'm madder than they are.'

'You're very young, David. I know that it's often idealism that inspires acts like yours. I won't call it youthful folly. It's serious. But is it worth dying for?'

'I don't think I've got a choice about that. And in any case, I won't betray what I believe and will die for. And killed for. If that's the choice, I'm a murderer, not a madman.'

Piet Kreer, Tertius Keyter, Hans Breitenbach, Jacob Arndt, Louis Spaarman, Pretorius Eybers, Peter Venter, Andrew Smith.

If he was mad, he could live.

If he was mad he could escape the stone that had begun to crush him from the first weeks he knew Joan and went about with her friends, and began to see what he had never seen before, the servants, the women who sat all night on the pavement outside the Non-European hospital, and the people who went to prison.

He had not asked to see these things. It was Joan who saw them, and Aviva and Michael who couldn't keep away from the excitement they'd felt the day of the arrests. When the trial itself began, they went to the opening. Waiting for their eyes to be hurt. For what they saw to make them mad.

They arranged to meet at the Drill Hall for the preliminary hearings. Michael, who had a nose for news and friends in the press, warned that they should come early because of the crowds.

In the morning streets, where few shops had opened, David looked at the natives he passed. He had come to notice them so recently, he did not know whether today imposed a special importance for them. A few looked at him in a friendly way that might have had as much to do with the pleasant sunlight filtering through summer plane trees as with his sense that that he was connected to their side now. As he came near the Drill Hall, he saw more natives. Some were wearing black, green and gold rosettes, and one or two were dressed wholly in these Congress colours. They seemed happy, excited, prepared for some significant event. He was surprised to find how thick the crowd became near the Drill Hall. Here was the world he had not seen before, the invisible city that always surrounded him. He felt elated to see it, and partly to share in it.

The others also seemed elated.

'That's the reporter for *Time*.' Michael pointed to a man in one of the groups talking in the courtyard of the brick hall. The whole day, Michael would be the one in the know. He was narrowing down to his journalistic vocation with the zest of learning and giving information that made him relish his work even when he hated what he learnt and told.

'There's Jacoby,' Aviva pointed. 'They're lucky he's willing to take this case. It could be risky.'

'I don't think so,' Michael argued. 'Look what he stands to gain. We're getting international attention.' He waved to someone in another group. Later he pointed out members from a delegation of observers sent by the International Commission of Jurists.

'Look they're taking films,' Aviva pointed to a crew of cameramen, but as they watched, a policeman came up to them and the film crew moved away. Policemen stood guard at every gate and door, and out in the street where the natives were now beginning to press. Someone David recognized from the Discussion Club meeting joined them. Aviva introduced him as Tony. He listened to their conversation a while, chewing dirty fingernails.

'I think the government's just fools. Harry says everyone's using this time in prison together to have a conference. It's terrific.'

Fired by imaginary triumph, Michael cried, '*Mayebuye!*' the Congress cry David would hear from the crowd all day.

The sun was shining, there was the press, the observers

from all over the world. It was like his father's dream of history.

Policemen locked the gates and shouts of anger rose from the crowd.

'Just look at them, the bastards,' Aviva complained. But David could see that she also felt herself in the eye of history.

Only Joan seemed downcast. Occasionally David saw her looking at him thoughtfully. But then the excitement and the crowds, the sun flickering in the poplar trees across the street, the feeling that this was history distracted him.

But it was going to be a long day when they would do little but move into the hall and out. The press table remained empty. For a while someone sat at the table set aside for the three judges, and people came to talk to him, but then he left. Joan's friends attached themselves now to this group, now to that. He felt apart from them all, even from himself, and watched their confluence and separation as if looking at pond organisms under a microscope.

A confused clamour of shouting and singing rose from the crowd. People in the yard pressed back into the doorway of the hall, people in the hall pressed to the windows and door. Several large police vans had arrived. Prisoners showed their hands through the wire netting, their thumbs raised in the Congress salute. *'Mayebuye! Mayebuye!'* Voices from the crowds inside and outside joined in the Congress songs, joyful and fervent. The police hustled their prisoners along, but the singing and the cries only grew louder.

He did not know any of their songs.

When the singing died down, Aviva said, 'It's hot,' and they went inside again. A policeman told them not to sit on that side of the hall. The inner block of seats was reserved for non-Europeans.

'Well then, why don't they let them in?' Aviva fulminated, 'They're not even letting in relatives.'

'Father Knowles is talking to them,' Edward pointed. David had heard of Father Knowles as one of those interfering missionaries who thought they knew more about race relations after ten years in the country, than people who'd been born in South Africa. The policeman seemed to be refusing his request. They saw that he moved to a group Michael had identified as reporters. Edward went to greet Father Knowles, a friend of his parents.

'He tried to persuade them that it would look bad overseas, but they don't care.'

It seemed to David that, like the crowd outside, they reflected their anger to each other. History was taking too long. It was tedious, and he was hungry, impatient, irritable.

Eventually Aviva said, 'I've just got to have lunch. I'm starving.'

Men in the crowd helped the girls climb out over a low fence of brick and cast iron.

At the small café where David sat next to Joan, holding her hand under the table, although he could still feel a constraint in her he did not understand, Aviva marvelled, 'There must be five thousand people here.'

'It's magnificent!' Michael took up her enthusiasm.

Although Edward shared their excitement, he did not forget the fleshly scrape of injustice that had brought the crowd here, and the pain likely to spill out at any moment. 'I hope there won't be trouble. I don't think the police expected a crowd like this.'

'Everyone's so friendly,' Aviva disputed his foreboding. Although she protested, again and again that the government was unreasonable, she never quite expected it to behave unreasonably.

When they came back to the Drill Hall, and the crowd again helped the girls over the fence, David wondered why they didn't simply break through themselves.

The afternoon hours passed like the morning's, empty. Tony suggested that the hearings had been delayed because the microphones weren't working.

'I think we should leave.' Edward sounded as though he had made the suggestion before.

'Just another half-an-hour' Aviva argued. 'We've been here all day.'

David took Joan out into the courtyard. 'What's the matter?' he asked.

'I phoned you last night. Did your mother tell you?' she asked.

'I'm not living there any more.'

'Oh. They didn't tell me.'

'What did they tell you?'

'Nothing very pleasant,' she said. 'In fact, they really attacked me, and said I was ruining your life, and all sorts of things. I don't even like to think of it. What's going on, David?'

'I'm sorry. They probably blame you for a lot of things that've got nothing to do with you, like my leaving home.'

'Why have you left?'

A coke bottle shattered at their feet. Fragments of glass shot up at Joan. She looked up, surprised. He stepped between her and the street. There was a small commotion in the crowd where the bottle thrower must be. Joan said, 'Please God, don't let it be a riot.'

'I think it's all right now.' He put an arm over her shoulder. 'It was only one person.'

Before he could guide her back into the hall, a policeman was asking for an account of the incident. They could tell him little.

'Let's go and get something to drink.'

Joan nodded, and they went inside to tell the others they were leaving.

When they came back into the yard, policemen were trying to clear a way for the prisoner vans, but the press of the crowd was too great.

Using their batons, policemen started to beat people away from the gates. Four policemen pushed each wing of the gate to force it open.

'Careful there,' they heard someone in the yard. 'That woman's pregnant.' But the policemen continued angrily forcing the gates and beating the crowd away. Singing prisoners were led into the first van, where again they pressed against the wire netting at the back, showing their raised thumbs. The van moved forwards slowly. 'Get out of the way.' 'Move.' Slowly the crowd retreated, and the freedom songs carried before the vans, up Twist Street, towards Hillbrow. Towards the Fort.

They walked away from the Drill Hall and the disintegrating, deflated crowd in the streets. They came to a silent part of town where small shops neighboured flats and doctors' offices. A few geraniums bloomed on balconies where pensioners had come out to sit in the afternoon sun and watch the quiet streets. A drunk veered from gutter to shop window, a dog sniffed at walls and light poles. Soon they came to larger shops and offices where the afternoon rush was beginning. No one seemed to know about the encysted mass of people at the Drill Hall. Natives acted like their everyday selves. Delivery boys on bicycles whistled hit parade tunes, errand boys pushed the glass doors of the new Post Office so that the sun flashed and the street blinked. A fat old women sat on the pavement selling peaches. A beggar offered his felt hat. Nothing had changed. The banners of evening newspapers announced a quiet day at the treason hearings.

Joan was looking at him over the small table. The Indian waiter who had brought their tea was spreading linen cloths, and setting cutlery out for dinner. The cashier sitting near the door stared straight ahead, an absent expression on her powdered face.

'What's been happening, David?'
'My parents didn't want me to see you again.'
'Why? What do they know about me?'
'Nothing. They didn't want me to see anyone, I mean, any girl. They have other plans for me. My father's got my whole life worked out. The only trouble is that I want to live my own life.'
'But can't you talk about it, work it out with them?'
'No. It's not easy to talk in my family.'
'What are you going to do?'
'I don't know. I don't even want to make too many plans, right now. That's what my father does. He's had me all set to win a Rhodes Scholarship and become the kind of man he should have been. I don't know what's going to happen, but I want to let things unfold naturally, without deciding too soon

whether it's good or bad, or what I'm going to do about things.'

'How do they know you were seeing me at all?'

'I came home late after the Discussion Club meeting, and I didn't come home to supper the day of the arrests — you remember, we waited for Gerald at Aviva's.'

'Yes.'

'When I came home that night we had a big row, and the next day I just left.'

'So of course they think it's to do with me. Why didn't you tell me about all this?'

'I didn't want you to feel that it does have to do with you. It was probably going to happen someday, one way or another. If you thought I left home because of you, it'd put a kind of pressure on you that I don't want. You know what I feel about you. I want you to have time to know what you feel about me.'

'What do you feel about me?'

He took her hand on the table between them, and turned the palm up. He put his palm over hers, and said 'I don't trust words, Joan. I think you know that everything in my life has changed since I met you. But I don't want to rush you. You don't have to feel that you must say, Yes, I love you too, or No, this is too much, too soon. We could just leave it, and see what happens.' He looked at their hands on the table. 'Though perhaps it's too late now, and I've told you.'

'I'm glad. I wanted to hear it. I do love you too.'

He stroked her wrist, and looked into her golden, green eyes.

'I don't know what's going to happen in my future,' he said.

'You know that you're going to finish your B.A. How're you going to manage it?'

'I've got a scholarship, and I've been working nights at Pop's café. Pop'll take me again next year, and he's renting me a room.'

'Will you come to visit my family at Christmas?' she asked.

'Yes.' She looked down, and he saw the golden fringe of lashes edging her pale lids.

'I want to show you my place at Pop's. Will you come with me?'

'Yes.'

As they walked through the empty city and over the railway bridge, he felt again that he was seeing the city he lived in for the first time, the empty evening streets, the orange glint of sun on the railway tracks as they crossed the bridge. He was alive and saw everything through Joan, close beside him.

When he kissed her, in his room, her lips were soft and dry. He stroked her golden hair. He touched her neck with the tips of his fingers, wondering.

'We'd better leave now. I'll walk with you to Aviva's.' Again his sense of the city and his sense of Joan came together. They passed gardens and walls, the cast iron fence of the zoo, and the willows of the Zoo Lake.

'I won't come to the house with you.' He touched her temple, where a curl of hair had fallen. He did not know anything that would happen in his life, but he felt that it would all be right. At the corner he turned back to wave, but Joan had gone inside the gate and did not see him.

The next day, he woke eagerly. Nothing could be more happy than the water he splashed on his face, the smooth feel of his skin when he had shaved, the taste of the peach he ate for breakfast. He rubbed the hair on his chest before he buttoned his shirt. Out in the sunshine, walking towards the Drill Hall, he whistled. As he approached the Parade Grounds opposite the Drill Hall he saw that the crowd was even larger than the day before, and there were more policemen. They were forming a line across Twist Street. The shopkeepers and pedestrians seemed subdued, afraid. The line of police in Twist Street started to move forward. He saw that they were beating the crowd back with their batons again. He was walking quickly. Natives ran towards him. There were screams and shouts. Pedestrians retreated into shops and shop entrances. More natives fled past him. In the empty lot near the hall a few crouched behind parked cars. Some picked up stones and broken bricks, and threw them at the line of approaching police. Now there were shots, and a storm of stones, bottles, bullets, bodies, hurtling towards him. Leaning, as if against a rainstorm, he ran towards the Drill Hall. He saw Michael crouching near the fence. The clatter of bullets and missiles, screams, natives stampeding from the police, others running back towards the melée, dust and glare, tumbled about him.

'Where's Joan?' he shouted at Michael. But Michael also seemed deafened. David turned away, running, calling, 'Joan, Joan, Joan, Joan, Joan.' He ran back to Michael.

'Where's Joan? Where's Joan?'

A scream sounded close to his ear. He saw that the woman's hand was dripping off her arm. She was staring at the place where it had been, yelling. He put an arm around her shoulders and pulled the arm out of her line of sight. Her weight felt like Sina's. He propped her against a wall, pulled his shirt off, bit, and ripped. He wound the bandage as tight as he could near the gory wrist. The dark flesh bulged over his rough tourniquet. He tried to wad the rest of the shirt where it would stanch the mess of blood still pouring out.

He left the woman. Michael had disappeared. He ran back towards the gates. Bullets were still making it hard to see. There was the film crew they had noticed yesterday. Joan. He turned back to look for her. Someone grabbed his hand. Joan! He tried to pull her away, but the stampede was too thick. He felt that she was pulling back, and turned to see why. Her face was pale. He led her to the edge of the pavement and made her sit with her heads between her knees. He sat next to her, holding her.

In the gutter, trickles and small puddles of blood mixed with stones, cigarette stubs, glass and paper. Smudges of blood tracked the street and pavement. He stroked Joan's hair. He watched the ambulance that drove down Twist Street and parked in the Parade Grounds. Michael had climbed onto the bonnet of a car near the ambulance and was addressing a small group. A policeman came to him, and he climbed down. He saw that several groups of Red Cross workers were scavenging for wounded and dead. He recognized Father Knowles.

'There's an ambulance, Joan. I'll take you to a doctor.' She shook her head without raising it.

Edward found them, and sat on the kerb next to David.

'What's the matter with Joan?'

'I don't know. Shock, I suppose.'

'Have you seen Aviva?'

'No. Were you together?'

'She was looking for Michael.'

'I saw him a minute ago, over there.' Edward went off to look, and soon came back.

'He's O.K. Let's take Joan to the ambulance.' Again she shook her head, but they both supported her and led her across the street. Natives stepped aside for them with closed looks. A Red Cross worker helped them lay Joan on a stretcher. She was the only person in the ambulance. He looked round for the other hurt people, and saw their stretchers laid out on the ground, in the dappled shade of the summer poplar trees. They were all natives, and would have to wait for a native ambulance.

'You look as if you need help yourself,' the nurse said to him. Blood had dripped over his khaki shorts.

'It's not my blood,' he said.

Although Joan seemed unconscious, he turned to her and touched her shoulder, 'Joan, I'll be back in a minute.' He searched for the woman he had propped against a wall. He looked at the natives lying on stretchers. She was not there. He saw horny feet, whitened with callouses and cracked. Sina. Some had stepped into blood and the dark lines seeped up the cracks.

He went back to the ambulance.

'I'm going to look for Father Knowles,' Edward said. 'Maybe there's something I can do.'

'I'll stay with Joan.'

David sat on the step of the ambulance looking out at the dusty Parade Grounds. Joan's friends were voyeurs. He hated them. Michael on the car, the police, the scavengers and the reporters. He hated the feet, the woman who poured blood all over him, the people who put stretchers for natives on the ground, Sina, Hungary. He hated everything that tied his love into a tissue of death and terror. He wanted nothing to do with history, nothing to do with politics. He wanted to take Joan back with him, into the world he had woken to that morning, where, a lifetime ago, he had splashed water on his face and the world had seemed to be full of light.

*Pretoria*

If ever there would be an end to the world, it would be preceded by a universal Pretoria. Everyone would be rich or starving, big in the belly with fat or hunger. Everyone would be tyrant or victim. All the air would smell of cars and putrefaction, inorganic and organic processes of destruction. Noise would be interminable and intolerable. Brakes, gears, motorcycles, shrieks, juke boxes, marches, planes, commands, mobs, pneumatic drills biting streets, shovels, cranes, balls punching walls, concrete mixers. No speaking voice would be heard. No voice would be allowed to speak. Prudence, caution, fear, exhaustion, satiety, sun, exercise, concerts, rallies, patriotic displays and duplicity would embalm the living flesh. Everyone would be calm. Electric lights flickering too fast to be watched would snag where one globe was broken. Distracted eyes would bury that distraction. Concentration would be impossible. No one would be able to resist degradation.

But the most abominable thing about Pretoria was that there would be no end to the world. Pretoria would survive with impunity. Survive, flourish, and destroy. It would swallow Johannesburg and Sweetwaters and the Long Kloof. It would replace the sun and bring drought to the whole country, from the Limpopo to Cape Aghulas. South and north, east and west, it would assimilate the British Protectorates, Basutoland, Swaziland and Bechuanaland. It would establish concealed empire in Mozambique and Angola. Rhodesia would become its northern province. Missionaries and entrepreneurs would spread Pretoria further, into black Africa, into the bowels of Europe and America and Japan. Pretoria would extract from the world a moral submission as glorious as gold and diamonds, first carriers of the disease into foreign bloodstreams. Communicating with the whole world by its secretions, Pretoria would emit its enzymes: gold, diamonds, uranium, platinum, apartheid, baaskap, the purity of the white race, pilchards, oranges, sherry, grapes. And the more poisoned the world, the more it would call for diamonds, gold, uranium, apartheid, titanium, white leadership, flowers in December, peaches, apricots, race purity, karakul, rock lobster, tobacco — every pusilanimous luxury that could be squeezed from mothers with flaccid breasts, men with dagga breath and yellow eyes, *kias* without men, compounds without women, kraals where mongrels ran about sniffing for masters.

He had been mad to let Pretoria get him down. He couldn't save the world. He had known that. That was what depressed him. The world followed its own appetites.

He had been reading the Bible because there was nothing else to read in the Fort but cowboy stories. David found himself preferring the crabbed collection of ancient writings that the Nationalists thought supported their cause. Although large stretches of the Bible seemed downright unreadable, others comically vindictive and preening, other parts demanded justice with a fury like his own, and showed him something of what Joan had found there. He saw why she had been happy when Muller had proclaimed aloud, for all his church to hear, that the Bible opposed apartheid. They would have to listen to Muller. He was one of their own, not only a *dominee* but the professor of theology at the University of Pretoria who had translated the New Testament into Afrikaans. But for all Muller's standing and learning, for all his severely righteous Calvinist mien, his face deeply lined and unflinching, unambiguous over the stiff white collar and stiff black suit, he had accomplished nothing. His truthfulness had provoked only obstinate anger and denial.

In any case, only prisoners read the Bible.

Living alone in its dust and noise, he tried not to hear Pretoria. He read the English newspaper and ate fried eggs and bacon. People who tried to curb the world's appetites were fools. They thought they could force South Africa to decency by trade boycotts. He read about their attempts and drank his tea. What! Would they make Pretoria bankrupt when her very shit was full of precious metals? Bankrupt the world's greatest producer of gold? The United Nations resolved a boycott. Of course Britain and America and Japan and France did not support it. They had too much trade with South Africa. Portugal and Spain also had their reasons. What had the sponsors expected? Why did they waste their time and spill the patience of the oppressed? If they were serious, they would do something serious.

Sometimes he saw Michael's name signed to articles supporting the boycott. As though Michael had not really understood what South Africa was, and had not talked that way with him in Pretoria. Their discovery of each other had come too late, but it assured David that Pretoria *was* the hell he thought it was. That he was not really mad.

Rifkin thought he was mad. Lippert might have thought so too, but Kaplan hadn't mentioned Lippert again. It was Rifkin who would do the job, certify him, and let him live. Rifkin said little. He took notes. David watched his thin hands. A cast in one eye gave him a secretive look. To Rifkin, Pretoria was hell only in David's sick mind. Talking to him was like being back in solitary. Or in Pretoria.

But Michael had known. They'd had that conversation. It was strange that they had never talked during the four years between the Treason Trial and Michael's time in solitary during the state of emergency after Sharpeville. Though perhaps not so strange, because David had, at first, hated the political certitude of Joan's friends. They knew too absolutely that they were right and the government was wrong. Or perhaps he had avoided them because he knew, after those opening days of the Treason Trial, that he saw too much now, and could be driven to madness.

Evasion had not helped him. He could not learn to not see. And seeing had poisoned his marriage until he and Joan separated. He could not separate his sense of the city from Joan and asked the Education Department to transfer him to a school outside Johannesburg. He tried to forget the bitter thing he cherished instead of love.

When Michael heard that David would be coming to Pretoria, he phoned and said, 'What a time for you to arrive in our nation's capital! Come and see me before I leave. I wish you'd been here last year, but if you come soon, I'll introduce you to a few people and show you where you can get a decent meal.'

So they had spent a day together. David met some of Michael's colleagues on the *Chronicle*, and Munira and Mr Moodley, and then they had lunch.

After coffee, Michael lit a cigarette.

'I'll have to give this up when I get to England. Can't afford it there.'

'Better for your health.'

'Everything'll be better for my health, and I'll miss South Africa like hell. God, this is a marvellous country, and I don't just mean cigarettes and swimming pools. I wonder if I'll ever find anything to match it.'

'Well if getting arrested in the middle of the night's what you like . . .'

'No! God it'll be good to get out! Even if I miss it like hell. I thought I'd never leave. Remember how we used to talk about it. But I'm forgetting how to live like a human being, in this country. Everything turns into politics, as if there's nothing else in life. I can't write any more. Last year I was doing the women's pass protests. It was the usual — policemen beat up woman carrying babies on their backs. How the fuck can I write about that again! It's hackneyed. I got a tiny piece on page four for it. Even if I'd done a better piece, it would've been page four. No one wants to hear that old stuff again.'

David knew that Michael was describing his own condition, but he said.

'There's no point in staying. You can't do anything now except go to jail again.'

'But that's it. I can't take another bout of solitary. I feel such an awful coward.'

'You know what you'd call yourself if you stayed in South

Africa so that you won't feel like a coward.'

'What?'

'A sado-masochistic martyr.'

Michael laughed. 'You're right, fuck it. I'd feel like Edward.'

'Edward?'

'I thought you knew. He's gone off with a bunch of missionaries to a godforsaken hole in the eastern Transvaal. Actually, Sekhukuniland. Just where I covered those women's protests.'

'You mean with the Ramsbottoms? Where there've been the Group Areas removals?'

'Ja. They haven't been removed yet, but it won't be long now.'

'What's Edward doing there?'

'God knows. Aviva says Father Knowles got hold of him and told him he should do something useful. Useful, my foot! Religious bladdy perversion, that's all it is. I was appalled.'

'Edward didn't tell you himself?'

'I was in solitary. He went in June.'

'Have you heard from him since?'

'Not much. He used to be my closest friend.' Michael picked up the red box of cigarettes on the table and turned it over so that the blank underside showed. 'It's too hard man. It's too hard. I'm going to miss too many people.'

David poured out the last wine. 'You'll make new friends.'

'Actually, Edward's been headed this way a long time.' Michael leaned back, savouring the blue smoke. David noticed that unconsciously, habitually, Michael was observing everyone else in the restaurant. 'Edward's always had a hankering for asceticism.'

'Remember the way he talked the day of the Treason Trial arrests? As though it's not right to listen to music because people are in prison?'

'Ja. I remember.' Michael lit one cigarette from the stub of another. He looked at David and acknowledged the name that lay between them. 'You know, while they were interrogating me, I kept wondering whether Joan was practising scales and Bach suites.' He laughed. 'It's bizarre.'

'She probably was.'

'Oh, I didn't doubt it.' Again Michael hesitated. 'Is it really finished between you?'

'I think so.'

'I'm sorry. I never expected it, and you know, one does, half the time, with a lot of people. I wouldn't talk like this if I weren't leaving.' He turned the cigarette box over again, 'I'm getting married myself, you know. I don't think you've met Ruth.'

'I hope you'll be happy.'

'Thanks.' Michael glanced away and then back at David. 'You know, you and Joan both looked extraordinary together — as though there wasn't really anything else in the world for either of you. I remember, at the Treason Trial, when they were shooting, you didn't seem to notice anything except Joan. You were full of blood yourself. I wonder if I'd ever forget myself that much for Ruth. For anyone.'

'I wasn't hurt. It wasn't my blood.'

David took a cigarette from Michael's box. Michael watched his unaccustomed gestures, lighting and drawing the smoke into his mouth.

'You stood up on a car and talked to the crowd.'

'Tried to.'

'I thought you were showing off then. I hated all of you for getting involved. But I wonder if I'll ever be that brave.'

'Oh, showing off might've been part of it.'

They fell silent again.

'You really hit it with that question about Joan.' David lit and puffed. 'It drives me mad that she keeps so calm, and nothing ever interferes with her work, and the way she talks to people like her relatives as though they're decent though she knows perfectly well how they treat the Africans on their farms. I just can't see how she separates everything like that. I'm like you, I don't know how to keep politics out of anything else in this country. How can she stand it, playing for whites?'

'You're beginning to sound like Edward. Or like Lenin. You know, he once said, let me see if I can remember it, I was very struck. He said, I can't listen to music too often. It affects your nerves, makes you want to say nice things and stroke the heads of people who create such beauty while living in this vile hell. And now you mustn't stroke anyone's head — you might get your hand bitten off. You have to hit them on the head without mercy . . .'

David laughed. 'That's a shocker.'

'Ja.'

'I don't think my hand'll be bitten off. That's not what bothers me. You remember Cato Manor? When I read the headlines, I thought, at last the Africans've begun to fight, now it's the policemen's turn to get killed. Those damn cops were asking to be donnered, raiding the location night after night. I don't know what I hoped for. I thought maybe it could be the beginning, the first real battle after the simmering last year — you know, all the pass protests and those damn stories on page four. All Joan thought was, how cruel.' He looked round, like Michael, at the people in the restaurant. 'I'm sick of cruelty.'

Michael grimaced, as though he knew that sickness, shared it.

'She wanted to tell me that you can't get justice by bloodshed. When we saw the pictures of Sharpeville it was the same kind of thing.' The cigarette tasted harsh and nauseating. David stubbed it out. 'You know Joan's friend Eugenie Tikos?'

'No.'

'Well, it doesn't really matter. She's Hungarian, and when the Russians invaded Budapest she was unhappy, but she was glad too. She said that now everyone would see what the Russians were like. I thought something like that. And it seemed for a while as if the world's attention would help. After all, the pass laws were suspended for a while. But to Joan it was only violence, like Cato Manor, as though all violence is the same.'

Michael was denting lines in his cigarette box with a knife. He set the knife down and looked at David. 'All right,' he answered. 'You feel differently about some things. But surely that's not enough to break everything between you.'

'It's been enough. It's been a year full of the things we feel differently about, Cato Manor, Sharpeville, the state of emergency and people like you being arrested in the middle of the night, like the Treason Trial again. This year has made me feel we'll never get out. Everything that's bad for the rest of the world is good for us. We get richer and richer. No one will ever destroy the government. We'll just go on for ever and ever, like Dante's hell.'

'Milton's is the one with all the gold and jewels.'

'That'll do. But you see, Joan doesn't think history's a prison. In some ways she thinks it's all planned and everyone'll go to heaven in the end, whatever that means.'

'But you've always known that Joan's a Catholic.'

'Yes, I'm the one who's changed.'

'Why didn't you ever join the Congress?'

'Oh, I don't know. I didn't feel as strongly about all this until last year . . . No, it's really that I can't stomach all the clichés about the people, and friendship and solidarity with Nkrumah and our brothers in Algeria, you know all that stuff. Remember that awful discussion when the party line was to defend the invasion of Hungary and Philip got angry and said that it had nothing to do with what's going on here? I felt he was right.'

'I want to see Philip before I leave,' Michael said thoughtfully. 'I'm going to miss so many people.' He took a pen from his jacket pocket and wrote 'P.B.' on the cigarette box. 'But,' he turned his attention back to David, 'You know, he really was naive. There is an alliance of interests that goes beyond this country both for and against apartheid. It was clear enough last year when the Americans saved us after Sharpeville, so that we could get back to normal and keep apartheid going. You teach history. You must know that this is true.

'Only half true. Whatever interests there may be outside, this is where the revolution's got to happen if it's going to happen. We've got to believe that this is our country, and that we've got the right to make decisions in it. That ideology business in the Congress is just playing the same game with Russia that Joan's parents in Natal play with England. Pretending that everything overseas is better.'

'But Congress has been the only white party in touch with the people.'

'What people? I'm sorry, Michael, but that just feels like another piece of jargon to me.'

So he put away his connection with the Congress people. When he read that the Treason Trial had ended he felt like a old man finding relics of his youth, now becoming history. He looked through a funnel of time to that morning almost five years before, when the dapple of popular leaves had fallen on the crowds of Congress supporters wearing black and gold and green. The colours were banned now. And the *Mayebuye!* the crowd had chanted, also banned. They had smiled at each other that day, sharing history. He would not smile again those green, hopeful smiles. Nor would they smile at him if he tried to join them now. Too many friends had betrayed them during these years. They would not trust strangers.

He felt old. Even his conversation with Michael had been a conversation of old men. They had been remembering a time before they knew they would not be able to change history, when they had still thought events susceptible to their will. But by the time they talked, they knew themselves shrunken. History did not need them for its grinding. Friends and lovers would follow purposes in which they had no say.

Sometimes David thought of writing to Michael now, but there was nothing to say.

Distance separated him from Michael. Bitterness separated him from Joan.

In Pretoria lassitude infected him like senility. He did not bother to put his name on the waiting list for a telephone. He did not bother to buy new clothes when his shirts frayed. He saw himself in the mirror, looking seedy. Like his father.

He tried to ignore the tremor that flickered on his right eyelid, distracting. It sometimes eased when he closed his eyes. He sat on the box with his head in his hands. Whether he liked it or not, his nerves were giving way. Rifkin had noticed the quiver, and asked whether he had any other tics. The questioning that would save him felt like something that would destroy him. He was as isolated here as he had been in Pretoria.

Michael had given him one contact and route to relief, the Asiatic Bazaar, where once a week, Mr Moodley drove him to the apartment behind his shop. There David would tutor him and Munira Ismael for the B.A.s they were taking by correspondence.

Munira wanted to teach. He did not know what Mr Moodley wanted. With them he allowed himself to comment, as he dared not in the classes at school, on the right answers given by the correspondence notes. Sometimes he asked wicked questions. He felt as if something like friendship was growing between them. Sometimes they invited him to a slide show about India, or the Ghandi Memorial Lecture, or a performance of *Shakuntala* at the Wits Great Hall.

Although Munira was plump and pretty, her features fine-boned and her expression full of patient sweetness, and Mr Moodley, darker, older, and beginning to show a weight of years, a man in his mid thirties who never talked about a wife or children, the friendship between the two seemed as asexual as their friendship with him. Munira was a Moslem, Mr Moodley a Hindu. Perhaps in a larger community, overseas, their religious differences would not have been so intractable. But Munira dared not escape like her older sister who had gone first to Kenya, then to England. Munira was now the only wage earner for her family. Her mother was dying of cancer, her grandmother was senile and blind. They lived with her in three rooms behind Mr Moodley's shop. When Munira told him that she was plagued with anaemia, David felt that he could not sympathize any more, as though a failure of artistic judgement had made her lay it on too thick . . .

In exchange for the tutoring, Mr Moodley wanted David to buy whatever he could in his shop, at wholesale prices. David walked among the counters of toothpaste and liver pills, tinned fruit and sardines, touched the rayon ties and cheap shirts, chose among buttons and shoe laces and writing pads, and admired the patterned blankets hanging from the ceiling. If he saw other purchasers in the aisles, he avoided them. He would rather do without buttons than hear an apology because their dark bodies blocked his white way.

Sometimes, happily, he needed nothing. Then, before the

curry supper that Munira cooked for him, he would wander in the Asiatic Bazaar, looking at the heaps of red and orange powders in shop windows, admiring the ornate richness of saris. He regretted the oleographs of Hindu gods and the Sacred Heart that showed him how a civilization as intricate, gorgeous and lavish as the saris implied, could yield to the garish shoddiness counted desirable in the Asiatic Bazaar because it seemed European. When fat mothers wearing a swathe of their saris over their hair brushed past him and he caught the glint of nose rubies and golden earrings, when shrill cries emitted by skinny boys playing ball in the street skimmed past him, when lozenges of odour in front of each shop door — incense and linen, curry and ghee — mixed with the street smell of dust and dry heat, when afternoon and evening glare were muted, falling kindly on dark eyes and shining hair, sari curves and finely boned features, in this forgotten slum of Pretoria, he felt that he had escaped to another country and other possibilities.

Mr Moodley's life was more opaque to David that Munira's. He did not talk about himself, and although he was irritatingly inclined to defer instead of asking questions when they talked about history, he held to his own opinions. Knowing little else about him, David knew that he was often consulted by members of the Indian community on questions of who should compose the welcoming committee when the Minister of Indian Affairs came to visit the Asiatic Bazaar, and how to resist eviction to Laudium.

'Why do you have a welcoming committee at all? Why don't you boycott the whole business?'
'We must cooperate. It's the best way.'
'Why?'
'There's no other way.'
'What about passive resistance, like Ghandi?'
'We tried passive resistance. Our leaders are in jail.'
'But if you joined the Africans?'
'We tried. It didn't work. And they're worse off than us.'
'One day they'll be free.'
'Then they'll make laws against us. It's happening in Kenya.'

'It's not a bright future.'

'We don't think of the future.'

So the Asiatic Bazaar was, after all another closed door. Its inheritance was division, caste, religion, race, and impotence. It had no future.

During his first months in Pretoria he invited Mr Moodley and Munira Ismail to visit his flat, and gave them supper. The next day, his landlord phoned to tell him that Non-Europeans weren't allowed.

'There's nothing about that in the lease.'

'I'm giving you a month's notice, Mr Miller. I can't afford to have your type in my building.'

'I'm surprised, Mr Kaminsky, that a Jew will support racial prejudice, after Nazi Germany.'

'I've got to look after my own interest.'

'I'm sure that's what the Nazis used to say.'

He heard the phone banged down.

A letter warned him that he would be evicted if he did not move. He found another flat. Munira and Mr Moodley refused subsequent invitations. Perhaps they had guessed why he moved.

The incident left him feeling that he did nothing in Pretoria without white permission. If he breathed, taught, read, caught a bus painted the colours that meant whites only, took clothes to a cleaner whose sign said, *Blankes Alleen,* ate in a café, he lived only as apartheid allowed him to live.

When he went to Johannesburg where he could find a newspaper from England in a bookstore, he bought it. Overseas, they knew that it was apartheid, not he, who was mad.

Very occasionally Rifkin asked a question that suggested how he must be cataloguing David's account.

'Did you ever do anything that made you feel less passive?'

David could not see where Rifkin's eye was looking, and the question irked him, also looking skew. He could have pretended to be more active, and even found a sphere of petty power for himself like Gardy, the geography teacher who presided over the Common Room at school. Gardy had his chair that no one else would sit in, and pretended that he was the one who ruled the school. There were infinite ways to be happy and forget who held the guns. David felt contempt for them all.

'Not much.'


While the Nationalists celebrated what they had wanted since the Boer War, while South Africa became a republic outside the Commonwealth, and all ties with the hated British rule of the past were broken or breaking, David hardly moved out of his flat. He didn't want to go to the café to buy eggs or bread in case he'd see soldiers in the street. The Afrikaners were full of pride and the world was not big enough for them. The streets were not big enough for them. Once David saw three soldiers push an old man into the gutter. Milk ran from the bottle he had been carrying and spilled like blood onto his clothes and naked feet. The soldiers laughed. When they had left, David helped the old man up, and gave him money to buy another bottle of milk.

'Dankie, baas. Dankie.'

It was unbearable. Next time he would protest.

Knowing his own cowardice, he read the papers with secret guilt as though he were drinking brandy before noon.

When the Muller trial broke into the headlines, he knew that Joan had also looked at the photograph of that righteous and severe face on the front page. Perhaps she was sitting at the table where the morning sun caught the checked cloth. Next to the bookcase with the African violets. Where she could look out over Hillbrow, the sun touching her left ear and making a cloud of light in the fine hairs springing into curls at the back of her neck . . .

He had scoffed at Muller when Joan first told him about his paper for the World Council of Churches.

'Of course he says that apartheid's contrary to Scripture. What else could he say to that kind of audience?'

'But don't you understand?' Joan said, 'Everyone in the

Dutch Reformed Church is going to know what he said. He's going to be attacked in every way they can do it.'

'You think they'll take any notice?'

A few weeks later, Joan told him that some of Muller's students were warning him to be careful.

'They don't know what's brewing, but they say it's going to be serious.'

'How serious can it be? David was not impressed.

'He can certainly be fired from the University.'

'Hasn't he got tenure?'

'They'll find a way.'

'Of course. We've seen what they think of academic freedom. But then someone else will give him a job, and he'll look like a hero. I'd be impressed if there was a chance he'd be sent off into banishment like an African.'

'Sometimes, David, I feel that you're so full of hatred . . .'

'I am, Joan.'

'It's monstrous.'

'Isn't what they do monstrous? Why has it taken Muller and his cronies so long to notice?'

'It takes everyone time, and some people never find out. Muller wouldn't have found out if he hadn't been asked to write that paper on the Scriptural basis for apartheid.'

'Why did he have to wait for that? Hasn't he got eyes? I trip over beggars wherever I go.'

'You didn't always know either.'

'When I was a child. Muller's forty years old. He's had time. And he's supposed to be a leader.'

'It takes courage, David. Muller wasn't the first choice to give that paper. I've heard that the other man refused, saying that he was old, just about to retire. He knew what he'd find, and didn't want to face the consequences.'

'Sometimes I hope you Christians are right, and there really is a hell. For people like that.'

'I can't judge.'

'Why not, Joan. Doesn't the Bible command him to bear witness to the truth?'

Muller was beginning to discover what bearing witness would bring. During a class on the Gospel according to St

John, three students stood to say that his interpretation of the cases of Greek nouns denigrated the Son in comparison to the Father. They recited the Apostles Creed in unison, accused Muller of heresy, and marched out. None of the other students in the class laughed. They all remained until the end of the lecture. Now the charge of heresy had been brought to the general synod of the church.

At the café where he ate breakfast, David lowered the paper and looked at other single men drinking tea and eating toast, at the refrigerator counter gleaming like a fish, the sallow owner counting boxes in a delivery of cigarettes, gleams of traffic in the street. Was this city, boastful of its modern buildings as though they proved that Afrikaners belonged in the modern world, going to be the setting for a Trinitarian heresy trial fit for the fourth century?

He followed the Muller trial as though in some magical way it could connect him to Joan again, or offer him a way to live. He saw the streets of Pretoria fill with dominees wearing black suits. A special fund had been raised to bring some of them from drought-stricken Platteland dorps. Dusty men who had not left their flocks these twenty years would sit in judgement on the theological purity of the professor whose comments on Greek grammar were dangerous to salvation. David saw their faces awed and pleased when they went into the hotel near his flat or examined the windows of department stores with dignified care so that they wouldn't make fools of themselves. He saw them cheerful and excited as they queued outside cinemas. They trooped into restaurants, sometimes in the charge of a city dominee who walked with greater confidence and knew his way. David wondered whether they sat up late hours at night to talk in rooms where the lights were electric and the power never shut off, like children who have permission to sleep away from home.

One night someone fired at Muller through a lighted window. A week later his wife was taken to hospital after an accident: the nuts holding her car's tyres had been loosened. David didn't want to see the country dominees in Pretoria who lost their way and asked policemen for directions.

Other country faces came to town, of the same lean and

hardened stock as the dominees. A fourth year of drought in the Transvaal was killing the cattle, and farmers were moving to the cities to look for work. There seemed to be none for these silent, sun eaten men. Their wives baked Boer delicacies and their sons hawked *koeksusters* from door to door. They did not beg. Frequently now, a ring at the door would call David from marking IVB's tests to meet a man with pale eyes and a khaki skin, or a boy wearing faded shorts, a shirt that had been washed too many times, and an air of indefinite confusion, reproach, and soapscrubbed frankness. He bought their rusks and *boerebeskuit* so that they could buy bread.

'Did you have any friends?' Rifkin asked.

'I saw a few people . . .' But his tone sounded doubtful.

For a while he had felt friendship growing between himself and Richard Cooke at school. They often fell into conversation in the Common Room, and one day Richard invited him to come home in the afternoon and stay to dinner.

'I've told my mother about you. She wants to meet you. She's formidable, but she usually likes people I like.'

Mrs Cooke was formidable. She carried herself with a straight back and examined David with assured curiosity.

'Take David to see the garden after tea," she told Richard. So they soon walked out towards the rockery and small orchard. 'I've just bought another plot of land. Come and see it.' They climbed over a rusted, sagging fence.

'It's so wild here I hardly want to touch it. I may just plant indigenous things to keep the wild feeling. Don't you agree?'

They picked their way along the bed of a waterless stream, and cut to where the trees grew so thick only a highlight of sunshine here and there drew the eye to a wrinkled trunk or dark feather of leaf. A stand of bluegums allowed more light through to a debris of pungent leaves and curved pieces of bark falling in long strips, white trunks and branches. Some bark, still peeling, lodged in crotches. They turned away from the stony declivity and came to an abandoned house. Its concrete stoep was littered with beer cans and broken bottles.

'I don't know what I'll do about this place,' Richard said.

'Shall we go inside?'

The dirty, echoing rooms seemed dark and surly, harbouring a smell of stale beer, urine, dust, dagga, decaying leaves. A crack in the concrete floor was shaped like lightning.

On the way back Richard stopped at the decaying fence bounding the established garden, and looked over the land he had just bought, to the valley, and the dry winter hills beyond.

'Magnificent view, don't you agree?' The thin light of approaching evening rendered the ochre hills indefinite and muted, faded, rich. Savouring the words, Richard recited,

'In me thou see'st the glowing of such fire,
That on the ashes of his youth doth lie,
As the death bed, whereon it must expire
Consum'd with that which it was nourished by.'

He looked towards the darking east, 'Shakespeare's so perfect. Don't you agree?'

Where Richard was looking, the more dense blue of smoke showed where there must be more houses. 'Where's that?' David pointed, 'What part of town?'

'I don't really know. The location? It's Garsfontein, I suppose.'

Garsfontein. Joan had given a recital there, in a mean and splintery mission school. Afterwards she invited the children to touch her 'cello and draw the bow themselves. When excitement and pleasure overcame their shyness, she hugged them. He had felt uncomfortable to see her touch their dark skin flaking white with dryness, their dusty hair redding with kwashiokor, their clothes whose colours had all gone under. The filth of the township's decrepit hovels, litter and refuse, surrounding the puny school in its drought-caked yard, burdened him as though it was all his responsibility.

The six German nuns who ran the mission complex had also established a maternity clinic. David followed Joan to the neat enclosure where flowers edged the paths. 'Ve haf our own vindmill, a chubby nun explained, 'So ve haf alvays vater for the hospital. Und also our own generator for the electricity.'

When they had seen the wards, where David saw a thin

Coloured woman sweating and concentrating on her labour, indifferent to their presence and everything outside her own body, the nun took him into a parlour to wait for Joan. He was not allowed into the ward where mothers might be nursing their infants. The nun offered him biscuits and tea, but a nunnish rule forbade her to eat in his presence. He asked conventional questions about how many cases the hospital handled, what they did in case of complications, how many babies lived. 'Vell, it is very sad. Many die in the first year. They haf not milk, und it is very dirty.' When Joan came back the nuns took her to the chapel to say a prayer before she left. At the door a box asked in gilded letters for 'Offerings for the Poor.' He put five rands in the box, resenting the inadequacy of the sum.

On the way home, Joan told him the nuns had been warned they might have to move because the location was a black area and they were white. He wondered whether they were still there in their black habits, rosaries at their belts and crucifixes over their stomachs, remembering *gemutlichkeit*, still sweeping the bare and sunny wards, and still keeping from the newborn the debris and filth of the world they were to inhabit.

'Have you ever been there?' he asked Richard.

'No. Have you?'

'Only once.'

'It's rather shameful that I've never noticed that it's in the view.'

'Oh, our lives are designed so that we won't notice.'

Richard's eyes were different colours, both pale, one green and one brown. David was surprised he had not seen the difference before. Perhaps something in the poetry Richard read and quoted had taught him shame that he had not noticed Garsfontein. Perhaps he had heard King Lear pray for poor naked wretches. His eyes of two colours troubled David.

'Draw the curtains, Richard,' Mrs Cooke commanded, and Richard closed the last colours of afterglow out of the room, obeying her with gentle deference. He filled David's glass of sherry again. David saw that Richard had inherited his mother's high cheekbones and long chin, but her eyes were both light brown.

'Richard tells me you're from Johannesburg.' David nodded.

'How do you like it here?'

'I'm getting used to it.'

'It always takes a while. Once you meet some nice girls...'

'Actually, I'm married.'

'Oh. Richard didn't tell me.'

'Perhaps I haven't mentioned it. My wife and I have separated, so I live rather a bachelor's life.'

Richard had turned to look at him, surprised and curious.

Mrs Cooke said, 'You do have a bachelor look about you.' It was obviously not a look she favoured.

'Come mother, you're giving David the third degree.' Richard reprimanded.

'I like to know who your friends are.'

And by the time coffee was served, David felt sure that she knew the answers to all the questions it had occurred to her to ask, either aloud or silently. He liked her decisiveness and efficiency. It had showed in the meal too. He had forgotten how, in white homes, every evening, unconscious of ceremony, there would be tables spread with heavy starched white cloths, polished silver and glasses, linen serviettes rolled in silver rings, salt and pepper in shakers, and butter in a butter dish with a butter knife. There would be bread plates, and mats to protect the table from warmed dinner plates, and a bell to summon meat platters, vegetable dishes, and the gravy boat. There would be a maid to remove these when the course was done, and to bring dessert dishes and take them away in due time, and bring in tea or coffee. He had forgotten how white people lived.

Soon after dinner Mrs Cooke went off to her own room, and then called Richard to her. Explaining that his mother needed some medicines from the pharmacy nearby, and that he'd be only a minute. Richard settled David with a record on the turntable, a book of Renaissance drawings to look at, and a glass of brandy.

David sat on a green armchair and listened to the music and the maid and man servant talking in the kitchen. Their small clatter of dishes and cutlery and gossipy, warm activity replayed the sounds he remembered from Sina and Samuel. Softened by the luxury of human society, and the memories of Joan and Garsfontein, he felt mournful for the life he had left.

The music flowed and bounded in a volume that seemed to open great spaces within him. His chest pulled tight. He stood quickly, and went to the bathroom at the end of the passage. He closed the door. Dry mechanical sobs lurched into him. Tears started, and then a feeling of grief. He tried to weep quietly so that Mrs Cooke and the servants would not hear him. He unrolled some toilet paper to sop up the tears. Gradually the tempo and harshness of his sobbing quietened. As the tide of weeping faded and renewed in fainter waves he did not try to stop it.

As involuntarily as the first sobs, a new series started, at first gently, then with the harsh contraction and pull of muscles that had clenched him before. This bout of weeping passed too. He washed and looked at the white tiles and shining chrome. He looked at his uncertain face in the mirror, and walked out. Mrs Cooke made no sound. The kitchen was quiet. The record had stopped.

When Richard brought him back to his flat that evening and he read the paper, he saw that another case had supplanted Muller's on the front page. An African prisoner released from the Bitterspruit prison claimed he had been tortured. Another African, arrested with him on suspicion of having stolen a bicycle, had died when the police forced him to drink water until he could drink no more, and then beat him with hosepipes. Msomi said that when Zwane died the police had stopped beating him, and threatened that if he ever told what had happened, they would kill him too. But, reporting the story, he said, 'I'm dead already.' The Bitterspruit police denied the accusation but the case had been brought to court.

David did not want to know what he had read. He bathed, ignored the dirty cup left in the kitchen sink, and tried to read. Instead of the English country house in the detective story, his imagination brought him to a party he'd been to in Cape Town soon after he had married Joan. In the garden overlooking the sea, Joan protested to Edward, 'I never see you any more Edward. What's happened to you?'

'It's been a foul year, Joan. I've been deciding what to do with my life.'

'What's it going to be?'

'I still don't know. I thought of law for a while, but then the thought of doing anything with the legal system in this country . . .' He had been holding a glass of wine, not drinking from it. He leaned forward and set it on the terrace's flagstone floor.

'It's the old story Joan.'

David watched coldly, annoyed that Edward was tapping his old intimacy with Joan.

'So what are you going to do next year?' she asked.

Edward leaned back in his chair and shielded his eyes as if from the sun's brilliance. His hand half-covered his mouth. 'Prolong my childhood. Hang on at varsity.' He spoke as though he tested the bitterness of his words more on himself than on her. 'Braithwaite's offered me a job in the maths department, but of course he wants me to go to England and collect more degrees. I can't see it. But I don't know what I can see.'

'I've missed you, Edward. You don't come to my concerts any more.'

'I don't listen to music much these days. It feels too much like maths.' He picked up his glass and drank the wine too quickly, his face puckering as though the wine had turned to vinegar.

'I don't understand what you mean,' but Joan's tone sounded foreboding, as though she knew what to expect.

'It's all a defence of the political statue quo.'

'That's ridiculous,' Joan said quietly, looking into Edward's eyes, 'And it hurts.'

'I know it hurts, Joan. It hurts me too. We talked about this the night of the Treason Trial arrests. I don't see how else to be consistent.'

'Why should you be consistent? You're not French.'

Edward laughed. He turned to David, 'Where are you going to be teaching?'

When the sun had set and the party moved indoors, David sat next to Edward again while he and Michael were having one of the long discussions they had indulged in while they were all still students, and everything they said had seemed true, and predictive of how they would live. The topic came round to music again.

'I don't trust it,' Edward said. 'There's a reason that music is the preeminent art of dictatorships.'

'Is it?' Michael challenged.

'Yes. Think of Germany. Think of Fascist Italy and opera. Think of the Afrikaans universities here, Stellenbosch and Pretoria — wherever there are educated Nationalists there are chamber music groups.'

'That sounds like a classic example of bad sampling and irrelevant correlation.'

'Not at all. You see, we human beings long for harmony and beauty. Even the most savage and primitive tribes make art. Even Nationalists.'

Michael laughed at Edward's jibe. 'Yes. So?'

'Say you live the way we live. Or like the Nazis. How can you make beauty of this filth?' Edward gestured to the party around them but he seemed not to see the people there, or even to notice David, listening. An abstraction in his mental eye imposed its vision between his senses and attention. 'You have to look away, and satisfy the aesthetic hunger with forms that have nothing to do with life, avoiding the imitation of reality. So you turn to abstract and intellectual forms of harmony. Maths and music. In that way, you can tolerate the conditions of life around you. You can even cooperate. You listen to Mozart with appreciation and it does not interfere with your duties as superintendent of the concentration camp.'

Michael set his glass down on the table with a thud for emphasis. 'That's an outrageous argument, Edward. I'd call you a philistine if I didn't know you better.'

'No, call me a philistine.'

'So what do you do to satisfy the aesthetic hunger? Or are you beyond that?'

'No, I cry for grace too. Almost the only thing that's made me feel happy this year has been inventing and solving elegant maths problems.'

'Shit, Edward, But what you say is *kaf*. Look at the visual arts . . .'

David began to feel his old impatience with their talk, arranging everything too neatly: consistent, systematic, full of words. He was known as the silent one in their group. He felt that words always fell somewhere else than their mark.

But now because he couldn't sleep, and had remembered Joan and Garsfontein, and listened to music and wept, and come home to read about how Zwane was killed by the policemen at Bitterspruit, the conversation caved in on him like a rockfall.

The morning paper carried the same story and added more about the Bitterspruit prison, electric wires attached to limbs, heads and testicles, near-suffocation in plastic bags, and a death rate even higher than in most South African jails. Again the authorities denied everything.

There was an article on Muller too, but David found himself impatient with Muller's heroism. Whatever Muller had endured he had risked, and in some way assented to. He was white. Protected. Like David himself.

All day he felt as if something in the air was hurting him. In the Common Room, when he thanked Richard and asked how his mother was feeling now, he noticed Matthew, the man, called boy, who brought the tea in, an extremely dark, round-faced, cheerful person who always greeted people with a wide smile. David liked him. Today he saw Matthew as vulnerable as Zwane.

'Did you see that article about Bitterspruit?' he asked Richard.

'Oh, I never read the news. These things aren't important.'

David went to the table where Matthew had set the tray of tea and scones.

When he came back to his chair, he found the Afrikaans teacher, Adrian Marais, talking with Richard. Adrian was another who should have been a friend. He had told David a little about Afrikaans poetry, saying that the language was at an exciting stage in its development, comparable to Shakespeare's time in England. Though most Afrikaans poetry, he said, was just growing out of sentimental and patriotic pieces. David noticed how Adrian carried a quiet humour in his face, softly lined, too marked for his years. He was sure Adrian wrote poetry himself.

Richard had been asking Adrian about his family.

'We've got a farm in the Long Kloof.'' So Adrian was one of the mad Marais Tannie van Zyl had talked about during David's visit with Joan.

'Is Lord Ford still alive?' David asked.

'Did you know Lord Ford! What a character!'

But no affectionate memory of the eccentrics of the Long Kloof could heal David's raw imagination. All through school that day, he heard rasping sounds — a suitcase carelessly lugged along the floor, the squeak of chalk, a desk top banged down, scuffing and kicking as the boys waited in corridors, the snap of metal clasps as the boys packed at the end of the day, sounds of careless and destructive contact. After school he packed textbooks and composition books into his own case. Outside, the superintendent was yelling at the Africans who scrubbed the floors. He always yelled at them. Every afternoon the school was full of those unanswered shouts, magnified and echoing in the empty spaces from wall to wall. It was impossible to know why the superintendent was always so angry.

David heard the white yells superimposed on those other sounds continually carried in the South African air, the crack of whips on flesh, screams, 'Thank you baas.' It was a dream of hell to walk through Pretoria's dusty streets, lowering his eyes against the glare of cars and dust. Winter jacarandah leaflets were sifting down like foliate excrement. The traffic set its metal anguish against his will to not hear.

During the weeks that followed, David could not tear his attention away from the Bitterspruit trial. The story developed as he had expected. All the officials denied Msomi's accusations. The judge warned Msomi that if the evidence went against him he could be jailed for perjury. Cabinet Ministers and Members of Parliament complained that the English press was making a fuss of the story to put South Africa in a bad light. Prime Minister Verwoerd said nothing, and neither did the Minister of Justice and Prisons, Vorster. David did not understand silence from these two and it oppressed him with impatient uneasiness.

His attention continually snagged on Bitterspruit. He set aside the book by Marc Bloch he had been reading and enjoying. He couldn't attend to it, although the detective stories he read instead could not numb his imagination. Images of van der Walt, an overgrown and loutish boy at the back of IVB, intruded into his mind. Hosepipes, that day at Garsfontein, a curve of road in the sunny Long Kloof, a location superintendent with thick grey eyebrows who had stopped Joan in Soweto to ask her business, the house on Richard's property, floated behind the butler's evidence and the witty detective. When he was teaching, telling unwilling adolescents the Seven Causes of the French Revolution, with van der Walt squeezing his pimples and playing poker at the back of the room with two admirers, Venter and Smit, David wondered about the Bastille. What noise did a man make when his stomach burst? Luminous declensions of sunlight among the desks and faces hardened into an airless amber where no sound carried.

In a few weeks the newspapers told him that the prison commandant and doctor at Bitterspruit had been found guilty of criminal negligence. They were sentenced to four years in jail, three suspended. The young constables, found guilty of manslaughter, were sentenced to eighteen months, six suspended. Outraged supporters throughout the country wrote letters to them sympathizing because the sentences were so severe. When the English newspapers called for a Parliamentary Commission to investigate prison conditions, Vorster replied that he saw no need for such an inquiry. He had made it clear, he said, that abuses like those at Bitterspruit would not be tolerated. Now David understood why Vorster had been so quiet.


If it had really been they who were mad, what did that mean about Rifkin's attitude to him? And his defence? He paced the cell. Guy Lechaptois, Piet Kreer, James King, Willem Schoeman, Jacob Arndt. The constipation and headaches that came with confinement were making it hard to think clearly.

'Hullo, Gericke.'

'Ja, David.'

'What's the time?'

'Three o'clock, maybe. The warders haven't changed shift yet.'

'What's the date, Gericke?'

'Twentieth of January? Why man?'

'Nothing. I don't know why I asked.'

'Ja.'

'You feeling bad, Gericke?'

'It's nothing, really, man. Just sometimes I don want to go on.'

'I know what you mean,' David said.

'Ja.'

'You think it's going to rain this afternoon?'

'Ja. It's the weather. When it rains we'll feel better. You'll see. On my brother's farm, this time of day in summer everyone goes to sleep. Then in the evening you *mos* fresh again, you go out en find girls. *Ag,* man, that's the way.'

'When were you there, on your brother's farm?'

'Well, it's really a long time ago. You know how it is. Time flies. It must've been ten years ago. No more. It was the year Danny Boy won the Durban July. You remember that, hey? I was lucky. I had a lot of money on that horse. The odds was sixteen to one . . .'

So Gericke cheered him. In prison he was learning to become as tolerant as Joan. In Pretoria he had not been able to manage it, not even with Adrian. David and Adrian discovered that they both played tennis, and arranged to meet once a week to use the school's courts. Adrian gave David some Afrikaans poems to read, and one day he showed David a new anthology that included six of his own poems. David congratulated him.

'What's it feel like to be famous?'

'This isn't famous. Hardly anyone'll see them.'

'Does it bother you that so few people speak Afrikaans?'

'A little.'

'Have you ever tried writing in English?'

'I don't feel at home in it.'

'But if you practised?'

'No. I don't believe anyone can write in English about South Africa. In English it always sounds like some other place. The language doesn't feel the country. It has no words for *kopjes*, or *veld*, or *khakibos*, or anything. If I say Weenen in English, no one knows that it is a place called Weeping. If I wrote in English it would cut me off from my people and my imagination.'

Adrian was lying on one elbow on the lawn next to the tennis court. With his free arm he tilted a ball on the strings of his racquet. Without looking at David, he added, 'Foreigners don't understand this country.'

The phrase was a political excuse, and David wondered why Adrian had chosen to touch this dangerous ground.

'What don't foreigners understand?'

'They think that every evil they see here is something we have done deliberately. I don't deny that there is some evil. In other countries too there is evil. But foreigners treat us as if we are all guilty, and only guilty.'

'Aren't we guilty?'

Adrian hestitated to accept the challenge he had provoked. He bounced his ball a few times on the racquet. 'Are we?'

David looked at Adrian on the lawn, slim in his white tennis clothes, brown, his face scribbled with premature lines. He did not want this fragile friendship to break. He tasted the bitterness that had poisoned his marriage. But he asked the question, in a gentle voice. 'Aren't we?'

'No. Every man is responsible for his own life. He is not responsible for actions beyond his control.'

'What if he condones?'

'Condoning is his own evil.'

David felt himself skidding towards open challenge.

'Are you a Christian?'

Adrian was surprised. He stopped playing with the ball and racquet. 'Yes.'

'So's my wife. She was very moved by Muller. His case seems a paradigm. He wouldn't condone, so he's in trouble.'

'I know in the English press Muller's a political martyr.

Most of the reporters are Jewish. What do they care about his orthodoxy?'

'Do you think anyone else really cares?' David asked. 'The theological point seems pretty obscure to me.'

'Are you a Christian?'

'No.'

Adrian sat up and hugged his knees. 'Then I don't know whether you can appreciate how even the most delicate points of theology can affect the whole life of the church.'

'The command to love your neighbour as yourself doesn't seem especially delicate or obscure. What happens to the church when it says, Don't let the black man be your neighbour, he must live in a separate group area?'

'That's not the church. That's the state's law,' said Adrian.

'Is it a law acceptable to Christians?'

'It could be. Christians must love everyone in the world, but they can't live next to everyone. Love is not a physical thing.'

'So Christians have nothing to say if the law forces people from their own homes and separates them from their families?'

Adrian turned his face away from David, 'I know that much suffering is caused by such laws, but they are needed to prevent worse suffering. Apartheid is the only way to avoid friction between the races. In America they try integration. Look how much trouble they have.'

'You think we have less friction here?'

'We've never had a lynching in South Africa.'

'I would call Sharpeville a kind of lynching.' Adrian was silent. 'In any case, some kinds of peace are worse than trouble. A corpse causes no trouble.'

Adrian turned to face him. 'You know, David, I like you too much. We shouldn't talk politics. You want me to agree with you, but there are many reasons that I won't. I have grown up all my life as an Afrikaner. I am troubled by many of these questions, but I also have a love for my people that is very deep, and I cannot let them be criticized by an outsider, even by a friend like you. We shouldn't talk politics.'

'No, we shouldn't.'

They smiled at each other. They played another set. But the

conversation left David bereaved, feeling that their friendship had died. Although they still met to play, once a week, and talked in the Common Room, the fissure between them seemed to deepen like a donga.

More and more David felt spent and alone, crumbling and drying out, like the veld during drought. Then, in September, three days fell on him like lashes from a sjambok.

On the Tuesday when the synod's final judgement was due in the Muller case, the school syllabus brought him to a history lesson about Dr Philip of the London Missionary Society. Dr Philip had caused a lot of trouble by preaching equality to the natives and agitating for the repeal of the pass laws. Then, when they were repealed in 1828, the land filled with lazy vagrants, and cattle theft increased on every side. The Boer resentment Dr Philip provoked, combined with other grievances like the abolition of slavery, eventually persuaded the Boers to leave for the interior, on the Great Trek.

As David, at the table in front of the class, talked about Dr Philip, van der Walt, at the back of the class, was talking with Venter and Smit in a voice hardly lowered as a gesture towards classroom decorum. David stopped talking and waited for silence. Van der Walt stopped, and David began the lesson again. Again van der Walt started.

David said 'I know that history bores you, van der Walt, but you'll need some to pass your matric. You might as well listen and let the rest of the class listen.' He felt that van der Walt, his face darkening with stubble and reddened with pimples, was the gross material that jail warders and policemen were made of. There was something curiously, ignorantly pitiful about van der Walt in his naive discomfort with learning, overwhelmed like the woman in labour at Garsfontein, with the needs of his own body. What need to fuel him with hatred of Dr Philip? 'Of course, passing matric is not the only reason for learning history. Many issues in history are still alive today. Dr Philip, who may seem a bore to you, is having half his case replayed in the Muller trial right now.'

Surprisingly, Muller did not seem a bore to van der Walt.

'Do you think he's guilty, sir?'

'I've no idea. If it's a theological question, the judgement will be made on theological grounds. It's difficult for a lay person to judge because the case is being tried in secret. But let's get back to Dr Philip.'

Venter, following van der Walt's lead, said, 'Sir, My father thinks Muller's a tool of the Communists.'

'Do you think he's a Communist?' van der Walt wanted to know.

David started to feel that there was something suspicious in all this sudden interest. 'The Communist Party didn't exist in 1828,' he said.

'But he was a foreigner. He didn't understand this country,' Venter said.

'Yes, Dr Philip was a foreigner,' David allowed himself to stray from the syllabus. 'And it explains a great deal about his troubles. There's a pattern in history that repeats itself. The city person and the country person won't agree. The Greeks have even given us words for this quarrel. Living in the *polis* made you *polite*. They called foreigners barbarians. The Romans thought the same. If you lived in the *city* you could be *civilized* and *civil*, the *urbs*, made you *urbane*, but if you lived in a *villa* in the country you became a *villain*. Have a look some time at the English word *boor*, closely related to our Afrikaans *boer*. Dr Philip came from the largest city in the world to a country where hardly anyone could read. It wouldn't have mattered whether his ideas were good or bad, as long as they were different.' He knew that he had gone too far, but it felt like a relief.

'We'd better get back to the syllabus. I'm going to dictate six points about Dr Philip. This could be an exam question.'


He felt angry with himself. If he couldn't talk with Adrian, why did he try to enlighten the likes of van der Walt? He dragged through the rest of the day, feeling depressed and inert, and when he came home in the afternoon he lay down and slept. After an hour he woke, suddenly feeling alive and drained of the poisons that had been clogging him. His teaching was a death and an abomination. At the end of the year, he would have paid off the loan from the Education Department that had paid for his B.A. He would be free to resign and stop teaching. He would leave, and find some other way to live.

He fell asleep again, happy as he had not been for a long time, and dreamed of palaces and civilizations growing out of each other in wonderful succession, the amazing sequence of human history. When he woke again, in the late afternoon, he felt that he longed for civilization. He wanted to live like a civilized person, tied to the decencies of cleanliness and decorum and the inheritance of self-discipline he had once loved in Joan. He made the bed, washed the dishes and cups that had accumulated in the sink, showered, dressed, and decided to find something better to read than the vile detective stories that cluttered the flat. He would cook himself a civilized meal. It was too late to get meat or fish, but he could still buy eggs at the corner café and make an omelet. Perhaps he would still be in time to buy some wine.

As he walked through Burger's Park feeling happy, free, the blurred rose of the afterglow was rising to the zenith.

He bought wine, and at the corner café he looked happily at the rows of tinned food. He could buy asparagus to put in the omelet, some tinned peaches for dessert. He could make himself a really decent meal. Why hadn't he done this before?

He picked up a newspaper and went to the counter to wait for service. A wizened old African was waiting already. The woman behind the counter turned to David.

'Yes?'

'This man was here first,' David gestured.

'Kaffirs must wait. What can I do for you?' David looked at her impatient, blowsy face. He wouldn't have guessed that she had the discipline to maintain a principle.

'Serve him first.'

He must have tapped some pent-up anger. 'Don'tchou tell me how to run my business,' she screamed. 'Filthy *kaffirboetjie*. I don't need your business. Get out!' She pointed to the African, 'You too!'

The man cringed and explained in a pleading tone that he

only wanted a penny matches, he didn't mean to make any trouble.

'Scram, both of you.!' She pointed at David. 'Don't you come back here, *kaffirboetjie* drunk!'

He put the newspaper back on the pile. The old African was still excusing himself to the womam, who seemed ready to be mollified.

David disgusted himself. What a futile gesture, to invite a scene and make himself feel good and civilized. And his omelet! What propaganda to guzzle and live easy! He wanted to play civilized, the English South African, so superior to the boorish Boers who didn't know what was going on in the world. They knew enough. The Nationalists knew who must pay for wine and guzzling in South Africa. If that was civilization, they knew how to get it.

He didn't know what to do with the wine. He put it under the kitchen sink. He felt hungry, but the only thing he could find in the flat was a tin of beans. He ate them cold out of the tin, standing in the kitchen, but afterwards he washed the spoon, making one gesture towards civilization. And he looked for the copy of Marc Bolch's *Feudal Society*, but when he read it, something about the clear and patient mind searching for order seemed painful to him, and he could not bear it. He tried a detective story.

In the morning paper he read that Muller had been found guilty of heresy.

Just after the lunch break Mrs Blake, the school secretary, sent a boy to fetch him from his classroom to take a 'phone call in her office. She busied herself with files while he was talking, but David felt that she was listening, wondering about this Indian woman who had phoned him.

'Mr Moodley cannot fetch you today,' Munira said. 'He's at the police station.'

'What's happened?'

'They arrested him in the shop this morning. They said they want to question him.'

David did not want to say too much in front of Mrs Blake,

but the matter seemed urgent. 'Has he got a lawyer?' Let Mrs Blake think this Indian woman called on him as African servants sometimes called on their masters for help with the police.

'No.'

'I'll get one, then.'

'Maybe he should not have a lawyer.' Munira's telephone voice sounded thin and high. 'The police don't like it. It is better not to annoy the police.'

'They've got no right to be annoyed.

Munira did not answer, and David realized that her silence was an argument against him. Mrs Blake was hardly pretending to look at her files.

'I'll come straight after school. Where are you?'

'At a 'phone near the shop. How will you come?'

'By taxi.'

'No. A taxi will make talk. I will ask someone to fetch you.'

'Make it half-past three.'

Mrs Blake had gone to another filing cabinet in the corner of the room.

'Perhaps you should not come.' Munira said. 'The police may be watching.'

'What for?'

'We do not know why the police have done anything.'

'Come and fetch me,' he told her.

'I will send someone.'

Yes, of course. They couldn't be alone in a car together because of the Immorality Act. David had once felt impatient of Mr Moodley's caution. He was coming to see how the terror that taught fear surrounded every moment of their lives.

A young Indian his own age came to fetch him. Mr Moodley's shop was dark, stricken, and shunned, as though word had gone out to all the customers that there was calamity and danger within. Munira was sitting in the small room at the back of the shop where they met when he tutored them for their B.As. He took her hand and pressed it. Her mother was sitting in the one large old armchair, flanked by two men he had seen before consulting Mr Moodley on community affairs. They nodded to each other, and Munira introduced him. Their group sat solemnly, like mourners meeting before a funeral. The conversation changed from Tamil to English, a courtesy to David, although sometimes one forgot, and came out with a sentence David did not understand. One of the men explained to David that the most likely reason for the police visit was some matter connected with the group areas removal to the new Indian township at Laudium. Mr Moodley had not been filling out the papers and returning them as he was supposed to. He had hoped to remain unnoticed. He had hoped that Munira could be allowed to stay in the rooms at the back of the shop.

David suggested a lawyer again, but they all demurred. Not knowing what else to do, like mourners repeating the incidents leading to death, they told him how the police had come at ten-to-eleven and taken Didi away in their van. (So Mr Moodley had a first name. Perhaps it was a nickname.) David imagined how courteously Mr Moodley would answer the police, and their contempt for his *koelie* tone.

They sat for a long time. In the centre of the room a brass vase on a doily was beginning to look like a spider waiting in its web. David felt that his presence was only a constraint. He wondered whether to ask for a lift home, but in a state of boredom, irritation, embarrassment and pity, he held to his hard seat.

'D'you know if they came for anyone else?' No one had heard of other arrests, though Mr Moodley's strategy to postpone removal must have been a common one.

It grew so dark in the little room that Munira switched on the light. Her mother pulled herself out of the obese armchair and went out. Soon sounds from the kitchen showed where she had gone. David felt that at a meal he would be even more uncomfortably an outsider and a white. He would ask to leave soon.

They heard voices in the shop, exclamations, questions and answers. Mr Moodley came in and they made their own exclamations. Munira called her mother, and Mr Moodley's friends embraced him. He did not touch Munira, but he shook

David's hand, looking solemnly into his face. The assistant who had guarded the till at the shop, stood at the door. Other people pushed past into the little room.

'How are you?' 'What did they want?' 'Are you all right?'

'It was a mistake. They wanted someone else. They got the names mixed up.'

'Did they treat you all right?'

'I'm fine. No, it was someone else they wanted. For sabotage.'

'Allah!' Munira exclaimed.

'It's all right now. They know it's not me.'

'But how could they make such a mistake?'

'So many Moodleys. It was a mistake. We won't talk about it any more.'

After the supper, a feast, Mr Moodley took David aside.

'I want you to know how much I appreciate it that you came. Now we know that you are a friend.'

'I'm sorry I couldn't do anything useful.'

'Friendship is like a rose. We don't love it because it is useful.' As Mr Moodley pressed his hand, David felt awkward. Indians were always talking about flowers in a sentimental way.

'Well, don't mention it.'


That was Wednesday.

On Thursday, he found a message in the Common Room. Spence, the principal, wanted to see him after school.

When the boys packed and the school emptied, and David heard the superintendent yelling at the African cleaners again, he went to Spence's door. The thin sound of his knock rebuked him.

'Yes?'

'It's Miller sir. You wanted to see me.'

'In a few minutes.'

He waited on a bench in the anteroom.

When Spence called him in, he did not ask David to sit. Throughout the interview he pressed the tips of his fingers together, and bent and straightened his fingers so that his hands moved with the slow rhythm of snake swallowing a large prey. Black hair grew on the backs of his hands.

'You are aware, Miller, of the law against politics in the classroom.'

'Yes, sir.'

'But you had a discussion about the Muller case in class?'

'I mentioned the Muller case, sir, because I was talking about Dr Philip and wanted to point out that some of the issues are still alive today.'

'Hmm. You mentioned the Communist Party.'

'One of the boys suggested that Dr Philip was a Communist. I pointed out that the idea was an anachronism.'

'I see. And I gather that you made some pejorative remarks about the Boers of Dr Philip's day. Something about their being uncivilized.'

Whoever had reported his remarks in class had understood them. The pupils weren't as dense as David might have guessed possible from IVB's dreary history compositions. 'My remarks weren't intended to be pejorative, sir. I was trying to explain some of the hostility Dr Philip felt and provoked. I was making a general comment on the suspicion often found between city and country people, and used some illustrations from etymology.'

'You find etymology part of history?'

'The history of words, sir, is a useful historical tool.'

'Ah.' The room waited. A large reproduction of Bellini's Doge hung on the wall. It was a surprising picture for Spence to choose. 'I think such refinements are beyond the boys' scope. That's why we have the syllabus, Miller. Too much sophistication may be too, ah, *urbane,* for the boys to understand.' Bellini's Doge looked at the world calmly. 'I cannot have teachers in my school breaking the law, Miller. There will be no politics in the classroom, and no material not specified in the syllabus.' A white balustrade separated the Venetian prince from the clammy threats that filled the space between Spence's hands, contracting and distending.

'That will be all, Miller.'

'What's wrong?' Richard asked when he came to fetch David to supper.

'I'll tell you later.' Several poppy petals were lying on the fresh-turned earth of a flowerbed outside the front door. A flower in a hurry to die. A cold wind sprang up.

'What's the matter with you, David,' Mrs Cooke demanded as they sat at tea. 'You're looking like a starved cat.'

'Mother!'

'I've been living too much like a bachelor,' David dodged.

'Then it's time you took your wife back. You've got no right to be looking so sickly at your age. Eat your cake, and make up your mind to live like a married man again.' David ate the cake.

After supper, a neighbour came to the door. Richard invited Dierdrechs in for coffee and for a while they all sat in front of the fire and talked neutrally. Dierdrech's face had lived too hard. There were pouches under his reddened eyes, and flaps at his jowls. His skin had burnt a hard red-brown, his nose was pitted. It was a face that warned against life. David couldn't follow his rapid Afrikaans and was left with an impression of violent gesture.

When Dierdrechs left, David heard him saying to Richard, at the door.

'Tomorrow is another day.' But then they had a long conversation in undertones. Afterwards, Richard told him, 'Dierdrechs wants me to join a commando the neighbours have organized to protect the ridge from attack.'

'Attack from whom?'

'There's been a lot of restlessness in Garsfontein. It's just down the valley you know. We'd be the first target in a riot.'

'Why do you think there's going to be a riot?'

'It's just a rumour.'

'So what's the commando for?'

'Just in case.'

'So will you join?'

'I don't want to, but Dierdrechs lives next door, and he says that if I won't protect myself, it just means he's got to look after us as well as his own family. I've told him I've got a gun, but I haven't practised shooting since high school cadets.'

If Richard heard a noise on the terrace and looked through the French window that faced east, where Garsfontein lay, and saw a pair of eyes, he would shoot. He had a gun. If women ran up the hill singing and ululating, the way they had at Cato Manor, he would shoot. Perhaps he would shoot a child born at the clinic where the German nuns taught the newborn that they were human before they could learn they were black. 'You're not asking him to protect you. You could tell him to go to hell.'

'It's easy to say that, David, if you've got no responsibilities. I've got my mother to look after. I can't think only of myself.' Like you, the unfinished accusation hung in the air.

'So you'd do it.'

Richard stared at David. He hadn't been stared at like that since he was a child and had played contests to see who must look away first. David stared back, and felt the whole world recede from the arena where their eyes locked like animals in a fight that could end only in victory or humiliation. There was nothing now but Richard's irises, different colours.

Richard looked away. 'Would you like some tea?'

'I'm rather tired. Would you mind if I leave early?'


Although he felt as exhausted as he had ever been, he could not sleep, feeling that Pretoria whirled him in a centrifuge that separated everyone according to race. Everyone fell into his proper place, whirled, whirling, African, Coloured, Asiatic, white.

Many hours later, as he was being drawn down into sleep at last, he heard car doors slam in the street. Soon after he heard banging, like wood on wood. Then screams.

He climbed out of bed and looked out of the window. The light behind him blinded the street. He switched them off. Across the street below him a flicker of torch shafts came down the alley between two blocks of flats. Angry voices and thuds sounded among the screams. He saw two policemen emerge from the alley dragging an African boy, perhaps a skinny man, between them. A third policeman walked behind them and kicked, making the large thuds David had heard.

He turned and ran out of his flat to the lift. The concrete floor was icy. The lift sighed and rustled up to his floor like a fat lady doing an unpleasant chore. It opened unwilling doors with metallic shuffles and clicks. As David reached the ground floor and ran out to the street he heard the van doors bang shut and the van driving off. He had not been able to see the numberplates.

His bare feet ached with cold and he went into the building again and waited for the lift to shuffle its doors open and take him upstairs. Its walls were padded with khaki matting and smelled of dagga. Under the shower where he washed the filth and cold of the street off his feet, he examined what he could do. He could phone the police and try to find out who had made the arrest. He could phone Michael's colleagues at the *Chronicle* — though what sort of story could he give them? What else? He could not think of anything.

He did not try to sleep. He tidied the flat and made his bed as though he were going to leave and did not want strangers to see the sordid misery he had lived in. Shaving, seeing his face in the mirror, he beat his head with his fists and banged it against the tiled wall. He went to the window and looked again at the alley he had seen lanced with torches. The sky had become deep and very blue now. The first glow of morning was rising into the darkness with impassive perfection.

When the city was ready to wake, he went out and bought a newspaper and scanned the front page. Muller had decided that for the sake of the many who had stood by him in a time of testing, and for the principles he believed in, he must contest the synod's judgement in a civil suit and an open court. He would have preferred silence and peace, but conscience demanded justice.

David counted his change and went to the public 'phone booth. The police could give him no information about the arrest. None of Michael's colleagues had come in to the *Chronicle*'s offices yet. Through the glass of the booth Pretoria's traffic showed sunny and metallic. His mind slept and knew nothing but sensation — the blue sky, the muffled shift of gears, the smell of urine and exhaust fumes. He sorted out the coins he would need for a call to Johannesburg.

'Hello. Joan? This is David.'
'Hello, David.'
'Can I see you again?'
'Yes.'
'This afternoon?'
'Yes.'

'Your reconciliation was successful?' Rifkin asked.
'Yes.'
'So why didn't you stay with your wife?'
'I couldn't.'
'If you were my patient, I'd say you wouldn't. But tell me about it. What was your fantasy?'
'You think everything I know is fantasy.' David could hear Rifkin's breathing and his own. 'You think I'm mad.'
'I think you've been very disturbed. It's perfectly understandable.'
'Answer me straight, dammit. You think I'm mad. It's not just what you're going to say in court. It's what you think, isn't it? It's what you think!'
'I'm a damn fool. Of course I'm mad. It's what I want you to say.' Rifkin probably called the screams a fantasy too. David put his hands to his face. He could feel his hair. He started to pull it. 'That's it! That's the point of it!'
Rifkin called Snyman in to handcuff David and take him back to the cell.
'You O.K., David?' Gericke asked him.
'Thanks, Gericke. I'll be O.K.'
But he was thinking, I can't go through with it. He was shuddering, and sweat was pouring from his whole body. He had played with the world. He hadn't believed that anyone would really think he was mad.

# *The Bomb*

A membrane thin as the skin inside an egg held him away from the glare and anger of Pretoria and the school. On weekends, while Joan practised, he marked compositions and prepared lessons near a sunny window that looked over the high skies and white mine dumps beyond the city. Afterwards they wandered among the small shops of Hillbrow where the owners came to expect them and the exchange of pleasant remarks about the weather and the state of things in general. They walked in Joubert Park, and booked a tennis court at a club where no one knew them. At Joan's rehearsals he sat near the back of the hall. They avoided old friends as through they feared for the fragility of their new marriage. They had no telephone yet.

One day Joan found a note from Aviva. 'Let me hear from you, dammit. I've got news.' The women met for lunch while David was in Pretoria, teaching.

'Aviva's married.' Joan told him that evening.

'Well! Who to?'

'It's really surprising. A friend of her parents, a businessman, older than her. Actually he's a widower, and there's a child.'

'Whew! That *is* surprising. What's he like?'

'She says we must come to visit soon, so we'll see. They've moved to a new house in Northcliffe.'

'It all sounds amazingly bourgeois for Aviva.'

'Yes, doesn't it. Imagine Aviva a stepmother!'

'That's easy enough. I've always found her rather formidable.'

Aviva's intrusion into their idyll opened a tear in the film that protected them. News came at him brutally again — raids, arrests, and the increasing ferocity of the drought. Because of a glut in the market, oranges were being allowed to rot on the farms. There were pictures of heaps like hills. The newspapers ran a campaign to collect money so that the oranges could be bought for children starving in the reserves and townships. There was talk of a new sabotage bill that would allow arrest and solitary confinement on suspicion, without need for a specific charge or trial, and, as if to justify these preparations, a government office in Pretoria blew up, but no serious damage was done.

Although the drought would not break, spring came on, the leaves on Christmas bushes fattened, and early fruit trees began to blossom.

'Let's go to Barberton during your Michaelmas holiday,' Joan said. 'I've never seen the daisies, and they're supposed to be spectacular.'

'I haven't either. It'll be good to get away.'

'Perhaps we'll stop on the way to see Edward. He's working at St Thérè's, a Catholic mission right nearby.'

'Has he become a Catholic?'

'No. He started out at the Ramsbottom's place, but when they were banned the Anglican mission was declared in a Black Area, and he had to get out. But whites are still allowed at St Thérèse's. I saw him while he was still with the Ramsbottoms, and he seemed happy, settled in some way. I'd love to see him again.'

'Yes, let's.'

She knew that somewhere Edward must have heard something like those screams in Pretoria. That was why, ripening for some dreadful act of abnegation, he couldn't listen to music, and couldn't play with mathematics. Perhaps Edward had found a way to live now.

When they drove out of the city, they saw that its urban, watered fertility had been a mask. The veld's starved thirst showed a world as dry as if it had never rained, as if the stalks of yellow grass fixed to the ground had grown from stone, or dust, or mineralized air. Discarded dongas filled their beds with stones. Dead thorn trees cast arid shade onto boulders and sand. Not even vultures flew in the opaque and dessicated sky. They passed through dorps whose half-mile main street became the road again. The blank, disheartened stare of dusty shops and sullen loungers forbade them to stop until they needed petrol. When they did stop, the rattling air attacked them like a bird of prey. Teenagers played irritated pinball machines in empty cafés, and adults accomplished their business in tindery, splintering voices.

In one of these dorps they stopped to 'phone Edward. He told them how to start on the road to St Thérèse's. Eleven miles on, they would see the buildings of a school on their right, and a row of trees. He would meet them there.

The dirt road led from the familiar dry, golden openness of the highveld to a new kind of earth, grey, breaking out occasionally into black scrub, boulders, ravines, and jutting knobs. Its funereal pallor and skeletal, angular coarseness threatened and warned. The highveld had seemed dead and inorganic. This land was a corpse.

The foreboding waste seem necessarily and totally uninhabited, but at a downbending curve in the road they twisted to the sight of several hundred tents pitched on barren arms of land clutching a donga. They could see no water among the round stones that littered its bed, but on the banks some children played, and among the tents human figures moved. As David slowed the car, picannins threw stones at them across the dead river. One stone hit metal, and an unhappy bang resounded between the dead earth and the dead sky. Joan's face took on the grey, killed look of the world around them. They drove on, past the encampment of walking corpses. Except for the hostile children, no one looked at them.

About three miles on, a high plume of dust coming towards them showed them where Edward was approaching. When the cars met and stopped, they all stepped out into the road. Edward embraced Joan and put a hand on David's shoulder.

'I'm so happy to see you both!' His skin was grey, and his faded hair also looked more drained of colour than fair. He had become as thin as if the cadaverous landscape had gnawed the youth off him to make him part of itself.

'We're going to have so much to talk about. Your room's all fixed and Sister Anna's baking a cake. One of you come with me.'

So Joan rode with Edward, and David followed close on their dusty trail. The landscape slowly rose from grey constrictions to rounded, dry hills. Near the mission, the valleys held swatches of poplar and willow, and evening light glanced sidelong over worked fields. Stone buildings, among them the church, scattered in the shallow valley.

Edward took them to a small, white room reserved for guests.

'Why don't you wash, and rest a bit?' He pointed to a pitcher and basin on the dresser. 'Supper's in about an hour. I'll come to fetch you.'

Lying on the white bed, David watched Joan brush her hair.

'Edward looks terribly tired,' she said. 'Downright haggard. Almost as bad as you.' Her arm moved with a strong, steady movement down, and away from the breast where she had laid the heavy, living tress of threads, down, away, up.

'Come here Joan.' She set the brush on the dresser and came to the side of the bed. Looking at him, she touched his forehead.

'Not that haggard.'

'Getting better.'

He pulled her down to him, feeling the firm and supple weight of her body. 'I love you.'

'I'm so happy, David. I'm so happy we're together again. I love you so much.' As they were making love, he felt that her face was wet with tears.

When Edward brought them to the dim, narrow room used as a dining room for lay people at the mission, they found a gaunt, dark man already at the table, eating before them.

'Dr Frank Kinley,' Edward introduced him.

Frank greeted them and then continued eating, methodically and with the air of someone who eats out of a sense of duty. He did not join the conversation. Though at one point David saw that his fork moved more slowly. He was listening with straightforward interest. David was asking about the encampment on the donga.

'Who are those people?'

'They're the people the Ramsbottoms were working with last year,' Edward's voice had the dry ring David recognized as the way he contained pain.

'Why are they out there, in the desert?'

'The police moved them there.'

'To punish them for resisting removal?'

'They were in a white area.'

'And what's the place they're in now?'

'That's their new homeland.'

'I read that their old one is fertile and beautiful.' Edward looked at him but did not answer. What was he trying to prove? Frank had turned his deeply lined face towards them and was stroking the lobe of his left ear.

'When were they moved?' David pursued.

'Above five months ago.'

'Just before winter?'

Again Edward said nothing but reached for a piece of bread. David understood that there was nothing to say, but like a child who cannot stop scratching at an itch, he let curiosity and horror drive him.

'Where do they get water?'

'From the river,' Edward answered.

'And when it's dry, like now.'

'It's not as dry as it looks. The water's more than four inches deep in some place. You probably couldn't see it from the car.'

David laughed. 'Four inches! That's handsome.' Frank had stopped eating. 'So you went to measure?' Edward did not answer. 'Did the children throw stones at you?'

Edward looked up. 'Did they throw stones at you?'

'Only one hit the car,' Joan answered.

'They're very bitter.' Edward's voice seemed to taste their bitterness. Then, resuming his duty, he offered vegetables to Joan and David, and took some himself.

David's curiosity picked at another question.

'What do they do about sewage?'

'There's the river,' Edward answered.

Frank poured himself a cup of coffee.

'Well, that should solve the problem, one way or another,' David could hear that he sounded like Michael, retreating into helpless irony.

After dinner Edward took them to a guest lounge where he lit a fire.

'I've got something I've been saving for a special occasion. Wait.' He came back with a bottle of brandy.

'K.W.V., Edward. You've got good connections.'

'It's a present from Father Knowles. He's got good connections.'

'Not what one usually imagines.'

'I suppose not, but he's very friendly with some cabinet ministers and Bantu Affairs officials. They can't understand how such a pleasant person can have such deplorable politics.' Edward laughed. 'And they're awfully good about warning him when they're going to close down one of his schools.'

'I don't know how people with such deplorable politics can be pleasant.' David's voice hardly sounded joking. 'I wonder how he stands them.'

'I suppose they're human, like anyone else.'

Now David laughed. 'Remember that farmer in the Long Kloof who used to say that about his pigs, Joan?' He felt happy with her, calmed, in spite of those children at the dry donga.

Edward was pouring the brandy, with careful pleasure, looking at the transparent liquid. When he had handed Joan and David their glasses he held his for a while, and sniffed its bouquet. David wondered at it. Edward had once seemed so indifferent to luxury.

Again, when he sat in a deep armchair, it was as though he yielded to unaccustomed comfort. Suddenly David recognized that his pleasure was an index of the austerity of his daily life.

'My best occasion,' Edward toasted them. He sipped his brandy slowly, 'Ah, that's good!' He leaned back. 'I think you've made a friend of Frank, David.'

'How did I do that?'

'He's just waiting for an order banning him from this area. The local magistrate warned him to stop interfering with the Pedi at the river. He's been taking food there and teaching them to boil the water before drinking it. Though they don't listen much to him. There isn't enough wood or dung for them to waste fire on things like that.'

'Of course. I can see that teaching them things like that could interfere with the whole idea.'

Edward stretched his legs in front of him and stared at them. 'I don't think Keyter really has a specific idea about the Pedi. He just doesn't like his arrangements criticized. He's defending his self-respect really.'

'You mean, he's also human.'

Edward sipped his brandy. 'There's been too much trouble with that tribe.'

'Yes. I remember reading about them. And Michael talked about them.'

'He talked to me too. He's the one who got me interested in coming here.' Edward smiled, recognizing the irony David made explicit.

'He'd be damn upset to know it,' David said.

'Oh, I know!'

'He felt hurt you didn't tell him.'

'He was in solitary.' Again that voice as pale as drought. 'And anyhow, I didn't want to argue about it. I knew what Michael would say. That's the trouble with good friends. I've been imagining you'd say the same things yourself.'

'You mean about why you shouldn't be here?'

'Yes.'

'No. I've got nothing to say. You live your own life. I've got nothing better to offer. I'm stuck.' David looked into the fire, trying to believe its warmth could resist the deep chill that had entered him.

A knock at the door brought Edward sharply out of his chair. He stepped outside and closed the door behind him. Joan came to David's chair and sat on the arm. He took her hand and kissed it. How was it that she could see all that he saw — she had been with him that afternoon when the stone banged on the car, and her face had gone grey — how was it that she could recover, become easy again? He caressed the callouses the 'cello had made on the ends of her fingers.

'I love you,' he said, feeling his difference, and his distance from her.

Edward came back carrying candles and matches.

'The generator stops at nine,' he explained. 'Did you bring your 'cello, Joan?'

'Of course. I've got a concert next week.'

'Could we fetch it? I need a benefit.'

So Joan played a Bach suite for Edward. Imperfectly visible in the irregular firelight and candlelight, she looked like a musician of another time. Her music brought their past and Europe into the room and told, in her other voice, of possibilities of being other than their own. It bound them to configurations of order and sound made for other audiences in other countries and other times. If the men who had composed these harmonious sounds had looked into the imperfect future, they could hardly have guessed their music would make men know their life anew in this bubble of fire set in the exposed and windy veld, dark and dry.

Another knock interrupted them, and again Edward closed the door behind him.

'They want me at the hospital,' he said, coming back. 'I'll show you to your room, if that's all right, and see you in the morning.'

But when morning came he was still busy, and asked one of the brothers at the mission to show them around.

Brother Isidor, a pink man with the face of a baby, showed them the fields and vegetable gardens, the carpenter's workshop, the anvil, the generator. The mission seemed much larger than it had looked in the evening light. He took them to the school, where the rooms were ranged with looms, sewing machines, more carpentry tools, and nutrition charts with gay pictures of meat, eggs, milk, and leafy green vegetables. There were few books.

'Is there a library?' David asked.

'No. The children look after their own text books. You know, they pay for them themselves, and that makes them more careful because they can sell them afterwards.' Brother

Isidor was garrulous. 'In any case, we don't do much with books. It's no use with natives. They can't come to school long. One, two years, sometimes three or four. That's the most, usually. So we don't bother with subjects they can't use. We stick to hygiene and crafts, some agriculture, woodwork for the boys, sewing for the girls. Of course we teach them a bit of reading and arithmetic. They need that too.'

It was clear that Brother Isidor agreed with the philosophy of Bantu Education, but David felt the school like a harsh prison closing the young in their own ignorance. Last night when Joan had played, she had bridged this remote mission to worlds beyond their own cramped time. She had taken them into a boundless company populating the future and the past. The children of this school set shallowly in their own world would learn no history, no geography, nothing to let them hear or speak to other men. He saw that his own school in Pretoria was the complement of this one. The history he taught was also a prison, the story of how God chose the white race to be guardians. His own school trained the warders, and was the brother of this one. Cain.

Again he promised he would stop teaching at the end of the year.

Edward had arranged to meet them after mass. David went with Joan. The dim and garish nave was crowded, men worshippers on the left, women on the right. Joan protested when two fat ladies waiting with an air of confident piety vacated seats for them, but they would not allow a white madam and baas to stand.

The church breathed and shuffled. Nuns brought candles to the altar and fussed with cloths. Acolytes wearing red and white robes performed errands in the area beyond the altar rails, and in the nave, women rose from reciting their rosaries in front of a statue of the Virgin, babies whimpered and cried until their mothers suckled them, and ushers admonished seated worshippers to crowd together on the benches. When the service began, African hymns overrode the Latin mumble at the altar. Women in the aisles pressed rosary beads through their fingers. After the sermon the worshippers in the aisles kneeled on the bare floor, but Joan and David sat until a bell rang and all the congregation, except David, slid to their knees for the consecration. With unbowed head, David looked at the fervent faces around him, the women with their eyes closed and Joan, like them, holding a reverent pause during the tinkling of more bells. Joan's expression was as attentive as the crone's whose high cheek bones and medieval lines of suffering spoke now so singly of worship that she became beautiful. He felt himself outside this company, alien in the church. If he had any company, it was invisible, single disbelievers, uncomfortable sceptics. Among the Africans, though not in this congregation, there must be a man like him, alien on his own soil, a stranger in the country he could never leave. He longed to meet that man.

Most of the other worshippers remained in the church after mass.

Edward, outside, explained, 'Some of them walk twenty miles to church. Once they're here they want a long service.'

On the dry lawn clumps of men and women sat talking. Children, a red jersey here, a blue doek there, gave the scene a gay and pleasant air, and David remembered Marc Bloch's *Feudal Society*. In that world too, the church had gathered people together like this. But here, something in the dry air, almost invisible, like candlelight in sunshine, reminded David of the hostility they had met on the dead river bank.

While Joan took time to practise after lunch, Edward offered to take David on a tour of the monastery. They walked in silence along a sunny causeway, and then on a narrow road bordered by fallow winter fields.

'How was your tour with Brother Isidor this morning?'

'Depressing. Brother Isidor doesn't seem to mind Bantu Education at work.'

'No. He's not very bright about some things. He's really a carpenter. He's done some fine work for the hopsital. You've got no idea how much that's worth when you're two hundred miles from anywhere.'

'Does he teach carpentry too?'

'A bit.'

'And you? What's your work here, Edward?'

'I'm a jack of all trades. Less useful than Brother Isidor. Mostly I help with administration.'

'Why?'

'Someone had to do it, and other people have different skills.'

'That's not what I'm asking.'

'I thought it might not be.' He kicked a stone off the road. 'I suppose it's because of Michael.' Edward paused and grimaced. 'When he was arrested I saw what was probably going to happen to all of us. I could've seen it before, it's happened to so many, but you know how close Michael and I were. At first I felt a hell of guilt because he'd been arrested and not me. I was jealous too.'

David gritted his teeth. So Edward had felt this too. When the police were holding Mr Moodley he had felt such jealousy, as though to be arrested would signify something valid in the way he had rejected apartheid.

'But', Edward continued, 'I knew I'd been doing much the same as Michael. Next time I'd be arrested too. So I began to think about it, and what would happen after. What do you do after prison? Go on as before, get arrested again? Some do, and it has a kind of usefulness. There're a few things you can do while you're out, though you've got to be careful not to incriminate other people — I mean, more careful each time. And there's something about a moral witness. It's O.K. But in the end, that kind of life wears out. Most of our friends've decided to leave after one or two rounds in prison. I'd probably do the same. So then you work overseas. I suppose it'll produce results some time. Sharpeville wouldn't've been the same without all the international horror. But since Sharpeville we've been back where we started from, and overseas opinion doesn't seem to make much difference after all. So what else, if you do the kind of things that get you into prison? You can turn state's witness, or informer, or slip out of the whole business and never think of justice again.'

They walked in silence. Afternoon heat bore down on them.

'You've said it,' David acknowledged. 'Those are the choices.'

'You've been thinking about them too.' Edward looked at David. His green eyes and fasted lips smiled out of a sadness that made David feel, for the first time, that Edward was closer to him than anyone he had ever known, perhaps closer even than Joan. They shared a weight that oppressed them like a secret.

'Yup,' David confessed, 'And I'm stuck.'

'I felt stuck.'

They walked on. Then Edward started again. 'You know, if I'd thought the revolution could come soon . . . But we know that it's not going to happen for ten years at least. I couldn't wait that long. It felt like a luxury. I could've gone to prison, satisfied my vanity and my guilt. I knew that was a waste of time.'

'So you've left the Congress?'

'I haven't had to do anything special. The Congress is banned now. But I came here.'

The pale winter sky and dry sun surrounded them. 'Tell me why this matters,' David asked.

'There *are* some absolutes. You teach a little. You're not allowed to teach much, and I'm not Brother Isidor, I find the school depressing too, but it's better than nothing. You feed the starving, and teach them a bit how to feed themselves. You teach them to boil water. O.K. They shouldn't be hungry in the first place, but if you don't feed them they won't last till the revolution. And you do what you can to heal the sick. That's also palliative, but sick people also can't wait for the revolution.'

'So you've given up on big change.'

'I can't wait for it, and I'm not strong enough to make it happen on my own.'

'But you could work for it.'

'Yes, and that'd get me into jail, and then out of the country, if not worse, and that'd be the end of that. I'm not even sure that I *could* work for the revolution. It's not going to come from us. It's going to come from the Africans.'

'I'm sure you know as well as I do that palliatives don't work.'

'No, I don't. If there's a child alive because I helped run the hospital, that'll be enough.'

'So he can die of malnutrition three years later? Or work in the mines when he grows up? And say, yes baas? You can't pretend that you can do anything outside politics.'

'I don't pretend that. You think it's not politics to feed the hungry and heal the sick? Look what's happening to Frank. I've just given up using the promise of revolution as an excuse to do nothing until it happens. But I know that it's a matter of time before the mission's closed, if we're doing any good.'

'And then?'

'I don't know. I'm going one step at a time.'

'Why's that better than waiting for prison to stop you?'

'Because I know that what I'm doing now is immediately useful. I repeat, there are some absolutes. Congress propaganda doesn't strike me as one of them.'

David did not answer. They walked further down the narrow road and turned back.

'I wish I knew something better,' Edward admitted.

'I'll agree that they're useful absolutes.'

'I'll agree that they're not satisfactory.' For the first time in their conversation, they laughed.

After their walk, Edward had to go off again, and again in the evening he was called away when Joan played for them. The next day too he left Joan and David to books and walks. David began to wonder whether his life was always so busy, or whether he had some reason to avoid them.

The mission was quieter without the medieval worshippers who had populated the Sunday landscape. Here and there, a single person walked among the buildings, and small sounds of carpentry and dogs sounded under the opaque sky. Outside the hospital they saw a small crowd of women. David took them for patients. They didn't speak to each other, hardly moved, did not look up, and when their glances randomly touched him and Joan, did not tender human recognition. They wore the absorbed look of people debilitated by sickness, drawn halfway into death. As before, at the church, he felt something he couldn't see. The sky was a skull.

Edward met them again at supper.

'I'm sorry my time's been so interrupted. A visit's rare enough, and yours has been like new life to me.'

'We've found plenty to do. You don't have to amuse us.'

'You'll see us when you come to Jo'burg,' Joan invited.

'You sound as if you're leaving.'

'We must soon, if we're going to go on to Barberton.'

'I'll miss you.' But David suspected relief.

'Where's Frank tonight?'

'He's still busy at the hospital.'

'I'd like to see the hospital, if it's not inconvenient.'

Edward set his knife and fork on his plate, still half full of stew. Holding his hands on the table, he looked at David. 'Let me tell you what's going on.' He bit his lower lip. 'We've got a ward with eighty children, mostly kwashiokor and gastro-enteritis. They share beds of course. One of them developed measles last week. Five children've died since. Some of the others are going to die soon. It might take the whole ward. We can't let any of them out because in no time there'll be measles all over the area, and hundred's'll die. The children's mothers have been begging us to let them out. They've been banging on the windows, trying to see their children. They won't leave.'

'I think I saw them, sitting outside.'

'We can't let them in, of course. I think we may have a riot on our hands soon. Perhaps next Sunday, when there're men here too.'

'But children don't die of measles,' Joan protested.

'They do if they're starving. Internal bleeding starts. If the sores open, there's some hope, but internal haemorrhage means they'll bleed to death. The ones who live'll probably be blind, or deaf, or retarded.'

'Is there really nothing you can do?'

'Nothing we know of. It's too late for them. We're just hoping it won't spread, but Frank found measles in one of the villages today. But when they saw what he was doing, the parents wouldn't let him near the child. They think we'll kill all the children we can get here.'

He poured coffee, and offered them some. 'Of course,

they're right, in a way. We've given up, really, for the children in the ward.'

'You weren't going to tell us, were you?' Joan asked. 'You were going to bear all this alone.'

Edward looked at her, and she at him. They were close to each other again, the way they had so often been. This time David did not feel excluded. They were all weighed down by the same helplessness.

Deliberately, Edward poured himself a second cup of coffee. He's expecting a long night, David thought. 'What'll you do if there's a riot?'

'We're holding a meeting to decide. Actually, in ten minutes. This may be the end of the mission.'

'I had no idea, yesterday.'

'Oh, yes. It's all horribly close.' Edward turned a dry grin to them. 'I'm glad I told you. It sounded too settled and worked out for me.'

'I'm glad you told us,' David answered.

Joan stood and went to Edward. She embraced him.

'You'll leave early,' he said, holding her by the shoulders and looking into her face. 'Anything could happen here, and it's pointless for you to be involved. I didn't think it was so serious until Frank found that case of measles today. And I don't like that stone-throwing you met when you came.'

'We'll leave early, Edward.'

'Do you want us to contact newspapers?' David asked. 'Perhaps they'd raise money for milk or something.'

'It's too late, and probably better for us to avoid publicity.'

'God. It's awful,' Joan said.

They both looked at her as though she had spoken out of character. Edward embraced her and kissed her on both cheeks. He pushed her away. He faced David. They put their hands on each other's shoulders.

'Thank you,' David said.

'Thank you.' He left them.

Driving past the hospital as they left in the morning, they passed the women, vague shapes under a row of lighted windows. Inside there must be nurses and nuns in a morning bustle of thermometers, charts, carts of medicine and water. And screens around silent cribs.

They did not go on to Barberton, but turned back to Johannesburg. They crossed the dead river again, and saw movements among the tents. Small figures moved among the river stones with inscrutable actions. The caked earth lay dumb on each side of the road.

Joan gradually moved out of the silence they had taken back from St Thérèse's. David watched her patience as though she had become a stranger to him. Somewhere she could endure these things, celebrate after Christmas with her God the Massacre of the Innocents. His own innocent death, and the intolerable piety of cripples singing hymns at Lourdes. Although he remembered how Edward had eaten, out of self-discipline, he could not eat. When Joan brought spring flowers home, and arranged daffodils in vases filled with water, he watched her from a dream. She had always known what these things cost and accepted 'those in prison for our sake'. She knew why she lived. Like Edward, who had instructed himself to keep alive, who knew that the children in the ward could not be kept alive. Joan and Edward knew that they must make the choice. Only he was naive and had never yet decided who must live. Who must be allowed to live.

He would have to change. Soon. He would have to decide about his life.

The Sunday they went out to visit Aviva, the wattle trees had come out in thick clouds of yellow flowers like mimosa, and the new spring leaves showed bright and green, as though the dead veld near St Thérèse's had been a dream. At the new house, they met Sidney, a heavy featured man with the confident bearing of success, and his son Cecil, about ten years old, still slight and somewhat shy. David wondered how Cecil felt about the new arrangements for his life. He seemed happy enough, set apart in his own world, playing with a red leather ball on the terrace where a maid brought sherry and biscuits.

Soon Aviva said to Joan, 'I want to show you the house. Or

should we start with the garden? It's in a terrible mess. The peri-urban board won't allow anyone to water until the drought's over, and you can't start a garden without water.'

Sidney, obviously as proud as Aviva of the new house, added, 'The swimming pool's been in two months, and we can't fill it. I don't know what we'll do if the drought doesn't end soon.'

David saw that Joan glanced at him. She knew the drought that threatened him.

'Let's go inside, Aviva. I'd like to see the house. Do you want to come David?'

He obeyed her wish to be alone with Aviva, and shook his head. Perhaps Joan would tell Aviva about St Thérèse's, and warn her of the bitterness that infected him now.

They went off and David accepted Sidney's offer of the Sunday papers. On the front page he read of another sabotage attempt in Cape Town. Three telephone booths in the suburbs had been blown up. It seemed a pitiful and ill-conceived act. Another front page story reported that the Dutch Reformed Church had issued a statement criticizing petty apartheid. It told the faithful not to address grown natives as Boy, Girl, or John, but to learn and use their real names. Christians should not be rude and shout when giving orders. Family servants should be allowed time to attend church on Sunday. In too many whites' homes they were kept busy with a big Sunday dinner instead. David set the papers aside. What more could he learn about apartheid, after St Thérèse's. He watched Cecil playing with his red leather ball. It was like a ball he had once played with. The ball had lodged in a gutter on the roof once, and months later he had found it, split, and with the stuffing pouring out, like froth from a rabid mouth. It had reminded him of a dead cat in the gutter, he'd seen once on the way to school.

The indistinguishable chatter of the women in the house moved nearer and flitted away. Once, when they must have been upstairs in a bedroom overlooking the terrace, he heard Aviva say, 'Ruth's been sending me books about the Lamaze method, but I'm not sure I'll be able to find someone here who'll let me have the baby that way. She says it was such a thrill for Michael too, to be with her, but I'm not sure that Sidney'd like that kind of thing.'

He could not hear Joan's answer, but from another room he imagined his own name in Aviva's questioning voice.

Soon, when the women came out into the sunny garden again, he saw that Aviva winked at Sidney as if to tell him that Joan knew. He felt all their happiness separated from his life as though one life must be an hallucination: his, where St Thérèse's children clutched his ankles to hold him in their desert, or theirs.

During dinner, a spread of roast beef, potatoes, and peas that might well be keeping the servants from church, Aviva asked Sidney about new medicines for measles. Joan must have told her about St Thérèse's. Sidney's business imported pharmaceutical supplies.

'It wouldn't be worth it. Measles is nothing these days, Cecil got over it in two days.'

'Joan's just been telling me a dreadful story.'

Joan said. 'We've just been at a mission in Sekhukhuniland where the children were dying of it. I could hardly believe it. I'd never heard of people dying of measles.'

'I'll have a look at some catalogues after lunch. But I don't think there's anything we import.'

'Have you heard from Edward since your visit?' Aviva asked.

'No. And of course, we're rather worried for him.'

'Isn't that just like Edward, though! You'll hear some time that he's moved on to a leprosy camp, or decided he'd rather waste his life looking after imbeciles or something.'

'He's not wasting his life, Aviva,' Joan defended Edward. 'He's running a hospital.'

'Oh pooh. He's got no right to run off to the *bundu* to run tuppeny-hapenny hospitals. Let the missionaries do that. They don't need Edward. It's time for him to grow up.'

'What's not grown up about running a hospital?' David asked.

'I've got nothing against the hospital. Let them have a hundred thousand hospitals. In fact, it's all money in our pocket, if one wants to be crude. But I'm fed up with Edward.'

'I still don't see why.'

'All that pity and agony. It's adolescent. It was all very well when we were students. Oh, those endless discussions we used to have. They were fine, in their time. It was very exciting too. But it was a game, and we knew it was a game.'

'It wasn't a game for all of us.'

'Let's be honest, David. We all went to the Treason Trial and things like that, as much for the excitement as for anything else.'

'Speak for yourself Aviva. And I don't find pity and agony childish. I think Edward's being more responsible than most people.'

'You know, I never used to understand what Aristotle meant about purging pity and terror. Terror, yes. One doesn't want to be a coward. But pity? I used to think everyone decent must feel pity. Well, I woke up when Edward went off to the *bundu* like that, just wallowing in pity. It's so damn unreal! It's silly, that's all. He's not going to *touch* apartheid that way.'

'What else do you recommend?'

'We're adults now. It's time to get on with our lives and do the things that adults do.'

'And what do adults do.'

'We get on with our lives. We get on with the work of the world.'

'Ignoring things like apartheid?'

'I'm not saying we can ignore it. We must do what we can. But within reason. The world's full of injustice and starvation and all that. You can't stop living because ten million people are dying in India.'

'Not in India, Aviva. Here.'

'Here then. It's the same thing. You can't stop living.'

Just when David felt that it was pointless to argue with Aviva, tainting the good meal set before them, Sidney rallied to defend her argument. 'Aviva's right. If you want to do something for the native you should get on with real work. The native doesn't want a hospital in the *bundu*. He's flocking to the cities, and even the government isn't going to stop that, for all their Bantustan nonsense. And why? It's because the cities have the highest standard of living. That's what the native wants, just like anyone else. And this country is where he gets it, apartheid or no apartheid. Why d'you think natives come here from all over Africa? I'll tell you. It's because we've got the highest standard of living, and that's what the native really cares about.' Meeting blank faces from Joan and David, Sidney continued, 'I'll tell you something. The economy's going to do more about apartheid than a million soft-headed liberals. The Afrikaner's getting into business now. Mark my words, once the Afrikaner's got a stake in the economy, apartheid'll just melt away. It just doesn't make economic sense.'

David raised his glass, 'Let's hope you're right, Sidney. It'll be a less bloody way than anything else in sight. Here's to adult life and economic determinism! Come on, Aviva. Aren't you going to drink with me?'

Aviva raised her glass, 'Life and work,' she toasted.

'Oh, yes. Even better. Life and work!' David drained his glass and held it out for more wine. He did not look at Joan, and did not join the conversation when she had steered it to the University Players' production of *The Cherry Orchard* and Aviva started to plan for them all to see it together.

When the meal was finished, Cecil was sent to practise his violin for an hour, and Sidney, apologizing about the pressure of work, and promising to look up his catalogues for Joan, went off to attend to some business inside, which David suspected was a nap. Joan, Aviva, and David went out to the terrace again.

A stuporous feeling of three o'clock on a Sunday afternoon numbed David with comfort as he sat near the bright flowers and new leaves, hearing the women talk. Near his hand, an early rosebud was flowering, red and spiral. In a dreamy haze, portentous and certain, he felt that Aviva was right, and wished that he could live like her. Humanly, the way people had always lived. The very crumbs of a life like hers became history. Through living like Aviva, archaeologists and historians who gave their wives gifts understood the brooches they found in tombs. Their children's discarded toys became evidence of human life and clues to each particular culture. The very trifles of Aviva's life, her pots and combs, intelligible to all humans, were the stuff of immortality that would survive ages of time lying upon them like the sod of graves. Only he was divorced from the web of common humanity. Knowing that a child playing with a ball was immortal, he refused children, comfortable meat, friends. And wife. He was chained to a desert where angry children threw stones at him. When they came home to the flat, after tea, he helped Joan off with her coat, but did not take off his jacket. She looked at him, waiting for words she seemed to know before he spoke them.

'I'm not going to stay, Joan.'

But as soon as he said them she became as white as if a machine had drawn all the blood out of her. She turned away and went to sit at the table near the window. He came to sit opposite her. She did not seem to see him. In the street below, an African was strumming a guitar and singing. The muted traffic of Kotze street rose between them. He heard the bells of a distant church, the almost indistinguishable clamour of a train, a recording from some building nearby of the Beethoven Ninth. Joan roused herself.

'Then go,' she said.

'I love you, Joan, but I'm not free.'

'Then go. Don't come back. Don't 'phone me.' Her voice and face were weary and cold. 'Don't torment me. Don't destroy me.'

'Joan, you know that I don't want to hurt you at all.'

Her hands formed fists on the table. 'Say what you do, or do what you say.'

'I can't stay. I'll hurt you if I stay.'

'Then don't stay. Leave. Leave.' He stood and left her at the table. Her hands were still clenched. She did not look at him. He closed the door without having touched her.


The cell's heavy walls closed round him. The smell of prison entered his lungs.

Piet Kreer, David Smith, Tertius Keyter, Hans Breitenbach, Jacob Arndt, Louis Spaarman, Pretorius Eybers, James King, Harold Isaacs, Willem Schoeman, Guy Lechaptois.

Kaplan told him that Rifkin would not need to see him any more.

'I know. He thinks I'm really mad.'

'Don't make everything so hard, David.'

David sat in his straight wooden chair and looked at the dark walls of the room, dark brown at the bottom, dirty cream at the top. The bars on the window blocked the world outside. There was nothing left of life. Only himself, in his mind, scolded by the older man who had his own reasons, his uncle in Russia. David did not know what was in his mind. Weariness filled him like a rod of pain that forced him to hold himself upright, though what he wanted was only to lie down. To be unconscious. Or not be.

They would give him what he wanted.

'Edward Guail will be coming to visit you tomorrow,' Kaplan said.

'Edward! I've been thinking a lot about him.'

'He thought you must be.'

'Have you spoken with him?'

Yes. He's a remarkable person.'

'Is he still in Sekhukhuniland.'

'No. He's going to England.'

'It's happened so soon. Poor Edward.'

Kaplan said nothing, as though he knew that David's words had not been spoken to him.

They had little more to say, and Snyman soon led David back to the cell.


Piet Kreer, David Smith, Tertius Keyter, Hans Breitenbach, Jacob Arndt, Louis Spaarman, Pretorius Eybers, James King, Harold Isaacs, Willem Schoeman, Guy Lechaptois.


As Prinsloo led them out to exercise, he saw a group of African prisoners being hustled away. It was a common prison sight, but suddenly he remembered an afternoon when he must have been about seven, when they had just moved to Bramley. He had watched African prisoners paving the new street outside his house. They made hot tar and mixed it with gravel, they poured it on the road, and beat it smooth with flat bottomed staves. They were singing. A leader carried the line of song and alternated with the chorus. It was a hot afternoon, and the smell of tar carried all over the sunshine. The convicts sang in complicated African harmonies, and beat the tar in the rhythm of their song. He knew only a few words of the kitchen kaffir his mother used, and did not understand what they were singing about, but their voices and movements, rhythmic and continuous, felt natural and perpetual. A mirage of water hovered over the barrel of hot tar and rippled over the road, and the white policemen who supervised the work kept shouting out in irritable hot voices. The song did not pause, the staves lifted and fell, the beat smoothed the road, the tar smelt pleasant and black, and when the workmen left, he went to feel the road with naked, inquisitive toes. When he came back home Sina was sitting on the back steps shelling peas and gossiping with the girl next door. She exclaimed at his dirty feet and told him to wash before his mother came home. The shadows of a fig tree dappled leaves down a whitewashed wall.

The memory made him happy now, retrieving a state in which he was not guilty to either black or white. He was alive. He was who he had been, a prisoner too now, marched into the courtyard with Gericke to walk his set course under the brilliant sky. He was not mad. He had done what he could for the children at St Thérèse's and those women sitting there on the ground, the way Sina sat.

Snyman took him to see Edward. In this room there was more light than in the office where he met Kaplan. The room was bigger, and divided half-way by a shallow wall and a grille of heavy wire mesh. A bar held him away from the grille. On the table near the back of the room, where Synman sat to guard him, a tape recorder wound slowly with a low hiss.

When Edward came in, on the other side of the mesh, David saw that he had put on weight. He looked rested, and sad. He had not seemed sad at St Thérèse's.

'Thank you for coming, Edward. You're the only visitor I've had.'

'Joan will come soon. She hasn't been strong enough yet.

But she asked me to tell you that she'll be coming very soon.'

'I'm glad you've seen her. How is she?'

'It's been a hard year, of course.'

'Did she have a nervous breakdown? Is that what it is?'

'No, she was just exhausted, overstrained. She's staying with Aviva now and they're looking after her. She's fine. You'll see her soon.'

'I don't know what to say.'

'It doesn't matter.'

'I suppose it doesn't.'

Even through the coarse wire mesh David could see Edward's truthful, green eyes. 'I hear you're leaving South Africa.'

'Yes. St Thérèse's closed down.'

'Was it that measles epidemic?'

'That, and the Group Areas Act.'

'It's come so soon for you.'

'For both of us.'

Again silence joined them, full of things they could not mention in this prison room, with the tape recorder listening to their words.

'I've come to say goodbye, David.'

'When are you leaving?'

'Tomorrow night.'

David felt his eyelid twitch. He put his hand to his cheek to hide it.

'We won't see each other again.' Edward had always been able to speak the truth.

David looked at him through the metal veil. 'My lawyer says there's a chance they won't hang me.'

'My God, David.' Tears were coming out of Edward's eyes.

Terror flashed through David. His indrawn breath sounded like a gasp. 'Ah!' His body pulled back and he clenched his fists into his thighs. He felt his palms become damp, wet, and then drops of sweat falling off his forehead. His shirt was clinging to his chest, wet with fear. Another gasp wrenched through him and came out like a sob.

'David.' Their eyes met in shame.

'I want to tell you,' Edward stopped, not able to talk. He

breathed deeply, and David waited. 'I want you to know that I would never have done what you've done. But I know that you did it for the same reason I've done everything.' Again Edward stopped to take breath. 'They don't leave us other ways.'

David gestured to the tape recorder on the table behind him. Edward nodded.

'I want you to know how much I admire your courage. I know that my way can't last. It'll come to your way.' Edward stopped and sighed. 'Oh God! Oh God! I know you'd have done anything else, if there'd been anything else to do.' He did not hide the tears pouring down his face. He held empty hands towards David, like a beggar who shows that he has nothing.

David also held out his hands, and then let them fall slack in his lap allowing Edward to see his tears and the sweat running off his forehead and cheeks.

When Snyman touched him to take him away, he stood. But at the door he turned back to say. 'Live well, Edward,' and waved, and smiled.

Walking back to the cell he held himself very straight and with a fierce expression on his face that denied the tears.


Piet Kreer, David Smith, Tertius Keyter, Hans Breitenbach, Jacob Arndt, Louis Spaarman, Pretorius Eybers, James King, Harold Isaacs, Willem Schoeman, Guy Lechaptois.


He tried to calm himself with pacing, exercises. He tried to read, but the Bible's language pulled him back to the fierce emotions of Edward's visit.

When night came, he could not sleep. He heard the cars of the city outside. Hillbrow was still awake. He closed himself in the blanket. Edward knew they would put him to death, and madness would not save him. The traffic ebbed. Trains shunted back and forth in the night. He had done what he must.

All they had done was in vain.

At first, when he left Joan, still searching for what he would do, he had thought about sabotage. The few botched efforts of recent months disheartened him. What was the use of blowing up telephone booths in the suburbs? He wanted something stringent and irresistible, something to reach the mine owners in Johannesburg and the government officials in Pretoria, something to rip under the hypocrisies of Parliament and make the whites see that they had made South Africa a barbarous terror. The whites brazened it like gods, but they were mortal. He wanted something simple but portentous, impossible to deny, radiant with terror for the whites and hope for the Africans. He wanted something possible for one man. It must be a crack to breach open the whole dam of retribution to be poured over the government and all its allies. Something to undo them all and bring irresistible justice to Pretoria. Something . . . but he did not yet know what.

He wrote to Michael and told him that he had left Pretoria and come back again. He told him about the screams in the night and St Thérèse's.

While he waited to hear from Michael, Pretoria seemed translucent to him, the lightning of impending justice shone through it. The school, the policemen, the persistent image of the Voortrekker Monument filled him with joy. The new sabotage laws thrilled him with justification.

As before, Mrs Blake listened to the 'phone call that came for him at school.

'Michael Henderson wanted me to give you a message. Could I meet you this afternoon?'

'I teach until three.'

'Three-thirty then. I've got your address.' The 'phone clicked. David set it back in its cradle. 'Thank you, Mrs Blake.'

'Mr Spence doesn't like private calls at school. That's the second time.'

'I'll warn people.'

'It's not you personally, you understand, but if everybody does it.'

'I'll try to see that it doesn't happen again.'

In his dingy Pretoria hotel he marked compositions on the Discovery of Diamonds at the Cape. He did not know what he hoped for. If this was one of Michael's Congress friends he wouldn't be squeamish about their ideology or self-righteousness now. Whoever was not against him would be for him. Once it occurred to him that the man might simply be a friend Michael had sent to comfort him, so that he could bear, sanely, what had made him mad. No. He would not be sane. He would not bear his country's madness any more. He would not lose this freedom and this joy.

When he opened the door and saw the man, they looked at each other for a few seconds. The long, sensual lips and face wore traces of discretion, humour and frequent, mobile use.

'François Marais.'

Perhaps it was the name, or perhaps the thin build and dark complexion, the silence of the brown eyes — this man reminded him of Adrian.

In the lounge of the Ambassador Hotel, where the dominees had congregated after the sessions of the synod that judged Muller, they ordered drinks.

'Michael sends his best. I saw him in London three days ago.'

'How is he?' So François told him about Michael, his new-born baby girl, articles he'd been writing. He mentioned friends David had met at parties with Michael. He said that Michael was eager to hear more about Aviva, that he'd written to Edward at St Thérèse's. He did not mention Joan. David knew that he was presenting his credentials.

'Michael thought you might want to meet some of us.'

'Who's us?'

'He said you'd had a conversation before he left.' David waited. 'Do you remember Philip Brink?'

'Yes.'

'I asked him about you.' François smiled, acknowledging that he had been as careful about David's credentials as David about his.

'I'd be surprised if he remembers me.'

'He does. Very distinctly. He said he'd like to meet you again.'

'I'd like that too.'

'I'll fetch you on Saturday. Five o'clock. Outside Blystra's on Church Street.'

'I'll be there.'

'You know, the weather here may be bad for farming, but it's a great relief after England. I can't get over how much I miss the sun there.'

The first examination was over, though François would still be weighing him.

After a while David said, 'This may be silly, but do you know Adrian Marais?'

'You mean the poet? Looks like me a bit?' David nodded. 'He's my cousin. I haven't seen him for years.'

'He teaches at my school.'

'You like him.'

'I do, though I find it difficult . . .'

François completed his thought, 'Because of his politics?'

'Yes.'

'Michael said you were finding it difficult to have anything to do with Afrikaners. I'm an Afrikaner myself, you know. Adrian's politics could change. He feels uncomfortable with apartheid. But I don't know what could do it for him. His father's an elder of the church, treasurer of the party in the western Cape, you know, a pillar of the community, and Adrian's a very loyal person. He'd have a hard time if he went against the family.'

'Did you have a hard time?'

'I've been a black sheep for so many years no one expects anything of me now. It's much more convenient this way.' He laughed. 'But Adrian and I used to be very close. We used to be up to all sorts of tricks together as boys.'

'In the Long Kloof?'

'You know the Long Kloof.'

'Just slightly. I visited once for a few weeks.'

'You must've heard about Lord Ford.'

'Oh yes.'

'Adrian and I used to steal those wonderful apples he used to send the King of England and everyone. What a wonderful, crazy man! They were good apples! You won't tell Adrian you met me.'

'Of course not.'

On Saturday, François drove David to Soweto. David had never been able to find his way among the township's dim, small houses and unlit streets when he drove here with Joan. Of course there was no map for sale. Perhaps in some government office or police headquarters there would be a drawing of this invisible city, the white city's shadow, though separated from its own afflicted self by an armouring belt of empty veld. He felt strange at the party, where African men were drinking, laughing, a record played loud township jazz, and it seemed that no one feared a police raid. It was an unexpected relief to be among Africans instead of reading about them. Even at St Thérèse's everything had been in his mind.

He felt awkward at this party where no one knew him, and no one but François and he were white, but no one seemed to take notice. François shepherded him from group to group, introduced him to more people than he could remember, and watched, David thought, to see how he was received.

'Let's find Philip.'

He took David through a narrow passage, crowded with guests, to the kitchen at the back of the house, also crowded with guests. Philip was there talking with his chair tipped back against a wall. When he saw them he straightened his chair and waited.

'You two know each other,' François said.

Philip stood, and shook David's hand. 'I rather hoped we'd meet again.'

'I'm surprised you remembered me.'

'I remembered. You understood what I said though you didn't agree with it.'

'I've learnt more since that night.'

'Good.'

'But I don't know what to do about it.'

'What do you want to do?'

'I haven't worked out what would be most useful, but that's

what I'm thinking about.'

'Any ideas?'

They could not continue this conversation without risk. From this step he could be betrayed. Without this step he would have to act altogether alone.

'The usual risky things. But I don't care about risks now. They won't stop me.'

'What sort of risks?'

'Banning, exile, prison, torture, death. Some combination of the above. I don't think there's too much point in thinking about that. My real question is, what's worth doing now?'

'I knew I could get to like you,' Philip grinned. 'Let's meet again.' He looked at François, raising an eyebrow, and François nodded.

Soon after, they left the party.

'All right, David,' François said on the drive back to Pretoria. 'Could you meet me in Johannesburg on Wednesday, about six?'

'Yes.'

'Good. Make it outside St Mary's. Know where it is?'


Trevor Reed was the fourth at Wednesday's supper. David had been to exhibitions with Joan where Trevor's bright abstracts and drawings of nudes had fed gossip about his successive wives, mistresses, entanglements with actresses, heiresses and gallery owners.

'During this meal,' François warned, 'which I have cooked with my own hands, we will talk only about the weather and things like that. After dinner we can be less serious.'

So they talked about art exhibitions and plays, and some new buildings in Pretoria whose architecture amused Trevor.

When François seated them in the living room he put a Beatles record on the turntable and turned the volume very loud for a moment as though by mistake.

'Oops,' he twiddled the knobs, getting the highest volume a few more times. Then he set the music to a more tolerable level and turned to them with a wink.

'That's better. Let's start with you, David. Philip quotes you saying you don't trust whites.'

'With few exceptions.'

'Like us, I hope.'

'I hope so.'

'Do you trust Africans?'

'Yes. No one has to tell them what's wrong with this country, or to doubt their motives in wanting change. Of course, there are always a few Africans who could work with apartheid for some crazy reason. But if we're talking about groups in general . . .'

'So you'd be willing to work with Africans?'

'Of course. That's what it's about, isn't it. I think I'd find it a relief. Part of the whole insanity for me has been that I feel everything in a vacuum. I read about dying people, but I don't know them, about atrocities, but it's all words. But I don't know any Africans to work with. I hardly know you.'

'What were you thinking of doing?'

David sipped the brandy François had given him. They had examined him, but what did he know about them? No matter. He had decided to take this risk.

'Sabotage is one possibility.'

'You sound doubtful,' Trevor prodded.

'I am. Sabotage is so easy to ignore. I don't think many people are upset about the incidents we've had lately. It doesn't feel serious. At that rate we'll never have change. And when it comes to bombing telephone booths, it's comic! or lunatic!'

'If there were better targets?' Trevor pursued.'

'I'd feel better about it. I'd love to see the Voortrekker Monument blown up.'

'I don't see why that'd be better than a railway line,' Philip sounded quizzical, as though the idea appealed to him.

'The architecture is terrible,' Trevor agreed, 'But do you really think it's that bad.'

'Well David, it *is* our national shrine,' François smiled at the ambivalence of his situation, 'And we'd be furious to see it blown up, but railway lines and electric pylons make more sense to me.'

'Perhaps the Voortrekker Monument isn't a good idea if you don't see the point of it. But I feel that sabotage is really a way of saying something, and that to be convincing it's got to be said again and again, and on a wide scale. Can we manage anything like that?'

No one answered him.

'What're the other possibilities?' François asked.

'You *have* been thinking of others,' Philip pressed François's invitation, looking at David. And immediately it was like that night they'd first met at the Discussion Club, when Philip seemed able to draw out of David thoughts he had hardly dared to think. That night he had said he didn't trust whites; now he said, 'I have been thinking of one other way. It's simple, it's not going to be ignored, and it doesn't take many to start with. It'd show that we're as serious as we can get.' He hesitated, feeling it difficult to say what he must.'

'Well, tell us. The suspense's killing me," Philip joked.

'It worked in Kenya and in Palestine,' David said, still speaking elliptically.

But they understood. No one spoke.

Then as a deliberate act of leadership, François broke the silence. "What do you say, Philip?'

'It's worth thinking about.'

'Trevor?'

'No! It's murder! I don't want to commit murder!'

'Do you want to say anything to that, David?'

'Yes. We've got to know what we're trying to do.' He looked round. The others were listening, not so appalled by what he had said that they would not listen at all. He began to feel that he was happy. He had trusted them, and he was talking to them as he had not dared talk to anyone. He was not all alone in his hatred, and his need to do something about apartheid. 'What I want is a complete reversal of power in this country. In other words, revolution.' He looked at Trevor and Trevor nodded. Philip was leaning back in his chair watching, as though still curious about how far David had come. 'There's never been a revolution without people getting hurt and killed. I mean even innocent people, decent people, women and children. If we can't stomach that, we have to live with what we've got now. We can't change it without bloodshed.'

'I'm afraid that's true,' Philip agreed, and David felt happiness bursting out of every pore of his being. He had risked the bitterest thoughts of his mind, and Philip had understood him, and accepted the truth of what he saw. He was not alone.

David took up what he had been saying, looking at Philip. 'Of course innocent people are dying right now, women and children, because apartheid is a killer. Let's not pretend — doing nothing is murder in another way.'

'But it's not the same as deliberate murder,' Trevor protested. 'No. It's too horrible. And it'll only turn people against us.'

'Philip, what do you think?' François seemed to be the chairman of their group.

'I'd like to know how David thinks terrorism can do what sabotage won't.'

François gestured to David to speak. 'Fear,' David answered. 'The Mau Mau killed thirty-six people, and the British left Kenya. I'm not sure what the figures were in Palestine to get the British to leave there.'

'We're not going to leave, David.' François objected. I'm not a settler, or an Englishman. I'm an African.'

'Of course we're Africans. That's why we're in this. That's why we've got to take the country back for all of us. Our rulers call themselves Europeans.'

'Not in my language,' François retorted, *'Ons is Afrikaners!'*

'You really do identify with them.'

'Yes, dammit. I'm not an Englishman, and I'm not going to admit that I'm less than human because I'm Afrikaans. You damn Englishmen are always pushing us into that corner.'

'I say, chaps,' Philip interrupted. 'Let's not degenerate into white politics.'

'I apologize,' David said.

'It's all right,' François accepted. 'We inherit a difficult history.'

'Well, how do you feel about terrorism?' Philip drew François back to their topic.

'I also don't like it,' François answered, 'It's too hard to control. It's too easy to use for any reason, by anyone, against anyone — to settle old scores, to get a man's wife or his farm, or anything. In our situation it could release race war. It's too damn dangerous.'

'Actually,' Philip said, 'If the two of you feel that way, we should keep away from terrorism for the time being. We've got to work together. David's right — there's no way without bloodshed in the long run. But we may not be there yet. We don't have to set out to kill, though we may find ourselves coming to every extreme of violence in the end.'

'I do feel that patience is also bloodshed,' David said.

'If may be. But if François and Trevor feel strongly against terror we have to weigh that.'

David looked at Philip, feeling the joy of trusting him. 'You don't object on other grounds?'

'No. One doesn't resort to terror when there're other means, but when there aren't . . . We need to think about it more carefully.'

'I'll make some fresh coffee,' François said, 'Help yourself to the cognac. Trevor?'

'You certainly know how to live,' Trevor held out the goblet whose stem he'd been rolling between his fingers like a pencil.

'Gather ye rosebuds,' François joked. He reminded David of Edward, accepting petty luxuries because his whole life denied them.

Philip was standing near David now, and said in an undertone,' I wouldn't have guessed you'd come as far as this.'

'It *has* been quite a road,' David agreed, smiling slightly at their instant power to recognize each other's meaning. Philip knew what he had been thinking and feeling. Philip must have been feeling similar things himself. David looked into his face, 'Tell me, why did our discussion go the way it did? It felt as if you've never talked about these things before.'

'We haven't,' Philip answered.

'But how could you avoid it? You must have thought about it.'

'I think many things I don't talk about,' Philip answered in a sardonic voice, and raised his glass as if to toast David, as if to recognize that David too had much he did not say.

David raised his glass, to answer Philip's silent toast and make his own.

Two days later the Special Branch raided several homes in Johannesburg, Pretoria and the townships. David saw Trevor's name among the 'suspected Communists.' Their next meeting was in a flat Francois described as 'a friend's'.

Here too Francois put a record on the turntable, and set it to its full volume a few times before they started to talk. Then he turned to Trevor. 'Tell us about the raid.'

'It was just the usual. They took some books, none of them banned, and copies of the *New Statesman*. You know what really interested them? Government Gazettes.' Trevor laughed.'

'Why on earth did you have any?' David asked.

'I must have wanted to read the Suppression of Communism Bill years ago. I didn't even know I had these things.'

'Hmm. No one could have a good reason for wanting to read that stuff,' David joked.

'We'd better all go through our things and see that there's nothing interesting,' François suggested, and before the end of the evening, he asked David, when they were alone, 'Could I give you some papers? There's nothing dangerous in them, but the S.B. does have my name, and I'd rather not have these things around. You're still an unknown.'

When David looked round his hotel room, he hardly knew what to do with the papers. He did not want to leave the brown envelope in open view. The cupboards and desk seemed inanely obvious. He put the envelope in a suitcase with some old socks and underwear. Anyone could have found them easily, but he couldn't think of anything better. In the company of the others conspiratorial manners seemed natural. Alone, they felt unreal and melodramatic.

Either the police were intensifying their activity or David was being tested. François 'phoned at the hotel.

'Have you got a driving licence?'

'Yes.'

'You free this afternoon?'

'Yes.'

'I'll see you outside Hamiltons, Church Street, in ten

minutes.'

'Fifteen.' The 'phone clicked.

The hotel owner, sitting in a glass-walled office, looked up as David walked past. Could he see any change?

He went to the toilet, fetched his jacket and wallet, combed his hair and straightened his tie. He looked the same as he always looked in the mirror, beginning to resemble his father, but he had moved into a new world now, and it would upset the old.

François opened the back door of the car. Driving towards Fountains, he said, 'Norman, meet David. David, meet Norman. You'll be driving towards Basutoland. You could try to get some sleep on the back seat, David. Save these for the trip back.' He gave David two rolls of Lifesavers. 'Don't stop, and don't wait too long after Norman gets out. Drive back immediately. I'll hand over to you now.' He stopped near a clump of trees. David saw that his own car was parked under them. Norman took the wheel, and François walked away without a backward glance.

Lying at the back of the car, not able to sleep, David felt like a child. High clouds heaped over the Free State, and clustered like grapes in some inconceivable promised land, huge, godly, and weighty, pressing against the platter of air that held them up in the sky.

'If you're not sleeping,' Norman said, 'Let's change places.' They stopped in a stretch of veld. For a moment David heard the majestic silence, so still it seemed he could hear grass thrust against grass, earth clicking under the footfalls of small animals, the nearly imperceptible tick and rustle of stillness in living country.

Soon he heard Norman's soft snore.

In the small dorps of the Eastern Free State, churches and houses were built of sandstone. Their honey colour sheltered a few dahlias and roses. David wished the amplitude and noble dignity of this space and light could find some echo in the people who lived here. But this platteland was where the most pitiless Nationalists came from. Here they were as ignorant as stone, as obstinate as drought. These Afrikaners never expressed doubt, like those from the Cape, they knew nothing of the qualms David sensed in Adrian. Here they knew, with the assurance of the sun, that they were right.

He drove through dorps with an anger that fused into exultation as he remembered what *he* knew. Their day of judgement was at hand. In the highlands of Kenya, a golden land like this, the weak had overturned the strong and taught them that even though they were white, they were human, they were mortal. That day was coming here, and when it came, children would drink the milk their masters had wasted, and men would slaughter the cows they had tended. There would be feasting and singing. And after the joy, every man would work for his own good. He would build a house and live in it. He would plant a field and eat from it. The cattle he tended would be his wealth. The earth would replenish his life. He would govern the country for his children to be men in it.

Ah, he mocked himself, it wasn't going to be that easy. It wasn't going to be that good. He didn't know what society the Africans would construct after the revolution. He couldn't read whether Luthuli's generosity and Mandela's courage would rule, or whether there would be pettiness, squabbling, and a new tyranny after the old. It did not matter. Nothing could be worse than apartheid. He would open the gates. He would let the water through. Let history flow.

It was dark before they reached the border. Norman woke up.

'How do you feel about driving without lights until we get to the border?'

'I'll try.'

It was slow, but after about thirty minutes, Norman said, 'This'll be a good place.'

Through the open window, he shook David's hand, 'Give me a few minutes before you start the car again. Thanks.'

'My pleasure.'

High blanks of darkness that must be mountains blocked out the brilliant stars shining over a world David couldn't identify as the same in which this morning he had ignored van der Walt's talk at the back of the class, marked twenty compositions on the Discovery of Gold, and talked about upcoming exams with Richard and Adrian in the Common Room. The feel of seat leather under his tired torso, and a new hunger, assured him that this was the world he lived in. Perhaps the other was a dream. The stars were so bright he could see their burning colours, red and blue. There were galaxies aeons away. The world was infinite, and he felt extended to its depths.

He turned the car cautiously in the darkness. A few miles later he switched on the headlights. He could feel the bones in his back, the muscles in his neck, hunger grinding his stomach. He wanted to sleep now, and forbade himself to stop at a café for a cup of coffee. Once, he stopped to urinate.

By the time he reached the thickening neon signs and garages that showed Johannesburg was near he felt more impatient to squeeze the time short, to stop, to rest, to eat. Unobserved light sweetened the sky, and the sun suddenly flashed in the rearview mirror. As he turned through the sleeping streets of the smoky city, reflections ran along the dashboard. It was the new day.

François seemed to know his happiness as if he had expected it.

'Hullo,' he shook David's hand as though he must touch him. 'Coffee's ready. Come into the kitchen and sit down.'

'I'll stand, if you don't mind.'

'You want to shower first or to eat?'

Water brought his naked skin to life again. It poured over his head, face and body. He pressed the lather to himself, he rubbed himself dry. Everything was new, alive, clean.

'How many slices of toast?' Francois asked.

'Ten, but I'll start with two.'

'I didn't like giving you a job like that without warning, but you were the best person I could find in a hurry, especially because you don't know Norman so you can't tell anything about him.' François handed him a mug of coffee and set a plate of eggs and ham on the table.

'I'd like another egg, please.'

'What time did you drop him?'

'I don't know. It was dark.'

'Better get a luminous watch.' François did not ask about coffee before he poured. 'And a car.'

'I might be out of a job at the end of the year. I'd better tell you about it, but not now.'

'Here.' François brought another plateful of eggs and ham.

Teaching after the sleepless night was strenuous, but his custom of silence stood him in good stead. He wondered how the boys would think of him if they guessed. Perhaps his new sense of power showed, in spite of his tiredness. Van der Walt gave him no trouble in IVB's class on the Jameson Raid. In the Common Room, Adrian said, 'You look tired. I'll bring your tea.' He felt himself tempted to say, You're just like your cousin. He forbade himself to think of the connection.

The four arranged their meetings around visits to bioscopes, picnics, swimming and tennis, so that there would seem nothing but inane pleasure in the time they spent together. There were no more parties in townships, but once or twice David met Africans at François's flat. In the large building accommodating divorcees, homosexuals, and artists, no one made trouble about François's guests. Once David met Mabotoana, when he had expected François to be alone. François introduced him as 'one of us'. He was surprised that François should be so open.

'Don't worry, I've known him for years, and he may work with us some time.' David wondered why he had never met François among Michael's friends, the people Joan knew. Perhaps there were more people than he knew about in this world that had been invisible to him.

They decided against terrorism. For the time being, they would aim for a series of explosions on railway lines all over the country to give them an appearance of popular strength. They would not endanger human life. They would leave red flags to warn approaching trains. School holidays would be coming soon, and it would be a good time to scatter and examine their sites. David bought a car and moved to a flat where he could be sure of greater privacy. And François invited them to spend a weekend with him near Hartebeestpoort Dam. They would seem to spend their time swimming, reading, and climbing the kopjies.

The dynamite magazine was in a small cave in one of those kopjies.

When David handled the sticks, they seemed curiously inadequate, wrapped in heavy brown paper, twelve inches long, not particularly dangerous. François showed them where to insert the detonator in the hub of neat triangular folds of paper at the base of each cylinder.

David held a stick to his nose to smell them. François watched him, quizzically. Immediately David felt how the smell, like chemical fertilizer, began to make him feel sick. Dynamite was not as passive as he'd thought. It maintained a purr of violence all the time.

The detonators, in another magazine, were less interesting, bright caps on two legs of electric wire sheathed with plastic, like toys. They practised exploding a few, using torch batteries. David remembered an advertising sign in Soweto, 'Freedom from fear. Eveready batteries.'

At the house they practised timing with clocks, batteries and electric wires. They worked in silence. Their secrecy hid them from their own eyes. Hours of pretended leisure spent in a dazzle off the dam's water, under the unconcerned blank of the sky, wrapped them in isolation. Several times they swam, and the water washed dry concentration off them, refreshed them with living sweetness.

At sunset they built a fire and cooked a braaivleis. Afterwards they sat round the fire singing songs David had first heard at the Treason Trial, songs from the Defiance Campaign and the Congress, from the Civil Rights movement in America that flagged a signal to them they were not alone, songs remembered from childhood and scouts and picnics, school hymns, Gilbert and Sullivan, musicals. Nostalgia and resolution drew them into a bond as impenetrable as their silence had been.

In sleep that night, Trevor cried out, gave his name, said 'I want to see my lawyer,' and cried out again, 'Aaah.' Then his words became an indecipherable suppressed appeal. François switched on the light.

'Don't hit me. Don't!' Trevor sat up, still dreaming.

'Wake up, Trevor. It's O.K. There's no one here.'

Trevor's wide, blank stare focussed and gave way to recognition.

'I'm sorry. It was a dream.'

'Yes, we know. There's nothing to be sorry about,' François assured him. 'We can't prevent our dreams.'

But afterwards, lying sleepless, hearing each other's breathing, they all listened to the night.

As if to confirm Trevor's nightmare, a neighbour came next day to find out what was happening on the Celliers' farm. They watched the long dust trail of his car coming near. When he stopped the car he found them all sunning and reading.

'Hullo. Botha's the name. I was jes wondering who's on Franz Celliers' land.'

'Hullo, Oom Paul. You don't remember me? I'm Hennie's nephew, François Marais. We met at Karl Lamprecht's wedding. Remember?'

Botha said he remembered, and François took him through a long, genealogical conversation about the Celliers and Marais clans. David noticed that reminscences and jokes did not prevent Botha from letting his eyes, only apparently vague, wander over the props they had prepared for him, the coloured towels, sun tan lotion, cigarettes, sandals, magazines — all symptoms of careless idleness. When Botha left, François walked where he had walked and sat where he had been sitting. Finding the beer bottle Botha had emptied he smashed it vehemently on the ring of stones round the fire's ashes. They each had their own rage and terror. He was not alone.

'We should probably talk about what happens if we get caught,' François said. 'Why don't you say a few things, Philip.'

So Philip told them about the characteristic team of harsh and friendly warders and interrogators, about the temptation to feel guilty.

'Do you want to talk about torture,' François prompted.

'Not my favourite subject. But yes. I'll say this. There's not much point in describing what they do — it gets better and they change it all the time — but they've got techniques now that always work. There's no point in trying to resist. In fact, it's probably better to break quickly, when you might still be able to control what you say a bit.'

'Anything else?' François insisted.

'No. It's impossible to foresee too much. Everything'll change. Your whole sense of reality dissolves. You can't remember or concentrate. You feel worthless and depressed. And then if they torture you . . . the main thing is to remember not to feel guilty, not to try to be heroic. I don't think we should think too much about these things.'

'O.K.' François said. So they swam again, and made a fire, and a braaivleis, and sang watching the sparks die as they flew up to the stars.

Before they set out the next day, François had them check their code for contacting each other during the two weeks when they would not meet, and gave them directions on the escape route through Basutoland.

'If you need it, one of Mabotoana's friends will get in touch with you at this house in T.Y. Learn the map and then destroy it. This is only for an emergency, if we have to get to England. We shouldn't need it. We'll be in touch again on the twelfth. O.K.?'

They shook hands before they parted.

Spence told David which classes he'd be teaching next year. David did not resign. Teaching was irrelevant now. The school felt like a museum, displaying a life already past.

On Thursday night someone knocked on David's door. The police! But they weren't banging! How could he escape? Should he escape? There was nothing damaging in the flat. He'd hidden the dynamite and detonators in the abandoned house on Richard's property. There were François's papers, but he'd said they weren't particularly incriminating. The knock came again. In despair about doing anything else, David opened the door. Philip slipped in and closed the door quickly.

'They've got François and Trevor.'

'When?'

'Tonight.'

'How did you hear?'

'Mabotoana sent a friend to warn me.'

'What'll we do?'

'I'm driving to Basutoland.'

'Do you think we can still use that route?'

'Yes. François set it up so that it wouldn't need him. But we've got to use it quickly.'

'O.K. Have you changed your numberplates yet?'

'No. I wanted to warn you first.'

He looked at Philip. In the church at St Thérèse's he had longed to meet another man in his company, to have a friend like this.

He felt himself standing straighter with happiness, meeting Philip's eyes.

'Let's go.' He took François's papers and packed the rest of the suitcase. They looked over the flat. Nothing except the haste of leaving, the bed unmade, food in the fridge, clothes left behind, would betray him. If the police came at all, it would mean they already knew too much. He wrote a note for the man who cleaned the flat, left ten rands as a Christmas box. He wrote another note to the building superintendent explaining that a family illness had called him away suddenly, and that he'd probably be back before New Year. He noticed his alarm clock and took it.

'Whose car shall we leave behind?' Philip asked.

'Mine. But we'd better drive to a place I know to change the plates.' He led the way to Richard's abandoned house. They worked without speaking.

'Better drive your car to somewhere it'll look innocuous parked for a few days,' Philip suggested. 'I'll follow you.'

'I'll come later. I'll meet you in T.Y. I'm going to do something.'

'What?'

'I'm not sure yet. It's a waste to leave without doing anything.'

'You can't go ahead with the old plan.'

'No, I see that.'

'I think we should just get out. Quickly. Before the escape route's cut off too.'

'Look. Don't wait for me. I'll come.'

'Do you want me to stay?'

Again David felt the happiness Philip's friendship was bringing him.

'No. We've agreed always to work alone.'

'If they get you, it's the last thing.' Philip looked at him. David knew they both weighed their danger. He had made his decision. He could not turn away from action any longer.

'It may be the last thing anyhow.'

'I'll stay with you,' Philip offered.

'I don't want you to.' He looked at Philip, insisting on his own will, smiling, insisting on their friendship. There would be time for more later. Philip smiled. 'I'll see you in Basutoland,' he consented. They did not need more words with each other but before parting they stood for a moment with their arms on each other's shoulders.

David waved as Philip drove away. He decided to change his own number plates later. First he must empty the suitcase, pack the dynamite, remove the glass from the clock face, fix the wires, the battery, the detonator. He worked quickly, listening to his own breathing, unconsciously noticing and remembering the crack in the concrete floor, hearing his own steps, the click of objects as he set them down, the significant tick of the clock. When he wiped the glass face clean and shattered it, he remembered how François had smashed Botha's beer bottle. He carried the suitcase to the boot of the car. He hid the envelope of papers François had given him under the spare tyre. The sky was deepening, birds stirred, morning was coming. He felt very calm and acute. He would have time to change the plates. By the time he had finished, sharp rays reached through the trees and sank into him. The fire of the sun met a fire inside him.

Daily traffic thickened on the road to Johannesburg. He passed the Voortrekker Monument and the Air Force base, desultory farms and cafés. He must do it in Johannesburg. In Pretoria he did not feel comfortable, could not trust himself to know what stood behind each corner. He had to know and be calm and confident, honed by rehearsal, like Joan before a performance. He passed Alexandra Township, smokey on his left. Tonight his act would be known there and would shine like a beacon. Let the whole land tremble. The future was being born, in blood, as it had to come. The time was coming. He carried it. It smelled like fertilizer. Louis Botha Avenue was jammed with cars and buses. The Africans were still coming into town in packed green buses and bicycles, but white's cars were coming now too. David looked at the faces of drivers, thoughtless in their capsules. Their time was coming. He looked at white faces at bus stops. Schoolboys were gathering for the last inane day. Soon he would phone Mrs Blake with an excuse that he was not well and could not teach today. But he was well. He was well. All was well and would be better. He laughed behind the wheel.

He drove into the centre of town and looked for a parking place. A south side would be best, so the sun wouldn't shine on the car and heat it. He would do everything neatly. Today he would be meticulous. He paid the meter and listened to the whirl and click that registered his legitimacy. He walked to a café. He ordered breakfast and bought a newspaper. There was nothing in it about François or Trevor. Perhaps they had been arrested too late. Perhaps no one had told the papers. A small item caught his attention. During the night, police had conducted raids in the townships. He passed over the other stories, a front-page article on children looking forward to the holidays, predictions of greater prosperity in the coming year, the ninety-day bill winning a fierce way through Parliament. He 'phoned the school and left a message with Mrs Blake, reverting to the story of a sudden illness in the family. He finished breakfast. He wanted to wait until town was more full. He wanted a time when any white person would think, 'I could have been there.' He would create a universal vulnerability today. He could wait for the ripest time.

In the library, the reading room was peaceful and almost empty. There were no university students. Exams must be over for them too. He carried books by Marc Bloch among the gleaming desks. He was going to enjoy this silent morning, the sun coming in quietly from high windows, the mannerly librarians who would bring him, if he asked for them, obscure and learned texts from the stacks. Evidence of past civilization. Connections to others who had been alive.

In the middle of the morning he left the library to buy a

portable radio. He would want to hear the news. He took it to the car and drove to a new parking place. Today he would commit no offences. At lunch time he went out again, bought sandwiches and took them to the car to eat later. He opened the boot and carried the suitcase to the men's room in the library. He wound the clock and set the wires so that in half-an-hour they would make a closed circuit. What a leap of fire it would be! What a flash of justice! He snapped the suitcase shut, delighted with the precision of the click.

Down the cool dimness of the interior stairs, down the shallow steps of the main entrance, past the thin shade of the library gardens, past the glare of buses and tram rails, past the Indian flower-sellers near the Cenotaph, past the drab City Hall, past the planting on Rissik Street where political meetings used to be held, where his father had marched in the Torch Commando. At the intersection he had to wait for the light to change. It was a brilliant noon. He passed the Post Office. He came to the shops of Eloff Street. He turned left. Elegant dresses peered at him. Jewellery. Glazed fruit. Pianos. They deserved it. They deserved everything they would get. The station waited for him.

He followed the signs, *Blankes Alleen: Whites Only*. They gave him permission to go where he was going. A policeman was loitering in the entrance of the new whites' concourse. He walked past, confidently. Today he would use his rights as a white man joyfully. Near a sign marked *Information* he stopped with the suitcase. He pretended to look as if he was waiting. Leaving the suitcase, he went to a window displaying African curios for sale. The time was getting close. He walked out towards the platforms, and then turned towards a side entrance, moving quickly like a man who has important business to do. There were 'phones on the other side of the street. He found it difficult to focus on the numbers in the directory. He forced himself. He dialled. He smelt urine and dead cigarettes. He watched the traffic through the glass.

'Hello, *Star* office,' the woman said.
'This is the beginning,' he told her.

The rich boom of the explosion reached him, almost lost in city noises. He put the 'phone down.

A crowd was beginning to form, pressing to see the commotion. He waited, walked to it, allowed himself to be carried with it towards the station, to be pushed behind the throng, to peer in from the edges, to see nothing, give up and walk away, to find the car, to take the road to Basutoland.

*Judgement*

As soon as they brought him into court where the judge wore red and the barristers wore black, and policemen crowded around him, and the wooden galleries pressed down, he knew it would be death. His life had sent him to this blood and blackness, and his father sitting in the gallery, waiting, with the others, to condemn him.

Kaplan, beside him, assured him that he was lucky to get Justice Kok who had a reputation for fairness and mild sentences. David saw the room, wooden as a church, the benches like pews, heard the oaths administered, and knew that they brought God and the law together against him. He looked for Joan. She was wearing the dark dress, like mourning, she wore when she visited him. It had become her habit. Her darkness also condemned him.

He had waited for her first visit as if it were a threat. So much rubble lay between them. He didn't know who she would find him to be in the wreckage. A lunatic? A murderer? What else could he be?

When Snyman took him to the room he said, 'I'll stand here at the door. I don't have to come in.'

'Thank you. I appreciate it.' But he dreaded the privacy Snyman had taken care to give him. He waited for Joan.

She hesitated at the door, as though she also feared their meeting, or couldn't see where to move. Immediately he recognized that his fears had been a fig leaf of false pain put on to protect him from this — no protection after all. Her body walked as though it had learned to have a set place. The surfeit of life that had always enveloped her every gesture had been drained, not the way a child's illness drains, still promising recovery, but by an erosion she would never recover from. At the chair, she hesitated a hair's breadth, as though a film over her eyes was beginning to make her blind and hesitant. He saw how she bent to put her bag on the floor. It was a movement he would never have noticed. Now it seemed middle aged; and her hands, when she held them loose in her lap, seemed powerless and empty.

But there were no lines in her face. It was only the way she moved that proved him completely accused, judged, guilty, and sentenced. He waited for her to adjust to the dim, bare room, the grille, and him on the other side.

'Are you feeling better?' he asked.

'Yes. I'm quite strong now.'

'You've lost weight.'

'Aviva says I'm lucky.'

'How is she?'

'Putting on weight.'

'You're still staying with them.'

'Yes. I don't like being alone.'

'I'm sorry.'

She shrugged, as though there was no way to deal with his apology.

'You've also lost weight.'

He nodded. 'Will you go to England or Europe afterwards?'

'I don't know.'

'Wouldn't it be better?'

'I don't know.'

Mr Moodley had said. 'We don't think of the future," He had cramped her into that dilemma.

They both waited for a new sentence.

'How's Sidney?'

'Fine. Also excited about the baby. Cecil too, though he's a quiet child, and it's hard to tell.'

'What've you been doing?'

'Practising, as I always do.' She made a noise that would have been a laugh before. 'Michael wrote to me. He's written to you too, but they say you're not allowed letters.'

'They didn't tell me.'

'He asked me to say that when you were in Pretoria you talked about being brave — he thinks you *have* been brave.'

'Will you thank him, for me. He must know how much it means to hear from him here.'

'He does. He said it's one of the hardest things since he's left, that he can't visit you now.'

'When I thought I'd get out, I wanted to see Michael.'

'Edward's told him about seeing you. He told me too.'

At Edward's visit terror had soaked him. Now, he could feel nothing but a distant sadness because Joan had been quenched.

When she visited again she brought more messages that suggested support, or sympathy, or understanding. She never said what she felt. She told him news of the world outside, but he found the life where people would still be marrying and catching buses, hearing music, harder and harder to imagine. The prison was his normal life. His world had become Prinsloo, Snyman, Gericke, Kaplan, the books Kaplan had brought for him languishing in the front office, Joan visiting, wearing her dark dresses.

The last visit before the trial he said, 'You don't have to come to court, Joan.'

'I know.'

But she did not say whether she would protect herself from the stares and the reporters.

They brought their witnesses out, people he had known and people who had stood in the periphery of the action. All testified, all would concur. Although he was dead in their judgement, while they compelled him to wait they kept him mercilessly alive, and every day in the courtroom they unravelled the meanings of his life. He stood in the evidence piling round him like litter. Strange wrappings, words he had not remembered, fragmented conversations, fell around him as though he had become, like them, something for the dustbin, the coffin. They would not dispense with this ceremony, although they had already judged him. They needed the ritual to exonerate them — so they enacted contest: mercy, understanding, and forgiveness on the side of the defence; justice, order, peace, respect, safety, decency and civilization on the side of the prosecution. David waited. Their ritual conceded a place for him to speak. Without hope of revocation, he would speak, and pit his justice against their justice.

They called Mr Moodley and Munira against him, and he discovered that they had been imprisoned under the ninety-day act passed while he was in prison. Mr Moodley's hands trembled all the time. Munira's skeleton called for attention.

He had not thought about the passage that linked his life to theirs, or how, if his life collapsed, he would bring theirs down too, and tumble prison down on top of them like a rockfall.

He hardly heard what they said in court, crushed by other questions. What had happened to Munira's family without her protection? Without Mr Moodley's solicitude? Didi's friends had been so happy when the police released him. Now the police must feel justified.

The prosecutor asked what business they had had with David. Why did they want B.A.s? Were they dissatisfied with their lives? Had they ever discussed politics with David? What were their political views? How had David come to know them? They knew Michael too — did they know of his activities in London?

When David prompted Kaplan to object, Dietz insisted that he must demonstrate that David had long been associated with dangerous characters.

Munira? Mr Moodley?

They gave their answers with fearful politeness. At first, David thought they were afraid of the police, the judge, the court, the barristers, the crowds in the gallery. Then he realized that their faces were always turned away from him.

He wanted to repudiate their averted faces, to explain that he would never wish them any harm and could not hurt them. He, who had toppled prison onto them?

Munira was wearing a blue sari, although she usually wore European clothes. He recognized it. They had all three gone to see *Shakuntala* when an Indian dance company visited Wits, and Munira, proud to share her history with the dancers and the play, had worn the blue sari. He did not know why she wore it now. To hide the graceless protrusion of bones behind its lavish folds? Or because she robed herself like the judge and barristers for the ceremony of condemnation? He was glad to see it, as he had been glad to see the saris and Indian features of the Asiatic Bazaar. At times, when she was giving evidence, he was filled with such tenderness he wanted to stroke Munira's face or put his arms around her, to protect her from the injuries he had brought upon her.

He felt the same weeping warmth with Mr Moodley, whose trembling hands he wanted to hold still, whose face he wanted to turn towards him so that he could look with a clear feeling that would take away all the pain. But Mr Moodley would not look at him.

Until that aversion, David felt, he had not tasted his guilt in his own mouth. The others found him guilty: he was honoured by their condemnation. His nausea now tasted of himself.

The courtroom lights increased his nausea and he half closed his eyes. How condescendingly he had offered his love and pity. They were right not to look at him. How repulsively he had wished to save them and protect them. He was no better than the Nationalists who, no doubt, had the same benign feelings for the Africans, their charges.

They trembled because of him, and he, incurably white, wanted them to look at him and accept his love. His love — now he knew its taste — white, white as Spence, who was in the witness stand now, white as maggots, white as mould, white as tape-worms, white as all secret, disgusting creatures that never see light. It would be better for everyone if he did not think of them, inflicting his noble feelings on them. It would be better for them if he had never lived.

At first he had been disappointed that the Non-European gallery was so empty — only a few Indians when Munira and Mr Moodley had testified, and for the rest, only a few African men who might have been reporters. He had flattered himself that Africans must take precautions against showing sympathy, or even too much interest in the case. They were wise. They were not interested in his pity and noble feelings.

His salvation was not wanted, he had nothing to do with them, he was a European. Nothing could exonerate him from the whiteness he shared with Spence, who also had fine feelings and had chosen Bellini's Doge to hang on his office wall. Slowly, pushing upwards like a plant that had been germinating underground and presses towards the surface, something he had known, or could have known — in a luminous sweetness, he remembered Sina lying on the concrete floor of the balcony outside Ward Eighteen, shaking her head at the chocolate he had brought her, feigning no gratitude at his concern.

He could not conceive the boy Sina must have known, angry that his shirts weren't ironed yet, stupid with youth, staring at her breasts, casually kind perhaps when he was in a good mood. He must have been like other white boys. A pompous, unintelligible impulse had brought him to her with a bar of chocolate in his hand. What did she care? She was dying. He didn't even know her husband's name or that she had children. She wasn't interested in his kindness or his prurience. She knew him too well. She was busy with her own death.

He was interminably alive. Kaplan prompted his attention. 'Here's your friend who likes poetry,' and he saw Richard, in his turn, take the stand, his eyes two colours, pale, to tell the court about the abandoned house he had shown David (a crack in the concrete floor like lightning). None of them understood each other. David's nausea clung to him as though he were continually rehandling the dynamite he had used. He asked Kaplan for aspirin.

His cell sheltered him like a cave. He tried to think about Munira and Mr Moodley and Sina, but his attention flinched, and he could not concentrate. The coarse food and prison shouts relieved him. Continuous and independent, they existed without him, guilty or innocent and had become predictable, familiar, and lulling, like his regular pacing between the grey walls. His headache would go away. His nausea would diminish.

Piet Kreer, Tertius Keyter, Hans Breitenbach, Karl Borcherds, Guy Lechaptois, Duncan Campbell, Johannes Pereira, David Miller. I'm sick of clink. Women is the root of all evil. He did not imagine who had left their names to keep him company, who had reached forwards, wanting to be remembered by their successors, who had established this frail memorial for themselves, who had not wanted to be lost anonymously in history, to whom he joined his name. He read the names emptily, habitually. They also lulled him. Prison was a kindly drug.

They took him away from prison to bring him before the court again. Mrs McMullan described her mother, who had been killed instantly in the explosion. Mrs Blackmun had been standing very near the bomb, waiting for the train to Cape Town where she would visit her grandchild. So it was inhuman that he had blown her to bits.

He could not concentrate on the testimony. He had never known the woman and couldn't imagine her, though Mrs McMullan mentioned that she had been wearing a blue dress that matched her eyes. Instead, the taste of guilt flooded his mouth again, and he remembered the feel of Mrs Cooke's aged hand when she greeted him. Her skin was loose and slipped around her fragile bones as though decay was loosening her before her death. So he had killed an old woman, like Mrs Cooke who had offered him chicken and tea. How curiously stupid he had been. He hadn't imagined the people he would kill. He was like the policemen at Bitterspruit. After all, he was white too.

The next witness was Mrs Bekker. She used a lace handkerchief when she cried. David wondered who had given it to her. Or had she bought it for the trial or used it at the little girl's funeral. He hadn't noticed a child. He hadn't noticed anything. He hadn't noticed the colour of his own skin and mind.

The day was cloudy and the courtroom seemed dark and

full of varnished wood like a church. They would rehearse the whole tedious business again and again; they would drag him through time as at a horse's tail, before they hanged him. They would parade their justice. It was part of his punishment.

His cell was kind. It kept him among the condemned and offered him the names of companions. An impulse of castigation made him stop in his pacing and scratch new names under his own — Mary Blackmun, Freda Bekker, Munira Isamail, Didi Moodley, Joan Miller. Later prisoners would wonder how they had found themselves in the same cell as him. White and black. Women too. Their contiguity had been unfortunate, an accident of prison life.

During the night he woke suddenly. Murderer. Murderer. It didn't mean anything. He would go back to sleep. Murderer. Murderer.

Days of random, incomprehensible litter accumulated again. Other victims came to the stand. A man whose arm had been amputated. The pinned sleeve waggled a warning to David. A middle-aged brunette wore a patch where her eye had been. A portly businessman had been in bed four months, recovering from acute burns. David could not like him. In court, and pallid from months indoors, he lacked his cigars, his secretaries. The pretty shop assistant who had lost her leg, Lettie du Toit, limped now. How could he pay attention to all the ramifications? Feel sorry that no one would take her dancing now? He was busy with his own death.

The nights were shreds, waking and recoiling from faces and names and accusations. They would put him to death for the old lady's hand and bits of flesh scattered in the rubble, clots of hair and blue rag, an arm still bleeding while the dust settled, fragments of marble and splinters of varnished wood like bone shining with blood.

Weekends filled the prison with drunks and assault charges. The noisy prisoners shouted and sang drunken songs. Gericke's confidence about a short sentence had dissipated, and he was depressed now. He complained that the bladdy racket was getting on his nerves, man. David asked Snyman to give him some of the fruit Joan had brought.

'It'll be O.K., Gericke, you'll see,' he muttered during their exercise time.

One night he woke as he had been waking but this time he had the answer. He hadn't known what he was doing. He was not responsible. He had been depressed in Pretoria, and then, with Francois and the others, euphoric. Why, if he'd been able to think, he would have known all along that the venture was crazy. Michael's friends had been talking about revolution for years. He'd never taken them seriously before. He wasn't responsible. It was obvious. Anyone could see that. Kok was a fair judge. Rifkin's evidence and Kaplan would keep him alive.

Distant and calm with acknowledged madness, he saw Trevor take the stand. Trevor had told them everything. Kaplan had shown him the statement, half-translated into Afrikaans illiteracies by the man who had written it down, but accurate about the details and the names.

'You're disappointed,' Kaplan said, 'aren't you.'

'Not at all. Why should I be disappointed. Van der Merwe told me he'd talked. I knew all about it. They brought him in to see me. I told you. What's the point?'

'I can see your face.'

'It doesn't matter. I don't feel anything. I knew he'd talked, otherwise they wouldn't have brought me here would they? They'd've kept me in ninety-days until *I* talked. I'm grateful. There you are.'

'You understand that he'll be a state's witness.'

'Of course. Otherwise they'd hang him too. I'm not upset. We agreed to talk if they tortured us.'

'They didn't torture him. The night they came to arrest him they found that he'd been drinking ever since he'd heard about the explosion. He talked as soon as they asked him.'

David looked at the papers in his hand. So neither Trevor nor François had been arrested. Philip's scare had been for nothing. For Trevor, it must have seemed like his nightmare again to hear that knocking, to hear it, drunk, with no one to wake him from this dream. He looked at Kaplan. 'We could've guessed he'd break. Anyhow, he's not responsible for what I did. He opposed killing. As he says.' He found the section in

Trevor's statement where he reported their discussion.

'I wish you hadn't talked about it,' Kaplan said, 'It makes our case more difficult.'

'You don't have to save my life. I don't care.'

'I do care. I said more difficult. Not impossible. Rifkin will testify that you were temporarily insane.'

'Temporarily? Will I get better?'

Kaplan looked away and tapped his pencil with an irregular beat. Waltz time.

'My great uncle was betrayed.'

'Our cases have nothing in common. Trevor hasn't betrayed me. It was only a matter of time. He doesn't have to give his life for me. Isn't it enough? How many corpses do I have to carry?'

On the stand, Trevor was swept by sudden pallors and flushes. His hands also shook. Sometimes he leaned forwards to clutch the wooden rail of the witness stand. Sometimes he squeezed his hands into fists. At times he stammered, as though some judgement within him resisted giving testimony like a traitor.

Kaplan harped on the nerve of his pain.

'Please explain to the court why you have decided to give evidence for the state.'

Dietz objected, and Kaplan retracted.

'You knew the accused well. You were friends.'

'We knew each other for only a few months.'

'But you knew each other well enough to plot sabotage together?'

'Yes.'

'Which means well enough to trust your lives to each other?'

'Yes.'

'That seems fairly well.'

Trevor waited. Kaplan attacked again. 'According to Captain van der Merwe, whom I shall call to the stand shortly, you were rather eager to pin the blame on the accused. How could you be so certain he was responsible?'

'We were all prepared to blow up installations,' Trevor's voice changed pitch, became shrill, 'but we never wanted to kill people. We weren't murderers. He was the only one who wanted to shed blood. It's horrible. Horrible!' He covered his face and then dropped his hands. He regained control of his voice. 'Excuse me.'

'How did you know it was not another member of your group?'

'He was the only one who wanted to do something like that. He s-s-s-spoke about it the first time we met. He s-s-s-said sabotage wasn't enough. He s-s-s-said we should k-k-k-kill people.'

'When did you have this discussion?'

'Right at the beginning. It must've been October.'

'So, from the first you gave the impression that these were ideas you might seriously consider yourself.'

'No. I said right away I didn't agree. We didn't agree to it.' Dark rings had appeared under Trevor's eyes during the short time he had been on the stand.

'All of you?'

'I s-s-s-suppose I spoke most s-s-s-strongly. We didn't agree to it.' Trevor was flushing now. 'He used us.'

'Do you mean that he planned terrorism even when he seemed to agree that you would only commit sabotage against installations?'

Trevor took a moment to think about his answer, and then spoke slowly and almost inaudibly, 'No. He was sincere. It probably just occurred to him when he thought he was the only one left.'

'Ah. That's something you didn't mention in the statement you were so eager to give the police when they found you in a drunken stupor.'

Dietz tensed to protect his witness, 'Objection, your honour.'

'Objection sustained.'

Kaplan did not seem to mind. 'Mr Reed, you admit that your state of mind was not quite, er, normal, at the time you gave this statement to the police?'

'I was shocked.'

'I am sure you would not perjure yourself to injure a friend out of simple malice,' Kaplan admitted. 'I wonder how long your, er-unusual state of mind had existed. Would you say from the time you heard about the bomb's explosion? Before? How long before?'

'I was shocked when I heard.'

'And before? You were also planning an act of sabotage. What was your own state of mind?'

Dietz looked perturbed, ready to object again, but he said nothing. Trevor was looking down at his hands clasped round the wooden bar of the stand.

'I wasn't feeling as usual.'

'You would agree that the defendant's state of mind could also have been unusual? Over-excited? Tense?'

Trevor looked up. 'I don't know. I hadn't s-s-seen him for a few days.'

'But you think it possible.'

'Yes.' Trevor had become extremely pale again.

'Do you think his state of mind could be considered insanity?'

Now Dietz objected that a judgement like that needed an expert's opinion. Kaplan promised that he would call experts to testify later. 'But taking into account that I'm not asking for a scientific judgement, just an impression, you understand, would you consider the defendant in an unusual state of mind? Perhaps even temporarily insane?'

'Yes.' Now Trevor sounded surprisingly calm.

'You seem very certain. Can you explain why?'

'Sane people don't act that way.' This reply did not seem to satisfy Kaplan.

'Did you think him insane before the act?'

'No. We wouldn't have worked with him if we'd thought that.'

'But now you do think he might have been insane, or in an unusual state of mind before committing the act.'

Again Trevor paused to think before he answered. 'He was always very quiet. It was difficult to know what he was thinking. Our discussion at the beginning was the only time we really talked much. We all thought we understood one another.' At this moment Trevor carelessly looked up at David, and their eyes met. He suddenly paled again. 'Yes. I did always think he could be mad. I was shocked when he s-s-spoke of terrorism. I felt he was capable of anything.' He stopped to render his perfect piece of honesty. 'It appalled me.'

Kaplan thanked Trevor and allowed him to leave the stand. Dietz's expression showed that he was, after all, not pleased with his star witness.

David did not attend to van der Merwe's testimony, a corroborative account of how Trevor had given his written statement. He was angry for Kaplan. Trevor only wanted to live and save himself from the crimes of pity. Kaplan would have had nothing to say to him if he had lived peacefully like a white South African, painting his bright abstracts and enjoying the gentle sun. But because Trevor had felt pity and been sucked into madness like David's own, Kaplan, who had never played the brave matador who flaunts a cape at dangerous dilemmas, jeered that Trevor was gored. Kaplan was stupid, as stupid as the rest. He implied that Trevor with his, er, unusual state of mind was mad too. It should have been usual for Trevor to live in sunshine and not notice that his eyes showed anything but designs and colours for abstract, pleasing canvases. He should have enjoyed fine brandy. Trevor appreciated flamboyant women and men who knew how to live. He should have clung to life's pleasures only, not to conspiracy and mortal risk, to wildernesses of fear that Kaplan knew nothing about.

Through the mesh window of the police van, he saw the leafy sunshine like honey, Indian flower-sellers on street corners among their brilliant wares, and women in bright dresses and shorts, as happy as if they had never heard of him. Trevor had chosen to walk back to the women, and the flower-sellers, and the city. To reject madness and blood.

As though a sac inside him had burst, want poured through David. He wanted life. He was young. He wanted to swim again and climb the mountains near Rustenburg, to eat peaches warm off the trees near Vereeniging, to walk under the oaks in Cape Town and hear the doves' long colloquy. He wanted to see Joan in a bright dress again, and to hold her, to live with her where they could love freely, she could look at him from the mirror where she sat brushing her hair he could see how she chose a dress in the morning, how she leaned forward to pour tea and the sun touched her head and made gold of her hair. He wanted to live. Not to die strangled by crowding, naked beggars, by skeletal children, by drought, by everything that made men mad.

Kaplan would save him. He would live. The van pulled into the prison and the metal doors shut behind him. In the other prison they would call him mad. The sadness he had felt for Trevor reflected back on himself, as his madness had reflected onto Trevor.

A new warder brought the mug of tea and two thick slices of bread and jam that served as supper. It was food his mother had given to odd-job boys. David had accustomed himself to prison food, but tonight he did not touch it. He paced and absorbed the familiar, subliminal litany of names on the walls.

Gericke was also silent, more depressed than David had ever known him. They started one conversation, but it soon died in gloom.

'Agh, man, don talk to me about my case. Tell me how it's going with you.'

'Oh, I don't know, Gericke. My lawyer's getting me down.'

'Ja, man. That's how it is sometimes. Sometimes I get so sick 'n tired of clink I don even care, you know that? I thinks, what the hell! If they let me out, I'll get back. If you're in once, you're in for life. You might's well give up right now. But you got to say, bugger it, it's not forever.'

The weekend brought relief with its clamour of petty arrests.

On Monday, Kaplan said, 'Dietz has asked for a few days' delay.'

'Why?'

'I don't know.'

At exercise time, Gericke said, 'They got your *boet*.'

'Who? François?'

'Philip Brink. He's your *boet* isn he?'

'When did they get him?'

'Las night. He was trying to get to Mozambique.'

'Where is he now?'

'Here in the Fort. Not with us whites, nachrilly. *Daardie kant.*' His thumb made a cautious gesture towards the Non-European section.

Gericke called Philip his *boet*, his brother. If they had Philip, they'd take him to be hanged with his *boet* in Pretoria Central. Unless Philip followed Trevor's example and turned state's evidence. Perhaps Philip had realized the choices already in Basutoland. Or had he been shocked like Trevor, sick like a white man at the smell of white blood?

After they walked round Prinsloo and the new warder, a bony man whose mouth, tight and wide, made David fear, David asked, 'What charge?'

'Nothing so far. It's ninety days.'

So his *boet* was in an hermetic room where time and sanity dissolved, like the one at Marshall Square where they had shown him Trevor and he had been grateful when van der Merwe interrogated him, because interrogation was a human contact outside the flux and tumbling of his own mind.

'Is there any way to get a message to him?'

'Don't be mad, man. In ninety days? Hang! Who you going to get to do something like that?' David felt half relieved. What could he say to Philip? Sorry, old chap?

The screams, next day, had no clear rhythm or cause. When strokes were given in the Fort, the screams were regular. There'd be a hiss — the lash — a thud, a yell. Sometimes, after a few strokes, a hiss, a thud, no yell — the prisoner had fainted. These screams rose and fell untiring.

The prison's noises stopped, as if every inmate held his breath when the chill of pity fastened on his bones. Behind the screams, the muffled city brought workers home in cars and buses. A telephone rang, warders locked doors and paced noisily in echoing corridors. The cells began to move and talk again.

'What're they doing to him?' David asked Gericke.

'I dunno. Shocks maybe.'

Snyman wouldn't talk when he brought their food, and

soon after, the screams died down. Before the sleep bell they began again. David bit his hand. Perhaps he was really mad. It was a fantasy in his imagination. No one had voice to scream so long.

'Gericke.'

'Ja.'

'I'm not imagining them?'

'Shut up man, and stop worrying. There's not a damn thing you can do.'

'Have you heard this kind of thing before?'

'No.'

It was impossible to do nothing. No matter what Philip felt about him, it must be some encouragement to know, if he could know anything at all, that other people could hear him. If sound could come out, it could go in.

As loudly as he could, David started to sing the freedom songs he had learnt at Hartebeestepoort Dam. Voices from the Non-European block joined his. The screams did not stop. The singing grew louder. When David exhausted the repertoire he had learned singing with Philip, he turned to the defiant promise from the *Messiah* he had sung driving to Basutoland. 'He shall crush them with a rod of iron. He shall crush them.' More prisoners joined them. Many seemed to know the *Messiah*. Perhaps some had belonged to the thousand-voice African choir Joan played with every year.

'He shall break them in pieces like a potter's vessel. In pieces. In pieces.' The screams paused. The Africans, turned now to themes of familiar piety, introduced new songs, most of them sad mission hymns. The screams began again. David hoped that Philip did not know how, for days before an execution, the condemned in the death block at Pretoria Central sang hymns, and carried their melodious piety to the gallows.

The singers did not stop in the intervals when the circuit of screams broke, or as the intervals of silence grew longer. If some slept, others woke to hold their song. When morning came, the warders changed shift, distributed breakfast, supervised the Africans polishing the passage floor on their knees, shouted loud commands to the gangs chained together to work outside.

In the cold, bright morning of the courtyard David and Gericke did not speak. Mournful harmonies wound round them, and screams whipped their faces.

After lunch he did not hear them anymore.

That night, because he could not sleep, David took his wooden stool and put it under the window. Standing on the stool he could look through the mesh and see a piece of the sky pale with the full moon. After some hours he thought morning must be near. He listened for the whirr of bicycles along Louis Botha Avenue and the first buses bringing Africans to work. Soon the prison would wake and fold night's grim thoughts to day's lethargy of accustomed impotence.

He climbed down from the box and slept.

On Wednesday, Kaplan saw him.

'We're going to court again on Monday.'

'They've got Philip Brink, haven't they?'

'Yes.'

'They've been torturing him. We heard the screams.'

'That's a serious allegation, David.'

'All morning yesterday, and the night before.'

Perhaps Kaplan thought David had fantasies about screams in the night. Perhaps Rifkin had corrupted his trust in David. Or David's in him.

'I'll investigate.'

But on Thursday Kaplan told him there was no entry to show that Philip had been admitted to the Fort.

'So they've faked the records, that's all. You know they've got him. Where are they keeping him?'

'I'll find out if I can. Dietz tells me he'll give evidence for the state.'

'Ask what they've been doing to him. In court, if necessary.'

'I'll do what I can, David, but you know questions like that often get us nowhere.'

'You've got to ask them.'

Until Monday, time locked him in its prison. He could not

reach forward to the hour when the court would meet, he would see Philip, and wrest truth out. At last Monday came, hot and drowsy, boding storm in the afternoon. In the courtroom the judge's face grew more severe and distant, the reporters thinned. David noticed that his father, extraordinarily aged now, kept dropping off until his head lolled and jerked, and he woke up again.

It was afternoon before Philip was brought to the stand. David wondered whether he had been given drugs, he looked so strange, his gestures were so slow, his speech so weighted. His face seemed bloated and rigid, as though injected with preservative, and one eyelid hung lower than the other so that he looked absurdly villainous.

Philip read a prepared statement.

'I met the accused the first time in 1956. This is at a subversive meeting of the Discussion Club. This is a liberalistic, Communistic organization. At this time we have discussed the white man in South Africa. The accused says he cannot trust the white man. After this I don't meet the accused no more, but I hear he is in the company of known Communists and Liberalists. I meet the accused again at a party. This is a mixed party and there is illegal drink. This is in 1962, at which time the accused says we must overthrow the government. Accordingly, we arrange to meet secretly and talk about this matter. At this time he suggests many violences, also terrorism. We don't agree about this. We think sabotage is better for our purposes. We work many weeks to study sabotages. All these occasions the accused is altogether calm. Four nights before our first sabotage, I get a message the police is after us. Accordingly, I go to the accused to escape altogether, but he is not interested in this course of action. He is altogether calm at this time. He helps me change the licence on the escape car. Next thing I hear on the wireless there is this explosion in Johannesburg. I hear people is being killed. Next thing, the accused is coming to me looking for shelter, but I kicks him out.'

David beamed at Philip and then looked down at the table. He wanted to laugh. How had Philip managed to produce such a magnificently vague statement in the extremity of torture?

'Could you please explain to the court the circumstances in which you agreed to give this evidence,' Kaplan began his questioning.

Dietz objected that the question was not relevant, but Kaplan held his ground.

'My client tells me that on the fourth and fifth of February he heard screams in the Fort and that he recognized the voice as Philip Brink's. At first I must admit, I was somewhat sceptical, but I notice that that this statement is dated the fourth of February.'

David was surprised. Had Philip given the statement first and been tortured afterwards? It didn't make sense.

'Does the witness have any comment on this coincidence?'

'I have no comment.'

'Is it a coincidence?'

'I'm not sure what you mean.'

'Were you in the Fort on the fourth and fifth of February?'

'No. I was in Ermelo.'

'I had the impression you might say that. You were admitted to Ermelo prison on the fifth of February. Where were you on the fourth?'

'I can't recall. I have been in prison, and perhaps my sense of time,' Philip hesitated, 'And place, may be confused.'

So. He *had* been in the Fort.

Kaplan seemed to understand what Philip just said too. And perhaps Judge Kok did too. 'There will be an investigation,' he ruled. 'Proceed with your questioning.'

'Thank you, your honour,' Kaplan turned back to Philip, 'I realize that your written statement is not given in exactly your own words,' telling Philip, as well as David, that he knew they came from torture. Oh, he was a good lawyer after all. 'I presume that an investigation will explain the discrepancy. But could you say more, in your own words, about the first occasion of your meeting my client. At the Discussion Club meeting, I believe it was. What was the subject of the discussion that night? And what did you say to Mr Miller that led to his statement that he didn't trust whites?'

David looked at Philip. The distant room in Monica's house where they had first met stood between them brilliant with its own lights. Budapest and mine accidents. David's confused exultation at being with Joan. Philip's anger with Aviva. The conversation about blacks and whites and who lives that had told Philip and David that each understood the other's meaning, the feeling of friendship they had felt immediately. Who they were to each other now had started there, though it led here. Philip smiled at David. David smiled back. Philip's smile deepened, but as though it took some peculiar effort, forced through resisting numbness in the bloated, tallow face with its drooping and piratical eye. Philip was sweating, David saw. He keeled over. He had fainted.

The court woke up. A policeman took water from a carafe on Dietz's table and washed Philip's face. David closed his eyes. Had they splashed Philip with water to revive him from torture before?

'You're not going to faint too, are you?' Kaplan was holding his arm. David shook his head.

Officers of the court crowded around the witness stand and spectators pushed forward in the galleries. Reporters edged for good vantage points. Kok banged his gavel, and in what silence he could gain, adjourned the proceedings. Perhaps because the ritual rules had been disturbed, the strong arms that hustled David to the van, pulled at him with rougher force than usual.

Heavy clouds darkened the city's office windows, and uneasy calm brooded in the trees near the Fort.


Gericke had been sentenced to ten years' hard labour.

'Hell man, I didn't expect it. *Jirre*. It's a long time. Jesus Christ! What bloody luck! What blood fucking luck!'

'Where'll you be?'

'I dunno, man. Some bloody place in the *bundu* where I'll *mos* rot away.'

'Maybe they'll send you to Pretoria Central with me.'

'No thanks, hey. Pretoria's bloody murder. You just wait. Anyhow, your lawyer'll get you off.'

'I'll miss you.'

'*Ag*, man, I'll miss you too. You're too bloody serious, but otherwise you're O.K. Anyhow, Prinsloo says I'll still be here a week or so, so you needn' say good'bye yet. Hell, I'm not in a hurry.'

The rain came down in heavy rushes. David heard thunder. His cell was too deep in the prison's embankment wall for him to see the lightning or smell the new air, cleared of dust, but he was happy. Whatever Philip's smile had meant, it could not be condemnation. The rain muffled the sharp sounds of prison. He took the stool to the window so that he could see drops clinging to the mesh, holding the grey light inverted and formed. Soon night overlaid the storm's darkness, and there was nothing to see but spills of radiance coming before thunder.

When Kaplan came to the prison on Wednesday, he told David that Philip had disappeared. There was talk of his having escaped from prison.

'So there'll be no investigation into whether he was tortured, I suppose.'
'Probably.'
'I don't want to drop the issue.'
'I'm not going to push it, David. It can only prejudice our case.'
'There's nothing to our case. We might as well prejudice it.'
'I represent you in court David, not every worthy cause. Let's keep to the business in hand. Dietz is going to be ending the first part of his presentation soon, and we'll start the argument for the defence. You might find this part of the trial hard. I know that it's all been telling on you.'
'It doesn't matter.' David refused his pity.

Gericke had heard the story too. 'So your *boet's* escaped.'
'Yes. Who told you?'
'Prinsloo. Lucky bastard. I wonder how he did it.' David did not tell him about Kaplan's embarrassing questions in court.

Instead he asked, 'You want some peaches?'

'Hell, the last lot was the best peaches I've ever eaten. Strue's God.'

But their conversation, hampered by the imminence of separation, felt sad.

He paced. So Kaplan wanted to forget about Philip and the question of torture, and not make too much fuss. He would conspire tacitly with van der Merwe or Dietz or whoever it was, to let Philip escape and the issue die. And perhaps the return would be to let David get off hanging because he was mad. That must be the arrangement they had come to, silently, without need for incriminating words.

Guy Lechaptois, 17th June 1955. How odd. He had never noticed the date before. It was the day Sina had died. That wasn't supposed to be what he was thinking about now.

Philip, then, would be implicated in his madness as Trevor had been. They had all worked together. But it was nonsense. Philip had been brave and calm. They had not been mad. Philip even less than Trevor. His only madness had been to be willing to take arms against an overwhelming power. But if that was madness, who was sane? Verwoerd. Vorster. The fools and madmen were those who did not survive, and those who pitied them, the silly women who sat on the ground outside hospitals, at St Thérèse's in the dim morning, and here, just across the street from the Fort, at the Non-European hospital. And the silly men who went into mines to pick up gold dust on their lungs and let the earth collapse on top of them. The silly nannies who tended their oppressors' children and sang them lullabies instead of strangling them before they grew up to become policemen and teachers and businessmen.

By that judgement, he must choose to be mad, but not mad to survive. He must reciprocate Philip's courage, and insist that apartheid, not he, was mad. Mad and guilty. So he must let the system of law he had offended put him to death — it was apartheid's law that made corpses by law, made laws to make corpses, made charnels, locations where, in spite of Ever Ready batteries, knives got you for a pair of secondhand shoes, laws that made reserves watered by dead rivers, mines where no one was responsible for explosions and rock falls, wages to kill children with starvation, passes to take wives from the husband's beds, children out of their mothers' hands, schools to take the eyes out of young heads, the brains out of their skulls, laws like plagues. The country was an abbatoir. Let it be known that he had died by its hand. Let them strangle him.

He leaned his head against a wall. Its hard cold mass assured him there was a world outside madness.

He could hear Gericke in the cell next door also pacing about, farting, going to the bucket to defecate. He waited a while and then went to the door. 'Gericke.'

'Coming. Just a minute.' David heard his steps. 'Ja, David, what is it?'

'Gericke, tell me about Pretoria Central.'

'*Ag* man, it's a *nare plek*. Hell man, you musn' let it get you down. Strue's God, your lawyer'll get you off.'

'No, man, tell me,' David insisted. 'Can you see the gallows?'

'Ag, man what'choo want to know for?'

'I want to know.'

Gericke hesitated, and began. 'You sees it when they admits you. When you comes in, there's this huge bladdy hall with a black floor. You looks right across where there's a notice. It says SILENCE. Hell! You looks underneath. That's it. That's where we go. Jesus!'

'And then?'

'There's nothing else.'

'Can you hear when they take them out?'

'Ja. They sings a long time before, and then when they opens the door, the singing gets very loud.'

'And then?'

'What else, man! *Jirre*. Hell man, David, I dunno what to say to you.'

'Tell me what happens after they open the door.'

'You hears them going down the passage, en then you hears the trap fall, en it *mos sort of* trembles everywhere.'

'I suppose you hear some of them crying and screaming.'

'*Ag*, man, it can't be so bad. You know, you comes the best time in your life. D'you know that! Jesus, things's crazy you know. You can't make sense of anything!'

He dreamed that he was underground, sweating, the walls of his mind chamber had caved in on him. They were watching him through the judas. It was their eyes that made him sweat. When he woke and stared at the electric light it zigzagged like lightning. A crack in the concrete floor of that house. The cracked feet of beggars and children bled like milk.

'Please baas.' He couldn't answer them. He was dead broke.

At the next discussion with Kaplan he felt a pang that he was going to break the comfort of their routine.

'I've got a rather difficult request to make.'

'You know I'd like to help you, David.'

'I want to change my plea. I'm not insane.'

'Of course not. That plea doesn't mean you are. It's a legal technique. We've been over this ground before, David.'

'I'm sorry. I can't make these fine distinctions between legal jargon and what people will really think words mean. I will not plead insanity.'

'Why? What's it this time.'

'Don't be patient with me, Mr Kaplan.'

'I thought we'd settled this issue.'

'It's come unsettled.'

'And why, may I ask?'

'I don't want the tone of the way the trial's going.'

'Please don't be ridiculous. You don't seem to realize that you're responsible for several deaths and other matters. I don't think you're in a position to be fastidious about tone.'

'I am responsible, and I'm going to take the responsibility.'

'What, exactly, are you objecting to?'

'That we're going to keep everything private and psychological — all about my state of mind and my father and that sort of thing. As though politics have really got nothing to do with it. And we needn't mention unpleasant things like torture. Philip was tortured. And you know it.'

'Yes, I think he was. You understand how it is that he escaped.'

'I'm grateful for that. I am.' He looked into Kaplan's brown eyes and felt the joy he he felt at their first meeting, when

Kaplan had called him Mr Miller, not mad dog, Kaplan was a decent, humane, reasonable man. And, as Gericke had told him, a good lawyer. Once again he felt sad that he must separate himself from the life that sufficed for others. The life he had seen Aviva choose. That he had acknowledged to be good.

Seeing his warm glance, Kaplan added, as if to placate him further, 'Kok's ordered an investigation.'

'Yes. He's probably fair, according to his lights.'

'Why won't you hope for life, David?'

'You know, I'm immensely touched that you don't treat me like a pariah.'

'You're far from that, David. I don't take you to be the hero that some people make you — oh, you didn't know about that. Well, of course, you're a political martyr. But I'm sure you're sensible enough not to be too swayed when you're used that way. So, I don't think you're that kind of hero. But . . .' Kaplan looked away, and then back at David, 'I want you to live. This is quite personal. I want you to live, and if you don't plead insanity, you'll be hanged.'

'If I do plead insanity, I'll be damned.'

'You're an atheist, David. What do you mean by being damned. No devil will come to poke a fork at you. Talk about reality, David. Live.'

'I want to talk about reality. Not to pretend that the reason for my actions is that I am, was, or could be considered crazy. My reason is apartheid. That's what's crazy! An abomination! I want to talk about the real reasons, the pass laws, the reserves, the prisons, the people who die in this country.'

'And what do you think you'll achieve if you have tirades in court?'

'How do think I'll live if I perjure my whole life and go on breathing in a lunatic asylum. It's not worth it. I have to tell the truth.'

'Everyone has his own truth.'

'I have to tell my truth.'

'I don't know what to say to you, David.'

They sat silent for a while, Kaplan picked up his pencil and started to tap the table with it.

'Let's not settle anything now, David. Dietz's going to call your father as his next witness, and that's about the end of his case. We'll talk after that.'
'All right.'
'I feel a great failure.'
'So do I.'

At Joan's next visit he told her, 'I'm changing my plea, Joan. I'm not going to let Kaplan use insanity.'
'I'm glad, David.'
He drew in his breath. He was not prepared for her to say that she was glad he would die.
'I've been hating your despair.'
'Despair?'
'That's what it was, wasn't it. You've looked so tired and bored in court, just sick of it all, waiting for it to end, you didn't care how.'
'Yes, that's how it's felt. How did you know I've changed?'
'I can see it. I can hear it in your voice. And, of course, in what you're telling me. Why would you accept responsibility if everything's just meaningless.'
'You've changed too, Joan.'
'Yes,' she paused, gathering her feelings into words, 'It's not very clear to me. I mean, it's clear, but hard to put into words. But I want to tell you about it.' She paused again, looking at him through the grille with an expression like pleading on her face. 'Michael's been writing to me. He thought I might not understand what you'd been feeling. He wanted me to know that you talked in Pretoria. He says that he feels terribly to blame. Not that he condemns you or anything like that. He's been describing you as heroic. But, though he knew that you felt you had to risk everything, he didn't foresee that it would come out the way it did when he sent François to you. He didn't want you to die.'
'No one foresaw how it would come out. Will you tell him that? I didn't know all I was doing. But it was my doing, not his guilt, or François's, or anyone else's. Will you tell him that, Joan?'

'Yes.' She was smiling at him, sitting more firmly, as though happiness could come back to her. 'At first his letters made me very angry. I felt you'd betrayed me the way you talked with him. I hated you.' She was looking at him directly, as if to challenge him, also bearing responsibility for what she had felt. 'I hated everything that reminded me of you. I was so full of hate I wanted to hurt everyone I talked to. I don't know how Aviva put up with me.'

Now Joan looked down at her hands in her lap. With a movement he had not seen in her before, she folded her arms across her body, holding the elbows, and rocked forward slightly as she spoke, 'Perhaps that's how I started to understand why you couldn't talk to me after St Thérèse's. I started to feel that there could be something horrible in the way I can keep calm, go on practising and playing.' She looked up, smiling ironically, 'Michael wrote to me about that. And I remembered how Edward used to feel. I saw a lot of Edward before he left.'

She would go to England. She would see Edward. She would live. 'You've always been able to talk to one another.'

'Yes. You and Edward are very alike, in some ways. You both let yourselves get hurt. I've protected myself so much. I was prepared for things to be cruel and unjust, because that's how they'd been for God. I didn't see that my faith's been upside down. It showed me that the whole world's a prison, but I didn't really see that Christ became a prisoner to show how to be free. All this comes in Christian images to me, David, but I could say it another way. I mean, I took it for granted that there would be injustice, in a way that protected me from being hurt by it, so I wouldn't do silly things like you or Edward.'

'Did you talk to Edward about this?'

'No, but I've been writing to him.'

For a moment David felt his own jealousy. He beat it down. Joan would have to live after he was dead.

'Will you tell Edward something for me?' She nodded. 'At St Thérèse's I said I couldn't accept what he was doing because it was only temporary.'

'Yes. We talked about that.'

'Well, I've come to see that everything in human life is only temporary. Nothing lasts longer than individual human lives. Not in any way to mean anything. I wanted to do away with death altogether. It can't be done.'

The terror of his own death coming so soon, flashed over him again, and he knew that he was sweating.

'He cares for you, he admires you, David.'

'He nodded.

'So does Michael.'

Again he nodded. When the spasm of terror had passed, and he could speak normally again, he asked, 'Does Michael really believe what he writes about me?'

'He thinks what you did a tragic waste.'

They listened to each other's silence.

'Who's paying Kaplan, Joan? The anti-apartheid movement, or someone else?'

'Aviva. Sidney, really, I suppose.'

David laughed. 'Tell me *I'm* crazy.'

'They don't want anyone to know.'

'Why're they doing it?'

'Friendship. Mostly for me, I think, but for you too. Aviva's very loyal. She was marvellous to Edward. She coddled him and made him eat and swim and rest. He put on twelve pounds during his visit.'

'She knows that he'll go on being silly.'

'That's got nothing to do with it, though she argued her head off with him.'

'Will you thank them. Kaplan's been a very good lawyer. Though he's upset about this decision of mine.'

'He also cares for you. He wants you to live.'

Silence fell into the space between them. He noticed the bars, the mesh, the barren prison walls.

'I love you, Joan.'


But in the cell again he knew that he was free of her, only his own self now. Alone. Even Gericke had gone. They would have no more conversations about the taste of peaches or his brother's farm.

Kaplan told him that in Dar-es-Salaam Philip had told reporters that he had been tortured.

'So it's come out. Good. Do you think there'll really be an investigation.'

'I respect Kok, David. He's going to try to get what he said he'd get. We should talk about you. Your father's on the stand tomorrow. Let's reassess our position after that.'

'O.K. Do you know what's happened to the books you've brought me?'

'I think they want to make sure we aren't using a secret code in them.'

'I wonder if they'll ever let me read Marc Bloch again.'

'I'll try, David.'

In the court Joan smiled at him, ignoring the reporters. He knew that he would die soon.

His father was wearing a suit that looked new, bought especially for this public occasion, but his tie lay awry, and a red nose and watery eyes bleared his aging features. He had become unkempt and shabby, almost like those drought-worn farmers whose sons had come to David's door in Pretoria selling *koeksusters*. The leathering of his own years of drought had given his face a South African cast. If he left for England again because he could not live in the country where his son's name, and thereby his own, meant shame, he would seem a foreigner again.

He took the oath, and Dietz invited him to tell the court about the character of the defendant. At first he talked wanderingly, but it all came out — his hopes, his ambitions for David, the ideals he had set up for him. Smuts and Churchill and Rhodes. He had supervised David's homework and encouraged him to read and play sports. 'But there was always a barrier. No matter what I did for him, he turned against me. Even when he was a little, he was like that. My wife used to set him against me. She was a difficult woman. She quarrelled with me in front of him. She insulted me in front of the child, and even in front of the servants. When he was cheeky and criticized me, she took his side, even when he contradicted me and flouted me. I blame her.

'But it didn't do her any good. He didn't like her any better than he liked me. He was always a cold, heartless child. When I told him my hopes for him he walked out saying he didn't want to hear my problems. Imagine that. He left home without a word of explanation or goodbye'. He's never had any heart, though this is a terrible thing to say about my own son.'

David heard the words enlarged and multiplied, as though these pleas and accusations had continued to sound in some unheard depth of his being, in a whispering gallery where all the originals and repetitions accumulated so that now, when time reversed and carried him back to his father's voice, he heard all in a claustrophobic foreground, a noise not wholly inside, not wholly outside his own seething mind. This was his father, his own flesh, whose face he had been afraid to see rise out of his own.

'Everyone who is a parent will understand how my heart is breaking now. All my life I did my best for him. He despised me, and he went wrong.

'I say that when a child dies, a parent experiences a tragedy. When a child is crippled it is a tragedy. But when a child goes wrong, I tell you, a father would prefer it if his child had died. I ask those of you who are parents to look in your own hearts: think of everything you suffered for your children; and think how lucky you are compared to me.'

The pressure and clamour in David collapsed, and he laughed with relief to find his father so reduced and comical. Why had his father seemed so large and resounding? He was puny and full of self-pity.

The court turned to stare at his laughing.

'What more do I need to say?' his father declaimed. 'You see for yourselves that he is heartless and feels no remorse. See how he laughs at his old father.

'But still, your honour, he is my son, and I hope the court will show him mercy.'

David laughed again.

Feeling the precious sun on his limbs as he exercised, congratulating Snyman, who said he was soon getting married, David realized that impending death had set him free. It had brought his father before him and released him from the injunction to make history. He could not struggle any longer with the world into which history had delivered him. History was utterly beyond his power. He could do nothing now but live what was left of his own life. Moving. Enjoying the sun.

Dietz concluded his case.

'What shall we do now, David?' Kaplan asked.

'I think I have to conduct my own defence now.'

'I'm sorry we're not going to finish this trial together. But I understand that you feel you have to do it this way.'

'I wish I could say something more than thank you. You've helped me keep sane here.'

In court Kaplan told Kok that David refused counsel now.

'Do you wish the court to assign other counsel?' Kok asked David.

'No. I feel that I have had the best possible counsel, but must conduct my defence myself now.' Kok consulted with Kaplan again, and then, appearing satisfied, asked 'What do you plead?'

'I don't plead anything. I have been found guilty already. What I plead will make no difference.'

'Be careful not to commit contempt. I repeat, what do you plead?'

'I do not plead.'

'Then I shall continue your first plea, not guilty by virtue of insanity.'

'If I am insane, it is because you are guilty. The crimes of the law you uphold are enough to make anyone mad with despair.'

'I have warned you that I can find you guilty of contempt.'

'If I'm guilty of contempt, it can only be because you consider me sane. It I am sane, I judge you guilty.'

Dietz rose. 'Objection, your honour. I submit that the accused is mocking the court.' Kok silenced him with a glance, and turned again to David. 'I must warn you that you are trying my patience.'

'No, your honour, I am trying your office. I find you guilty of upholding a system of law that perverts justice.'

Dietz objected again. 'Your honour, the accused is trying to use this trial to make political speeches. He is not being tried for politics. His crimes are heinous — treason, murder, and terrorism.'

'I committed them to accuse you too,' David retorted, 'of crimes committed in the name of the law, by officers of the state, and by everyone who abides within the law. The law itself, in this country, is criminal.'

'I will not allow this courtroom to be used as a political forum,' Kok ruled. 'If the accused persists in his offensive behaviour, I shall find him guilty of contempt.'

'How can you frighten me with penalties for contempt when I know that you plan to kill me?'

'The court is adjourned.'

Two policemen standing behind David grabbed his arms and hustled him out.

'Think you smart, hey!'

'Bloody Communist!' They pushed him into the van.

Kaplan had watched this performance, and came to see David. 'For the last time I ask you, behave reasonably.'

'I won't say another word. He can enter any plea he likes. I've said what I wanted.'


Joan was allowed to visit him next day.' Joan, I've been thinking about what Michael said, that it's all a tragic waste. You think so too, don't you?'

'Yes.'

'And you hate it for being so ruthless.'

'Yes!' Her reply was vehement.

'I wanted to say that even if it is a waste, I had to do it. Everything's been a waste. We haven't found anything yet to destroy apartheid. We don't know what'll work.'

'I know.' He heard her as if her words confessed that she had been assessing what to do.

'I don't think we'll know until we do what does work. I'm

not going to condemn what I did as a waste. It's only use may be to show that some ways are a dead end. All right, I'll die for that then.'

'And the others who died?'

'I haven't wanted to think about them. I don't know. I've said all along that the innocent and the guilty are caught together, and that acting and not acting are both bloody. But it feels even more complicated than that. I've been thinking about Aviva and Sidney paying Kaplan. About the way he's treated me. As is if there's something to me beyond my ideas, whether they agree with them or not, and even beyond what I've done. And that's fused with other things I've been feeling here. You can't guess how important physical things become in prison — the size of your cell and the food and the number of blankets. I don't think I even knew how many blankets I used outside. Everything real was in my head, in newspapers, in ideas, in hating apartheid. People started to seem to me just aspects of apartheid. There was a teacher in my school in Pretoria, I really liked him, but we couldn't talk to each other because he's a Nationalist. I was like a totalitarian system all inside myself just like apartheid. I couldn't've done what Aviva and Kaplan have done for me. You saw it. You told me I was becoming inhuman.'

Joan nodded, and he saw that tears were sliding down her face. 'I knew you were right, but in some way I felt I had to let it happen to me. Perhaps I was even trying to numb myself so that I wouldn't think about how everything else has failed, all those in prison and exile or worse, and the hopelessness of everything so far. I didn't want to be reasonable about things like those children at St Thérèse's. Maybe I did want to be a bit mad. Maybe it needs madmen to try to unlock justice.'

'I don't want to be mad.'

'That's why I wanted to say all this to you. I want you to go on playing music, whatever else you do, to hold on to your senses and to being human. You called it being complacent. It isn't. It's being sane. You'll never stop playing, will you?'

She laughed. 'It's a danger I've never considered.'

'You see how the imagination gets out of hand in prison.' They sat silent.

'We've got nothing to talk about now, have we,' she said.
'Are you sorry we were married, Joan?'
'No. Not, after all.' She looked down at her hands, 'I didn't want to cry.'
'All right. Come to your senses. Stand. Stretch up. Arms down. Up. Down. Jumping jacks.'
'What's going on here?' Snyman opened the door, looking dismayed.
'*Ag*, man, Snyman, these chairs are so hard we had to move our bones,' David told him. Still looking worried, Snyman nodded and stood aside at the door again so that they couldn't see him.
'I've brought the copy of the Marc Bloch book you wanted, but van der Merwe thinks *The Historian's Tools* might be subversive. Dangerous, anyhow. He says he has to check it first.'
'Try to visit me again in Pretoria.'
'I will.'

But when they legalized his guilt, and took him to Pretoria Central, and stripped him of his own clothes, and put him in their condemned uniform again, and shaved his hair against lice, and locked him up with Lewis Cope, another murderer in the same uniform, he fell into a vertigo in which he felt he could not bear another visit. She came in the first week, but they could not talk to each other. He asked questions about Aviva's newborn baby girl and Joan's own health as though they were distant relatives at a wedding or a funeral. He told her he shared a cell with Lewis Cope. She said that she had brought Marc Bloch's books now to Pretoria Central, but Captain Bultman also wanted to examine them before David could read them. David asked her to get permission to bring him a jersey.

The routine of Pretoria Central was more harsh and superficially irrational than the Fort's. They were wakened at four-thirty and ate dinner at three in the afternoon. They cleaned their buckets during exercise time, and collected their food in dixies washed under the same tap where they emptied their buckets. The body that had restored him to a feeling of sanity in the Fort, produced involuntary sequences of loathing and terror in him at Pretoria Central.

During the second week, when he and Cope were staring at the African prisoners who, on all fours, polished the black concrete hall outside their cell, he recognized an individuality of movement and a face.

'*Dumela*, Mabotoana,' he projected a loud whisper. The polisher lifted his head and moved towards the cells. David crouched.

'We didn't know you were here already,' Mabotoana said.

'What did they get you for, *Ntate*?'

'Furthering aims,' was Mabotoana's shorthand for furthering the aims of an unlawful organization.

'How long?'

'Fifteen.'

Looking into this gulf of time, David clutched his near death. He would not have to endure so long.

'*Khotso, Ntate*,' Mabotoana jerked his head to show that a warder was watching. They could not talk. David stood, wondering. Mabotoana had addressed him with the term of respect, *Ntate*, Father.

Mabotoana must have spread the news. During the next two days some of the white politicals contrived to walk past his cell. He recognized some from photographs in the papers, other from parties he had been to with Aviva's set at Wits. He recognized two, Barnard and Taylor, from the group that had committed sabotage in Cape Town, blowing up telephone booths. They had also been tried and found guilty of treason. Prison was no place to disagree with their tactics. He was free to accept their friendship. Perhaps they had been as appalled as Trevor at his act.

Mabotoana polished the floor again, and other African convicts greeted him. They dropped scraps of toilet paper with taut messages, 'Welcome,' 'Don't let the bastards get you down.' One dropped a cigarette, another two matches and a piece of matchbox to strike them on. When they passed, he whispered '*Mayebuye!*' and raised his thumb. Unobtrusively, they raised theirs. The government had given them all the same uniform, and they were giving him friendship until he died.

He gave the cigarette and matches to Cope, who thanked him and said nothing about David's welcome into a society that mined the whole prison. Or David's cry, every night at the moment the lights went out, when the whole prison fell silent and a voice called out, '*Amandhla?*' Whose is the power? The prison answered with a thousand voices out of all its blacks cells, '*Nagawethu!*' It is ours! And David's voice joined theirs. Cope put up with David's raised thumb and shout as another unchangeable condition of prison life tolerated because there was no alternative. But when Cope's death sentence was commuted by the President, and they told him they were taking him to serve hard labour in Rustenburg, he wouldn't shake hands with David. 'You're a traitor to your race!'

He was glad to have the large cell to himself for the few days left. The prison began to sing for him. African voices initiated hymns he had heard at St Thérèse's and other missions, he had visited with Joan, and in the Fort when they sang against Philip's torture. As always, singing hymns on the missions, or chants of hoeing and lifting loads and cracking stones and stamping roads, their voices divided into harmonies and descants, every melody opened out like a ray of light passed through a prism to show its colours. The plain hymns of protestant Britain and the bold chords of counter-reformation Catholicism became African, subtle, and complex. Their sad, intricate, courteous farewell sang him to death. New songs grew out of old, new harmonies sent out shoots and buds. Day after day they sang to him in African languages he had never learned although he had heard them from the first days when Sina gossiped with Samuel as she shelled peas, or with the maid next door as she ironed sheets and towels and pillowcases and folded them into dazzling order, when a fig tree cast shadows on the garden wall, and African convicts built a road outside his house, stamping it with staves, singing.

The harmonies sweeping round him eroded his separateness. They were singing for him as though he would die the death of an African convict. They were singing as though he lived his last days now with them, in their prison, their condition, their endurance, their patience, their unquenchable harmony and courtesy. Hour after hour their song held him and comforted him, and protected him from the clack of keys, steps, dixies, doors, metal and force. It was death, but they knew death. It was loneliness, but they knew the mine barracks and servants' *kias*. It was fear, but they knew the nights, the *tsotsis*, the hospitals, the police, the random white bullies. They knew the careless white madam, the farmer, who wanted convict labour, the location superintendent, the informer, the traders who gave no credit, the children who stopped crying, the prisoners who stopped screaming. It was oppression, it was early death. They had been into the mines. It was defeat. They had eaten the food white men doled them.

But, they assured him, the power was theirs. *Nagawethu*, They welcomed him. The power was his also. Their power was his power. They would take his power and save it. He had poured out his life. He had not reversed history. He had not broken the dam. But he was not lost.

He was all one man. He was who had slept in the sun, who had loved Joan, who had read Marc Bloch, who had looked at Sina's breasts, who had eaten with Eugenie, who had hated Spence. He was who had bought mimosa, seen an old man pushed into the gutter with milk spilling over his feet, been swimming in a mountain pool streaked with malachite. He was the son of his father. He was who loved saris, he was who had heard Gericke fart. He was whose friend had been tortured. He was his whole life. He was white in South Africa, and the Africans were singing for him. They made him himself and more than himself. They included him in their history. They found an echo of their lives in his life. Under one law. Like the spiral in a rose and a galaxy.

The last night, when the lights went out and the prison was silent, the cry asked, '*Amandhla*' and the darkness answered, '*Nagawethu!*' they waited for him to start the songs he wanted them to sing for him. He began the songs he'd learned at Hartebeestpoort Dam, and then '*Nkosi Sikelele Afrika*', the anthem the African choirs used to sing instead of the white anthems after performances of the *Messiah*. When he ran out of songs, the politicals who had sent him greetings offered songs of their causes, which he might not have made his causes, partisan songs of the defeated anarchists in the Spanish Civil War, of the Zionist Haganah, of the Russian Revolution, the *International* and the *Marseillaise*, and more Congress songs than he had ever known.

When Bultman and the other warders came to fetch him, the prison waited again, and he started the words promised by Handel. To catch other sounds through that exultant 'He shall break them', his hearing must have been abnormally clear, but through 'In pieces! In pieces!' he caught the sound of cocks in the prison yard. They had started to crow, and others all over Pretoria were answering them, although it was still night, and lions were roaring in the distant zoo.

238

# Afterword

In 1964, John Harris, a white South African, made a bomb and planted it in the Whites Only section of the Johannesburg railway station. An old woman was killed, a child was maimed, and several other people suffered minor injuries. John Harris was soon arrested, tried, and hanged. I know little more about this incident. I have avoided reading about John Harris because I wanted to write a work of fiction, not history. I have used the station bombing because it presented my imagination with an action that showed both the violence apartheid breeds, and the hopelessness I felt about changing apartheid when I left South Africa in 1964, a few weeks before John Harris made his bomb. Although I have used history for the central action of this book, I hope I have avoided other echoes of John Harris's story.

I have used other historical accounts to help me imagine South African prisons. These have been Harold Strachan's testimony about conditions in Pretoria Central, reported by Benjamin Pogrund in the *Rand Daily Mail*, the *Jail Diary of Albie Sachs* by Albie Sachs, *A Healthy Grave* by James Kantor, and *Bandiet* by Hugh Lewin.

I owe many debts of gratitude for help in writing this book: to Stanley Moss for much encouragement and support; to Sylvia Laws for typing an early draft; to Harris Dienstfrey and Jane Langton for meticulous reading and criticism, and a generous belief in the book's value; to innumerable South African friends I have consulted about details; to Douglas Blewett, Mark Edwards, Eleanore Lonske, Lorraine Keating and Eugene Ott of the Computer Science Centre at Wellesley College who helped me prepare the manuscript for publication.

R.M.